CHARMED BY A WILY LASS

OLIVER HEBER BOOKS

1

FIFTH, JUNE 1819

"Why the devil did you purchase a sapphire ring?" Kenneth Davenport mused aloud, noting the date on the invoice from Phillip's Jewelry Store happened to be one day prior to his brother's death.

Alfred, the seventh Viscount Berwick had perished in his bed nearly a fortnight ago, thus rendering Kenneth the eighth viscount. The attending physician had deemed the cause of death asphyxia brought on by intoxication, which was further confirmed by the coroner. But Kenneth believed differently. Not that Alfred didn't enjoy his liquor. Quite the contrary. However, the former viscount wasn't merely one-and-thirty, he had been fit and well in control of his faculties. Alfred had a passion for horse racing and had acquired the Kiedler Equine Estate in northern England, one of the foremost horse training facilities in the Kingdom. He was an accomplished rider and could handle a team as well as any coachman running the mail up the Great North Road. The former viscount had been shrewd, determined, and imposing.

Seated at his brother's writing table, which was now Kenneth's writing table, strategically placed by the south-facing window to take best advantage of daylight, he set the invoice for the sapphire ring onto the pile deemed "of interest" opposed to the pile which was not. He then tugged the bell pull.

Brown stepped inside and clasped his hands over his black coat, clearing his throat. "You rang, my lord?"

Kenneth shuddered. Never in all his days did he anticipate answering to "my lord." The title of viscount had fit Alfred so well. "I'm surprised to see you're still here," he replied dryly.

The butler's... or soon to be former butler's hedgerow of eyebrows slanted inward. "Sir?"

"What with your inheritance, I thought you'd have your valise packed by now."

"Not at all, sir."

"Are you planning to remain in service?" Kenneth asked, unphased by Brown's baffled expression. Alfred had bequeathed the man with a rather handsome sum. Though it wasn't unusual for an employer to provide their elderly servants with a pension, the former viscount had been exceedingly generous in this instance, which had moved the butler to the top of Kenneth's list of murder suspects.

"Service, sir?"

"Surely you cannot tell me you haven't plans for your inheritance?"

The man's shoulders fell as he sighed. "I've scarcely had time to consider your brother's generous bequest. Besides, I have no intention of doing anything with the coin until you are comfortably settled and content with my replacement."

Interesting, though such selflessness did not remove Brown from the list, especially since after a bit of investigation, there appeared to be no other servants who might have had a motive to dispatch their employer. "Tell me," Kenneth said, probing for any sign of guilt, "if I were to find a butler with whom I am satisfied in the next fortnight, what would you do? Where would you go?"

"Well, sir, as you are aware, I'm getting on in years and have always thought it would be nice to retire to the country—to Surrey where I spent my childhood. Perhaps purchase a small cottage and a dinghy."

"Dinghy?" Kenneth asked.

"For fishing."

A rather unpretentious endeavor over which to commit murder. But that wasn't why Kenneth had rung the bell. Honestly, he'd thought Mrs. Fielding the housekeeper would have answered his call, but that was neither here nor there. He gestured toward the invoice at the top of his "of interest" pile. "Were you aware Alfred purchased a sapphire ring the day before he died?"

Again, Brown appeared to be utterly bewildered. "A ring, sir?"

"That's what I said."

"For whom?"

Kenneth clenched his chair's armrests. "You're not aware? You served my brother for years, for heaven's sake."

Brown tapped a gnarled finger against his chin. "He did attend a great number of balls this Season. Far more than usual."

A-ha, perhaps he'd happened upon a tidbit of a clue. "Do you know if he was courting any young ladies?"

"It wasn't my place to pry, sir. And you are aware of how private His Lordship was. He rarely told me the specifics about where he might be off to, day or night.

Only by his attire and the reports in the newspaper did I surmise where he had been."

"What about Alfred's valet? He was not among the servants I interviewed upon my arrival in London." Which was a fortnight ago. As soon as Kenneth had received word of his brother's passing, he and his manservant hastened for London. And once he arrived, he hadn't a moment's rest what with the funeral arrangements and all the rigmarole necessary for assuming a peerage.

"He sailed for America six month's past," Brown replied.

"Did he depart service in good standing?"

"Quite good, I'd say. I believe the former viscount gave him two months' severance."

"Generous of him." Kenneth drummed his fingers. "Have you heard from the valet since he set sail?"

"Yes, sir. He wrote a fine letter to His Lordship, which he gave us to read below stairs. The chap met a woman on the ship and married her—purchased a bit of land in Delaware."

Clues be damned. "Did anyone step in as Alfred's valet?"

"I did, sir. After all, I was the valet to your father before I was promoted to butler."

Kenneth knew this, of course. And as far as he could recall, Brown had been a most loyal servant to the viscountcy. "Did doing so not deter you from your duties?"

"Not really. Lord Berwick the former only required the attention of a valet in the mornings and when he was planning to go out in the evening. He preferred to be left alone once he returned from his social engagements—*if* he returned. Moreover, since Lord Berwick the former was a bachelor, he rarely entertained.

Things have been rather quiet since your parents were laid to rest and the two of you flew the nest, as it were." Brown leaned forward as if he had a secret. "May I speak freely, sir?"

Hoping for a declaration of guilt, Kenneth leaned in as well. "Yes, please do."

"This whole unfortunate turn of events just doesn't seem plausible, does it? For your brother to perish in his bed—a man full of youth and vitality. I cannot understand it."

Neither could Kenneth. Hence the very reason for sifting through his brother's correspondence. And was why he critically was examining the character of the servants who had been in the employ of the viscountcy for years. "Hypothetically, let us assume skullduggery is afoot."

Brown gave a discerning nod while jowls reminiscent of a bloodhound jostled.

"Can you think of anyone who might have benefited from Alfred's death?"

The butler puzzled for a moment, then straightened and clapped a hand over his heart. "Surely, you do not think I had anything to do with His Lordship's passing?"

Kenneth narrowed his gaze. Why had Brown jumped to such a sudden conclusion? True, he had known the butler all his life and the man had served his family well. But no stone could be left unturned. "Were you aware Alfred had included you in his will —you and not one of the other servants?"

"No, sir. I had absolutely no idea until you told me yourself. Surely, you recall how astonished I was at the time of the reading—after all, it was only yesterday," Brown replied, his face utterly blanched.

True, the butler had been unduly shocked, or at

least it appeared that way. Now Kenneth wasn't entirely convinced. "I wonder… " he said, drumming his fingers against his lips. "Did my brother have a mistress?"

"No, sir."

"No?"

"No one of whom I was aware."

"Yet you are also unaware as to whether or not he was courting a young lady?"

"Correct, sir."

"Very well." Kenneth picked up the next bit of paper—an invoice for the stabling of Alfred's horse at the Epsom Derby which had been held in Surrey. "I was surprised to read in the papers that Venom didn't win the Derby this year. He was favored, was he not?"

"Yes, he was, sir. And I'll say His Lordship was very out of sorts afterward. Horses were one thing the viscount loved to discuss, especially when taking his breakfast."

Kenneth couldn't argue that, what with Alfred's purchase of Kiedler Equine. "Did you travel to Surrey for the race?"

"I did, at His Lordship's request."

Kenneth watched the butler's expression as he casually replied, "What a good opportunity to enquire about properties for sale."

A pinch formed between Brown's eyebrows. "I do not believe the viscount was looking to buy property."

"I wasn't referring to my brother—what with you planning to retire to Surrey with a dingy and whatnot."

Brown again clasped his hands over his coat, his white gloves pristine. "I assure you I had no prior knowledge of the monies bequeathed to me. We are all bereft. Perhaps you might feel better after a warm brandy or—"

"No. Thank you." For a moment, Kenneth mulled over whether or not to dismiss the butler forthwith and send him off to Surrey but decided against doing so. Of course, he could make do as he always had with his manservant, Welch. But until he uncovered the true cause of Alfred's death, he needed Brown close at hand, under close surveillance as well.

After the butler was dismissed, Kenneth locked the items from the "pile of interest" into the top drawer of the writing table. He then took it upon himself to rifle through every nook and cranny of the town house in search of the sapphire ring. When all else failed, he lowered himself to his hands and knees and peered under Alfred's enormous four-poster bed. To his chagrin, the cavern beneath was too dark to see a thing.

He stood and turned full circle, eyeing the copper bed warmer propped against the enormous black-marble hearth. He swiftly removed the wooden handle, then keeled again and swept the tool in an arc beneath the bed, first toward the headboard, and then toward the foot.

"I'll be damned," he said, sweeping a velvet box out from beneath the edge of the coverlet.

Kenneth's fingers trembled as he opened the oval box, the sight making every muscle in his body clench, his face burn with fire, and his eyes nearly bulge out of their sockets. "Alfred's death was no case of asphyxia." He enclosed the empty box in his fist. "And this bloody proves it!"

∼

Lady Modesty MacGalloway gathered Poseidon's reins in her left hand before climbing onto the mounting block.

"I think it is time for ye to start racing against an opponent," said Mr. Willett, her trainer—a man she had met at the Epsom Derby, and the only person she trusted to keep her secret—aside from her lady's maid, whom Modesty trusted with everything.

Before she mounted the bay thoroughbred, she glanced through the stable's long corridor, lined with stalls on either side, each one containing a prized racehorse. *An opponent?* "Are you training other women?"

"No, ye're the only one."

She bit her bottom lip. Modesty would give her right arm to race beside a proven jockey. But then again, allowing anyone aside from Mr. Willett to know her secret bore a monumental risk. "Do you reckon 'tis safe?"

"There are one or two fellas I trust, but aye. There would be a small fee, of course."

It was Sunday. At noon. Not only did jockeys rest on Sundays, all the stable hands took their nooning at the Lion's Den down the road a wee bit. This was the only day of the week upon which Modesty could train. The only hour as well. Women weren't allowed on the track. Not that anyone would know she was a woman by her snug-fitting white breeches, red silk shirt, and jockey's cap, which was tied beneath her chin with ribbon because she had far too much hair for the wee bonnet to fit snugly.

"Besides," said Mr. Willett, giving her knee a slap. "Ye look like a jockey. Ride better than most as well."

Modesty beamed. Ever since she had been given a pony at the age of five she had been enamored with horses. But only when the patriarch of the family, Martin MacGalloway, the Duke of Dunscaby, allowed her to accompany him to the track in Surrey did she realize she was already in love with racing. "Just dunna tell my brother—or Mama, for that matter. When it comes to behavior befitting young ladies, they both have no sense of humor whatsoever."

"I doubt I'll 'ave the honor. The only nobility who visit the practice track are those who are in the 'orse trade—though they mostly give their 'orses a cursory glance before leaving them in the hands of their trainers."

Modesty slipped the toes of her wellingtons into the iron stirrups. "Well, I endure my fill of nobility quite enough aside from our noon hours on Sundays."

"I imagine you do."

She raised the reins and cued Poseidon to walk on toward the track.

Mr. Willett kept pace alongside them. "What shall it be today? Eight Furlongs? Six?"

"The Derby is one-and-a-half miles," she said.

"One mile, four furlongs, and ten yards," Mr. Willett corrected.

She tossed her head. "Which is one-and-a-half miles, mind you."

"It is at that, milady." As they stopped on the track, he wrapped his fingers around Poseidon's bridle. "Tell me, what is the one thing upon which you need to focus?"

There were many things, actually, the first being not to fall off her tiny saddle, made smaller to keep the weight Poseidon must bear to a minimum. But Modesty's seat was sure. "Heels down, crouch low so the wind glides over my back, eyes straight ahead, and..." She chewed her bottom lip. Even if she was wearing jockey's clothing, it wasn't proper to speak of certain parts of one's anatomy.

"That was several things, all of which ye've mastered. If ye want to ride like the wind, keep your backside up." Mr. Willett smacked her hip. "I'll tell ye true, every jockey who 'as learned to raise his arse in the air increases his odds tenfold. Ye're training to be a jockey, are ye not?"

"Aye, sir."

"Then ye'd best ride like one else you may as well go back to your sidesaddle and parade through 'yde Park with the ladies."

Modesty chuckled to herself. The man always talked as if she actually did have a chance to become a jockey. She was certainly small enough. She didn't even need to bind her breasts because her corset took care of making her bosoms appear flat—unless she was dressing for a ball, at which time her lady's maid managed to miraculously produce cleavage. But small breasts or nay, she had engaged Mr. Willett to indulge in something for herself—something she'd dreamed about, something aside from the endless parade of balls, tea parties, soirees, recitals, the opera... though Modesty did find Shakespeare riveting.

Nonetheless, things had grown rather disconcerting when both she and her closest friend Kitty were introduced at court for the commencement of their first Season. It seemed everyone considered Kitty to be one of the darlings of the *ton* while the only callers Modesty had received were parasites on the hunt for an easy fortune. Well, she had no intention of allowing some ne'er-do-well to take her dowry and lose it at the card tables in a horrid gambling hell.

At the practice track, all thoughts of her rather disastrous first Season blew away on the wind as she took

Poseidon through his paces, warming up with a trot, gradually urging him faster until he transitioned to a canter. By the time the horse was ready to gallop, Mr. Willett had marched across the paddock to the half-mile mark, Modesty's cue to ride to the starting line.

Even without any competition, the thoroughbred snorted and tossed his head, skittering sideways in his excitement to break into a run. "Easy, laddie," she said, patting his neck and holding the reins firmly to prevent him from lurching forward.

With his pocket watch in hand, Mr. Willett blew his whistle while Modesty dug in her heels and slapped her crop, leaning over Poseidon's withers as she had been taught. Her eyes teared up with the force of the wind at her face but, by the stars, it felt liberating. Riding on the back of a horse with no restrictions and no hampering conventions was the closest thing to unabashed freedom Modesty had ever experienced. Years of lessons in etiquette sloughed away. The shackles of her highborn birth didn't matter. The circumstances of being the youngest of eight children was momentarily forgotten as the thrill of commanding the fastest animal ever to set hooves onto a racetrack rushed through her blood like a sip of whisky on an empty stomach (which she had nipped once from her brother's decanter).

"Get your arse up!" hollered Mr. Willett.

Jolting with her trainer's correction, she pushed her heels down, taking all her weight onto her thighs, the motion making her lurch so far forward, Poseidon's wind-blown mane tickled her chin.

"That's it!" he shouted as she thundered past, the thrill of his compliment bolstering her confidence, making her demand more speed.

As they galloped around the bend and headed

down the straight, a man stepped onto the track—not a worker, but a man dressed like a dandy—Wellington top hat, gleaming hessians over a pair of skintight pantaloons, and a double-breasted coat with tails.

Gasping, Modesty slowed Poseidon, though it was impossible to immediately make him stop. After her initial tug, she eased the reins, allowing the horse to naturally slow to a canter and then to a trot while Mr. Willett marched back across the paddock, fists tight at his sides. "What the devil are you doing Modesty—ah, er... *Master Modistie*," he improvised, obviously flummoxed at seeing the gentleman who so rudely interrupted her lesson.

Modesty clamped her lips shut and shrugged as she inclined her head toward the unwanted visitor.

"I beg your pardon, I hope I am not interrupting your practice," said the intruder. Was that ginger hair peeking beneath the rim of his hat? "I couldn't find anyone in the stables and I've come to enquire about my late brother's horse."

She pulled the brim of her cap lower as Mr. Willett slipped his watch into the pocket of his waistcoat. "If ye tell me the name of the 'orse, I might be able to 'elp ye, sir."

"Venom."

Modesty emitted a high-pitched gasp before she thought to hold it in. The gentleman shifted his gaze her way as she clapped a hand over her mouth. His eyes were pale blue, the intensity of his stare rather disconcerting. But then again, everyone knew this man's brother had recently passed away. Breaking the polarizing connection between their gazes, Modesty glanced to the black mourning ribbon around the man's arm. The papers had reported Alfred Davenport was survived by a younger brother.

So, this is the new viscount? He certainly is not as handsome as the former had been.

But the man's appearance aside, she had attended the Derby—and it was won by an outsider. Furthermore, the papers reported rumors indicating there might be skullduggery afoot, which were heartily refuted by the Jockey Club.

Mr. Willett bowed with a flourish. "Forgive me, Lord Berwick. Please accept my condolences for your loss."

"Thank you. Alfred's passing was met with quite a shock." His Lordship gestured toward the stables. "May I see the horse?"

"Of course, sir. Straightaway." The trainer leveled his gaze at Modesty. "I'm afraid we'll 'ave to cut your lesson short, mil—er—Master Mod—er—ah—istie."

Wonderful. Mr. Willett had suddenly turned into a numpty of the highest order. Unless she held forth with a modicum of confidence, every member of polite society might be made aware that a *woman* was seen putting a racehorse through his paces. "Aye, sir," she said, affecting a deep, masculine voice.

After waiting for the men to enter the barn first, Modesty made quick work of returning Poseidon to his stall. She removed the saddle—something always done by the grooms at home, though a task she loved doing herself. In truth, Modesty often felt more at ease in a barn than she did in a parlor or at a ball. Horses didn't judge a person by their appearance, they judged them by their character, and whether or not the beasties deemed their humans worthy of respect.

Fortunately, she and Poseidon had struck up an immediate bond as if he knew she was his human from the moment they'd said hello. When they were introduced, she didn't try to mount him or take charge, she just accepted the lead line from the groom and breathed in the horse's scent, whispering a hello, and complimenting his beauty. As Poseidon began to relax, she had rested her forehead against his shoulder, spending at least an hour stroking him, whispering compliments all the while.

After stowing the saddle, Modesty donned a leather work apron and set to brushing her horse while the conversation Mr. Willett was having with Lord Berwick carried through the walls.

"He's a beauty. My brother was confident he'd win the Derby."

"'Twas a fluke if ye ask me. Ye are aware the former Viscount Berwick asked the Jockey Club stewards to perform a tooth check after the race to confirm the winner's age."

Modesty's brush stilled. The papers hadn't elaborated about the specifics of His Lordship's concern. They'd merely insinuated the winner was an unknown and a last-minute substitution—which was enough cause for consternation in itself.

"I had no idea," responded the viscount, his voice quite deep, stirringly resonant as well. "How did the stewards respond?"

"They swept 'is Lordship's request aside—said it was bad form and whatnot."

"I'll wager Alfred wasn't happy to be refused."

"Furious 'e was, so he sacked Venom's jockey."

"Truly?" A heavy pause hung in the air. "Tell me, who owned the outsider?"

"That would be Mr. Ward Crockford—proprietor of Waiter's Gentleman's Club on Bolton Row. Do ye know of it?"

Modesty had certainly heard of the men's-only

haunt, run by a corrupt and deceitful fiend—according to the *Lady's Magazine*.

"A gambling hell?" asked the viscount, his inflection filled with disdain.

"Aye, but an 'ighbrow one. 'Crocky the Shark' was the son of a fishmonger—grew up among the squalid surrounds in Temple Bar but ye'd never know if ye 'ad a peek at the finery of Waiter's. I reckon 'tis as fancy as Carlton 'ouse."

While the men's conversation lingered on, Modesty slipped into her full-length pelisse and fastened the buttons, then removed her cap and replaced it with a bonnet. Once again dressed as herself, she hastened outside to a waiting hackney, which was driven by a man whom she paid handsomely to ferry her to and from the racetrack every Sunday. His payment, of course, was in lieu of his silence.

Before the hack got underway, however, Lord Berwick appeared on the footpath. Again their gazes met. Her initial gasp was quickly replaced by a schooled purse to her lips, and rather than allow His Lordship to stare, Modesty closed the curtain and blocked the man from her sight.

2

Modesty stood beside Kitty, or Lady Katherine Mansfield as she had been announced upon entering the Duke and Duchess of York's ballroom. The two dear friends had met when they were both twelve years of age, not long before Kitty's brother, who had labored as a butcher until he unexpectedly inherited the Earldom of Brixham, married Modesty's eldest sister.

"Look there," Kitty said behind her fan. "Who is the dandy with Philomina?"

The steward answered the question as though he replied directly to Kitty, belting, "Lord Melvin Carmichael and his sister Lady Philomena Carmichael."

"Where has *he* been all Season?" whispered Felicity with unfettered interest as their fellow debutante sidled beside Modesty.

"I believe he's been abroad," Modesty replied, though the papers hadn't mentioned His Lordship's return. And Modesty never missed a single issue, which she always read cover-to-cover. Every day as soon as Martin finished reading the *Gazette*, she nabbed the newspaper before anyone else could put their hands on it, especially the servants. Once Giles the butler took it below stairs, the coveted news ended up divided into pieces and eventually incinerated in Cook's gargantuan hob. After all, knowledge was power, and Modesty loathed being powerless.

"Where?" asked Kitty.

"France, I believe." Modesty looked to a brilliantly lit chandelier above—lit with at least a dozen candles. "Or was it Spain?"

Felicity tittered. "Well, then your mother simply must introduce us!"

At the mention of her mother, Modesty glanced over her shoulder, immediately spotting the Dowager Duchess of Dunscaby. The family's matriarch was chatting with the ball's hostess, the Duchess of York, seeming to pay no attention whatsoever to the arrivals. Which was an outright ruse. Her mother was forever introducing both of them to gentlemen, though the men's eyes always homed in on Kitty with her flawless skin, fair hair, and astonishing amber eyes. It was humiliating to stand out like a goose among a bank of swans. Alas, if only Modesty didn't have to suffer these dratted balls and all the fuss that went along with them.

"Mm hmm," she begrudgingly agreed, wishing for the power to render herself invisible before being subject to the inevitable introduction.

"I beg your pardon?" Kitty pinched her arm. "Why are you so glum all of the sudden? I've never seen you glum, yet for the past fortnight, you have been acting rather melancholy."

In truth, Modesty only felt miserable when she was at a ball being compared to her best friend. She hated to admit how insignificant she felt when they stood side-by-side, but how could she not? Kitty was an English rose and Modesty? Well, she was a prickly thistle. Honestly, her middle sister, Grace, had once referred to her as a dandelion! "You are exaggerating."

"I am not. Goodness, you are not only wearing your mother's diamonds, His Grace gave you the most stunning hair comb I've ever seen. It even received a mention in the society section of the *Gazette*. How many other ladies present have their coiffure adorned with famous diamonds? Twenty of them, no less."

As the steward continued to hold forth with introductions, Kitty's bravado did nothing to raise Modesty's spirits. Marty had given her the comb while Mama had looked on, her expression abounding with aristocratic approval. The duke said it was only fitting for the sister of the most powerful peer in Scotland to be thus bedecked when attending a royal ball. But to Modesty, the sparkly stones represented her family's efforts to make up for what she lacked in beauty. Aye, she might be impishly cute, which was entirely appropriate for a child.

Alas, as a debutant being paraded before the kingdom's nobility, society's expectations of beauty had escaped her. Now Modesty's mother was employing every trick of lady's couture to attract the right sort of gentlemen, which had completely produced the opposite results thus far. Worse, the gossipy "society pages" had ruefully reported that Modesty would be wearing the gaudy comb this very night. A fact that was certain to bring the diabolical fortune seekers out of the woodwork.

"The Viscount Berwick," the steward boomed over the throng of the growing crowd.

Immediately drawn from feeling sorry for herself, Modesty glanced toward the entry while Kitty nearly knocked her over in an effort to catch a glimpse of the new viscount. "I hear he's quite stern," Kitty said.

"Yes, and he is withdrawn," Felicity added.

"How did you come by such observations?" Modesty glanced between her two friends. "No such thing was printed in the newspaper."

Kitty tossed her curls. "Not everything is reported by the *Gazette*."

"Well, who would blame the man for being a tad stern and withdrawn?" Modesty asked. "His dear brother just passed away. Far before his time, mind you."

Felicity snapped her fan closed into the palm of her hand. "I say, you have a very good point."

"Agreed." Kitty giggled, giving Modesty's shoulder a wee nudge. "Perhaps Her Grace will introduce us to Lord Berwick as well."

This comment earned another glance back to the dowager who was now nowhere to be seen. After the *Master Modistie* incident at the racetrack, it might be best to steer clear of the viscount this evening.

"Do you find him fetching even though he is a ginger?" asked Felicity.

Kitty sniggered with a hint of condescension while Modesty wondered if she could tug down one of the blue velvet curtains and drape it over her outrageously ginger head. "Of course not."

Lady Philomina approached with her arms outstretched and a radiant smile. "Modesty, might I say you are looking particularly adorable this evening?"

Adorable? There it was. No amount of face powder hid the freckles. She wasn't lovely or fetching, she was *absurdly adorable*. Which was synonymous with impishly cute. Modesty managed a pleasant expression and curtsied. "You are verra thoughtful to say so."

"She does look stunning." Felicity urged Modesty to turn her back. "And have a look at all those diamonds."

"Oh my," said Philomina admiringly. "I simply adore the color of your hair. Even if it is not fashionable, with such bright tresses you do not need dozens of diamonds to stand out."

The lass has never uttered truer words. Modesty again faced her friends, her countenance now appropriately fixed in schooled sister-of-a-duke affability. *Not long now and my first Season will be over. Then I'll have time to figure out how to tell Mama I intend to remain a spinster.* "How kind of you to say, dear Philomina. Did you see Lord Berwick? He's a ginger as well."

But no one heard Modesty's question because the little gathering of ladies had turned their attention to Lord Melvin Carmichael who was an icon of handsome beauty with brown hair and soulful green eyes. Grasping her brother by the elbow, Philomina ushered the rather stiff heir to a marquess forward. "Please allow me to introduce the eldest Carmichael, Lord Melvin."

Modesty and her friends curtsied in unison while Philomina rattled off their names.

His Lordship executed a gallant bow. "It is a pleasure, ladies. May I sign your dance cards?"

Kitty produced hers first, along with a pencil. Of course, hers was nearly full already. "I do so ever love the minuet," she said, though she was lying through her teeth. She found the minuet boring and outdated.

"As do I," replied the lordling, signing his name to the requested line before he turned to Felicity. "And you, miss? What is your favorite dance?"

She tittered again, something she was very good at

doing. Annoying or not, she already had three dances claimed on her card. "I enjoy them all."

Modesty handed over her empty dance card. "We may as well begin with the Grand March. After all, the musicians are taking their places."

His eyebrows shot up as he took in her Scottish burr. Perhaps she shouldn't have rolled her R's quite so harshly. Perhaps she ought to have taken her sister Grace's advice and attended Northbourne Seminary for Young Ladies rather than remain at home with her governess. But then again, Modesty liked her Scottish brogue. The problem was they were not in Scotland at the moment.

But at least she didn't have to sit out the Grand March. As a fanfare played, Lord Melvin offered his elbow. "Shall we?"

Together they joined the queue of members of the *ton* on the floor of the ballroom while soft strains of Mozart soared above the whispering voices. The Duke and Duchess of York had spared no expense, festooning their gold moldings with drapes of scalloped ivory lace. Each of the three enormous chandeliers was glowing with brilliant candlelight made brighter by tiny mirrors and crystals.

Everyone was elegantly outfitted in finery at the height of fashion, the room was abuzz with excitement as they gathered to commence the opening march. After Their Graces took their positions at the front of the procession, a moment of silence swelled through the air. Then with an uplifting fanfare, the orchestra began Beethoven's Turkish March.

"Did you enjoy your time on the Continent?" Modesty asked.

"I did."

"France was it?"

"Spain."

Drat, she should have remembered. "And are you glad to be back in England?"

Lord Melvin glanced at her from the corner of his eye. "If you mean am I happy to once again be under my father's scrutiny, my reply would be no."

She shifted her gaze to the woman's peacock-plumed fascinator ahead. Perhaps His Lordship might ask her a question. When he didn't, unable to bear the awkwardness, Modesty decided to change the subject to something His Lordship might enjoy discussing. "Tell me, what did you find so diverting in Spain?"

"My father wasn't there."

"I suppose I canna blame you. At times my mother can be suffocating."

"Hence all the diamonds?" he mused, finally managing a semblance of a smile.

"I'm surprised you can see them for the fiery color of my hair."

He chuckled. "Well, 'tis good to hear you have a sense of humor, my lady. What with your hair and freckles, I'll wager drollery comes in quite handy."

A quick slap across those foppish cheeks came to mind. Modesty might have jested about her hair color, but his remarks bordered on ridicule. *How dare he?*

If her mother weren't looking on along with three quarters of polite society, she might very well yank her hand away and continue the Grand March toward the door and straight out to the carriage.

Instead, she pursed her lips, stared straight ahead at the ridiculous feathers, and ignored the fiend. At least until the march ended. After she curtsied and he bowed, she refused to take his arm and allow him to escort her from the dance floor.

"Come, my lady. I thought you had a sense of humor."

"I do. It is just that *you* do nothing to make it spry." She snapped open her fan and fluttered it in front of her face. "Might I recommend you return to Spain where your stench will be far enough away not to make my stomach roil!"

To her amusement, the lordling turned scarlet. He also pivoted on his heel and strode away. The nice thing about the march was the participants merely walked in a circle around the hall and it was relatively easy for Modesty to ease herself into the crowd without drawing notice. She watched as Lord Melvin stepped behind a fiscus, inclined his nose to his shoulder, and sniffed. Now she had a very good reason to laugh, the cad.

"There you are, my dear!" said Mama, sweeping beside her like a buzzing bee. "I was ever so delighted to see you promenading with Lord Melvin."

Modesty tucked her hand behind her back, thus hiding the dance card tied to her wrist. "He was kind enough to ask."

"And?"

"I discovered he's rather unfond of red hair and he emits a certain unpleasant odor."

Mama's smile fell. "Your hair is stunning. Especially tonight."

"I told you the diamonds would make no difference whatsoever."

"Did you provoke him?"

Of course, her mother would assume Modesty was up to mischief—it was the easiest conclusion at which to arrive. Well, she wasn't about to admit anything. She had fully been within her rights to insult the self-absorbed lordling. "Who?"

"You very well know who. Lord Melvin is wealthy. Furthermore, he's the heir to a marquess."

"And he told me it's a damn good thing I have a sense of humor what with my red hair and freckles."

"Modesty, your language!"

"Verra well, my sense of humor is a *dratted* good thing."

Mama huffed and oscillated her fan in a flurry of white lace. "He didn't actually utter such rubbish, did he?"

Modesty leveled a sober stare upon her mother. "I dunna lie. I dunna need to."

"The fiend," cursed Mama, her upper lip disappearing with the dowager's subtle expression of ire.

"Exactly my sentiments."

Mama grasped Modesty's elbow and tugged. "I say that ne'er-do-well is of no consequence. Come, there's someone I want you to meet."

Groaning, Modesty dragged her feet. "I thought you indicated His Lordship was a good catch?"

"Not if he's rude and unrefined. Not if he has the gall to say something inappropriate and callous to my youngest daughter whose brother happens to be one of the most powerful dukes in the kingdom. You shall henceforth have nothing to do with Lord Melvin Carmichael."

"Mayhap we should tell Marty. He'll challenge the lordling to a duel and shoot him in the kneecap."

"I'd prefer it if we henceforth avoided duels in this family," said Mama, weaving through the crush of people, their skirts rustling. "Here we are!"

As Modesty all but stumbled past the woman from the march wearing the ostrich feather fascinator, Mama stopped in front of Viscount Berwick and smiled brightly, all vestiges of temper forgotten. "Good evening, your lordship."

He bowed. "Your Grace."

Modesty took a keen interest in the silk ribbon tied above her waist. Mama always included Kitty in the introductions, why not now? Surely if Kitty were also in tow, the viscount would only have eyes for her.

"As promised, I am pleased to introduce my youngest daughter, Lady Modesty MacGalloway."

The man's pale eyes shifted her way as he reached for her gloved hand. "My lady," he said rather officiously as he stooped to plant a kiss behind her knuckles. Though his hair was red, the color was a shade or two lighter than Modesty's. He didn't appear to have freckles either. At least not on his face. Though his hands were appropriately hidden by white gloves.

"'Tis a pleasure, m'lord," she replied, accentuating her Scottish accent. If her hair didn't dissuade him, perhaps her accent might.

"Tell me, my lady, have we not met before?" he asked, staring at her, his gaze much too keen.

Oh, holy hedgehogs, he could not have possibly remembered her face from the track? After all, six days had passed since. "I dunna reckon so, m'lord. This is my first Season."

"She is a diamond of the first water, is she not?" Mama said, beaming as if her middle daughter, Grace were standing in Modesty's slippers.

"Adorned by them for certain," His Lordship replied, smiling. "May I have the honor of signing your dance card, my lady?"

With Modesty's hesitation, Mama grasped her wrist and gaped at all the empty spaces. "I do believe my daughter has been overcome by a sudden stroke of bashfulness."

"Forgive me," Modesty managed not to look into Berwick's eyes—anywhere but those assessing eyes. They seemed so entirely intelligent as if they missed nothing—like women dressed as jockeys galloping around a racetrack. Then again, he'd seen her from the window of the hackney as well.

Is that why he recognizes me?

"I read in the papers that you're joining the chess match at Waiter's on the morrow," Modesty said, hoping to shift his attention.

Berwick nodded, using a pencil to sign his name. "Are you fond of chess?"

"I am," she replied.

He released her wrist, those dratted eyes meeting hers, blast it all. "Then we have something in common."

She nearly laughed as he bowed and excused himself. It was rare when first meeting not to have anyone comment about her hair. Perhaps he did not because it would draw attention to his own coiffure?

Modesty glanced down at her card and gasped.

"What is it, my dear?" asked Mama.

She slipped her wrist behind her back. "Lord Berwick reserved the waltz."

"Oh heavens, how wonderful!"

How calamitous is more apt. What if he did recognize me from the track?

3

If there was one thing Kenneth detested, it was dancing. As the son of a viscount, he had been subjected to lessons with a dance master twice a week, which meant his skill was passable simply due to years of repetition. But Kenneth was a scientist. He'd studied biological inheritance at university. Until he was urgently summoned to London, he had been working on a project of selective breeding to create a new variety of sheep that produced more wool, milk, and meat. He also maintained one hundred and fifty beehives, which not only supplied a great deal of honey to the Kingdom, they required hours of his attention, even though he employed laborers to manage them.

But still, there he was, signing dance cards, skipping gaily, and pointing his toes. Yes, it was an exercise in self-flagellation, but attending the Duke of York's ball drew him one step closer to finding out why the devil Alfred had purchased the sapphire ring, and hopefully for whom it was intended, which then might lead to the identification of Alfred's murderer.

Kenneth's problem was he'd chatted with every young lady to whom he gained an introduction, and though all of them knew Alfred, not one mentioned being courted by him.

He also had another, rather more sinister reason for his presence in the hall. Actually, it wasn't really sinister, but he wanted it to appear that way. He had been fortuitous to discover Waiter's was hosting a chess match and when he inquired, they happened to have room for one more player. Over the past sennight, Kenneth had conducted his own little investigation into Ward Crockford's affairs. The word on the street was the proprietor of Waiter's had his fingers in every nefarious transaction in London. Though Crockford went to great lengths to give the appearance of being a respected businessman, rumors and hearsay stuck to the man like honey. And what better way for Kenneth to elbow his way into the exclusive gentlemen's club than to join a chess match hosted by the notorious Crocky the Shark? After all, Kenneth had won every tournament at Cambridge. Though he might be a tad rusty, he ought to be able to hold his own in a match of highbrows.

As the first call for the waltz was announced, he found Lady Modesty in the vestibule, facing a table displaying a vase filled with calla lilies. She studied the white blooms as if they were the most riveting flowers she'd ever seen.

He stepped beside her. "*Zantedeschia aethiopica* is a rhizomatous perennial native to southern Africa."

She startled, her blue-eyed gaze meeting his, then shifting away as if she'd been caught pinching one of the blooms. Was she shy, or was she embarrassed because he'd come across her at the racetrack? At the time, the trainer had made a dreadful bungle with her name. But by the way her satin breeches had hugged her hips, there was no question as to her gender.

"I beg your pardon?" she asked, keeping her eyes averted. Obviously she didn't want him to know she had been riding around a track where women were forbidden. Moreover, she not only had been riding astride but at breakneck speed. Good heavens, if that woman had been on the back of Venom she most likely would have won the Epsom Derby rather than Ward Crockford's Red Charlie.

Kenneth pointed to the flowers. "I was referring to the cala lilies. Are you partial to them?"

Frowning, Her Ladyship tapped one of the petals. "I'm more partial to dandelions."

"Excellent choice," he agreed, though it was astonishing to encounter any lady in this ballroom with an affinity for a flower considered to be a weed. "They are well suited for pollenating insects in early spring when other flowers are not yet in bloom."

"Pollinating insects?" She cocked her head to the side seeming to ponder his words. At the racetrack, the lass most likely hadn't been aware that several strands of glorious coppery hair had escaped her cap. "Are you referring to bees?"

"I am. Especially honeybees." He offered his elbow, smiling to himself at how her cap had fallen askew. Truly, if anyone had asked him to provide a one-word descriptor for her, it was adorably tousled... but then again, that was two words and he wasn't attending the ball to find anyone adorable. There were two very specific reasons for his presence at this pompous gathering of the *ton*. "They just made the second call for the waltz. If we don't go now, we'll miss it."

"Och," she groaned, sounding as if she'd just galloped down from the Scottish Highlands. "I'd never hear the end of it from my mother."

She wrapped her fingers around his arm, her touch light but firm in a way that said this was a woman who possessed far more confidence than she allowed anyone to see. He puzzled at her unspoken self-assuredness because, thus far, she had been very reserved about meeting his gaze. Her hair was brilliantly red and adorned with curls, so lustrous, there was no need for her to wear diamonds. But then again, Kenneth also had red hair. Most of his life he had been teased for being fair-haired. He'd heard it all— no carrot-topped chap could ever be handsome, or smart, or wealthy, or well-liked, or crafty, or lucky, etcetera. Kenneth was glad his hair had begun to thin. Perhaps one day in the future, he'd have his manservant shave his head and thus end the ludicrous insults.

They were among the last to arrive on the floor, Kenneth quickly finding a place in the enormous circle of dancers, spinning Lady Modesty toward him and placing his hand on her waist. A very petite waist. Warm as well.

The music began and he suddenly wasn't quite sure with which foot to begin.

Her Ladyship pulled him, her left foot sliding back, making him follow with his right. "How often do you waltz, m'lord?"

"As infrequently as possible."

"So, I assumed."

He let her lead for a moment. "Not to worry, I might be a tad out of practice, but I shan't step on your toes."

"You are most kind," she replied, her tone sardonic.

He quickly collected his composure and took charge, stepping in, stepping out and ushering her in a turn beneath his arm as required in the slow French waltz, which had only come to London two years prior.

"Well done," she said as they once again joined side by side, facing forward, hands around each other's waists. "Tell me, how do you find being a viscount?"

"It has been rather overwhelming, given the unexpected passing of my beloved brother."

"How awful for you. I have five brothers and I canna imagine losing a single one of them. But... ?" Her voice trailed off as they executed another turning combination.

"But?" he asked when they joined together again.

Her gaze trailed to the black ribbon around his upper arm. "I'm surprised to see you here considering you are in mourning."

"Hmm," he said noncommittedly. "I assumed it was the right thing to do, considering the invitation I received from the Duke of York."

"Of course." One two three, down, up, up. "Your brother had a racehorse, did he not?"

He glanced at the lass out of the corner of his eye. Perhaps it was time to ensure there was no question Lady Modesty became mindful of the fact he knew of her jockeying endeavors. "You are well aware that he did, *Master Modistie.*"

The young lady's entire body suddenly jolted upright, making her stumble forward, though with Kenneth's hand firmly on her waist, her footwork quickly resumed the three-count step. "Wheesht!" she hissed in a whisper. "You must never again refer to me thus, else I will flatly deny I was ever there."

Kenneth inclined his lips toward her ear as he deftly plucked the diamond comb from her hair, slipping the piece into his pocket as nimbly as he had removed it. "Not to worry, my lady. I shall keep your secret as long as you keep mine."

Her eyes met his directly. They weren't merely blue, they were enormous. Azure like a midwinter's sky. Clear and brilliant, flecked with facets of gold—far more dazzling than any diamond could ever be. "What is your secret?" she whispered.

He grinned, unable to look away. "You shall find out soon enough."

AFTER LORD BERWICK escorted her to the edge of the ballroom, Modesty watched as he disappeared into the crush of the crowd, most making their way toward the cloakroom, or saying their goodbyes. Mama was deep in conversation with Lord Roxburgh and appeared as if she was in no hurry to take her leave. Kitty was surrounded by giggling ladies, though when facing the option of joining her mother or her friend, Modesty headed toward Kitty, her hand absently patting the curls piled atop her head.

She stopped abruptly, her stomach dropping to the depths of her bowels. She scarcely drew a breath as her fingers frantically searched for the diamond comb her brother had given her—the only truly exquisite piece of jewelry in her trousseau. Kitty caught her eye just as Modesty shifted directions and hastened for the door.

For the love of St. Eligius, she wasn't about to let that thieving fiend leave the ball with those diamonds! Her lady's maid should have locked them in place with a chain. Perhaps a cage over her head would have given all the vindictive gossip mongers something to talk about.

As she turned into the entrance hall, she was blocked by a crush of people crowding the floor. "Viscount Berwick?" she said loudly, though no one even bothered to look her way.

Rising onto her toes, she strained to see over heads to no avail. "Pardon me," she said, trying to push into the mob, but getting nowhere.

"You'll have to wait your turn, madam," said a beak-nosed cur with a horrible overbite.

Scoffing, Modesty, shuffled to the wall in time to spot His Lordship's red hair right before he donned his Wellington top hat and took his coat from the butler.

"Lord Berwick!" Her shout was most unladylike, but her only option to catch the thief before he took his leave. "Your secret is not—" Modesty clamped her lips together as the viscount turned, met her gaze, and tipped his hat.

"The loathsome, despicable, cheating fiend!" she seethed under her breath.

"Modesty? Whatever is the matter?" asked Kitty, touching her arm.

Whipping around and facing her friend, dozens of explanations rifled through her head, though all she managed was a strangled cry.

Kitty slid her arm around Modesty's shoulders and ushered her into a nearby parlor, which was empty, thank the stars. "What on earth has you so upset?"

Secrets. She hated keeping secrets, yet she had her own because though Kitty meant well, at the most inopportune moments she sometimes managed to blurt out things that shouldn't be uttered. Kitty didn't even know about the jockey lessons. Modesty glanced at the closed door. "You must not tell a soul."

"Of course I will not. You know you can always count on my discretion."

That was the problem. Kitty was the most loving, kindest friend, but discretion was not her strong suit. "You will not repeat a word. Swear it or I will walk away this instant!"

Kitty offered her little finger and locked it with Modesty's. "You can trust me. Our bond is stronger than a fortress."

It was. Secrets aside, Modesty was closer to Miss Katherine Mansfield than she was to either of her sisters. She drew in a deep breath, then turned and presented the back of her coiffeur where the comb should be secured. "Lord Berwick pilfered my diamond hair comb!"

"Oh, my heavens! We must inform your mother straight away."

"Have you lost your mind? Marty just purchased it for me. He said it was an early wedding gift because he was certain it would bring me luck. I canna just tell him I lost it."

A pinch creased between Kitty's perfectly arched eyebrows. "But it was *stolen*."

"Aye, and I need a chance to get it back afore we go raising the MacGalloway regiment of foot."

"You intend to retrieve it? How?"

Modesty had already formulated a plan, but it wasn't something she could share with her dearest friend. It wasn't as though Kitty intentionally shared other people's secrets. The lass simply had a way of forgetting that things were told to her in confidence. Nonetheless, Kitty usually could be counted on to remember to keep mum for a day or two. "I have wee plan, and if that doesna work, I'll talk to His Grace, but not until I've faced the cur myself and demand he return my property."

"Oh dear, you are not planning to go to his house are you? If anyone were to see—"

"Of course not, are you daft? I'd be ruined for the rest of my days."

"But you do intend to confront Berwick?" Kitty asked, leaning in expression aghast.

As she shook her head, Modesty covered her mouth. No matter how much she wanted to tell her friend exactly what she must do on the morrow, she could not. "All I need is a day, then I shall tell you everything."

They hooked their little fingers once more, then Kitty took Modesty's hand and headed for the door. "You'd best don your cloak and pull up the hood before Her Grace notices your comb is missing."

4

———

Her hair unfashionably clubbed back, Modesty stepped out of the hackney and straightened her top hat. Actually, it was her eldest brother's hat, with a bit of cotton rolled up and wedged inside the inner band so the ridiculously gargantuan John Bull wouldn't fly off her head in a breeze. She was also wearing the Duchess of Dunscaby's suit of clothes which she'd discovered in a trunk in the attic at Newhailes, one of the ducal residences near Edinburgh.

A lady never knew when it would be fortuitous to dress as a man, an opinion which had been emphasized by Modesty's sister-in-law when she'd first come to the family to work as the duke's steward, proclaiming herself to be Jules Smallwood. Actually, at the time she was Julia St. Vincent, daughter of the (former) penniless Earl of Brixham. Regardless of her gender, Julia was the best steward Martin had ever employed. Though since marrying His Grace, she was far too busy with her duties as duchess to pay any mind to the running of vast the Dunscaby estates.

Confident with her disguise, from the footpath

Modesty gazed up at the building's ivory façade with its Corinthian columns and large windows. A mammoth doorman dressed in livery guarded the entry. From her vantage point, he appeared to be quite broad shouldered and so tall he most likely had to stoop whenever he crossed a threshold.

There was no need for a placard to be affixed to the wall. Everyone knew Waiter's occupied the corner of Piccadilly and Bolton Row. Everyone also knew it was a hallowed hall for gentlemen only—aside from women of easy virtue.

Which Modesty most decidedly was not.

After taking a deep breath, she climbed the stairs and addressed the doorman in her deepest voice. "Mr. MacFee, Esquire. Barrister to the Duke of Dunscaby here."

"'Ere for the chess match are ye?"

"Aye, as a spectator."

The man opened the door and gestured inside. "Welcome to Waiter's."

The entrance hall was hewn of marble with gilt iron railings leading up a half-dozen carpeted steps, beyond which came a hum of deep voices.

"May I help you, sir?" asked a steward, standing behind an ornately carved mahogany podium.

Modesty glanced back at the closed door. She'd already given her name and purpose. "I've come for the chess match."

The steward's eyes narrowed as he studied her. "Have you been to Waiter's before?"

Was this the sort of chap who never forgot a face? If she lied, he'd most likely feed her to the giant footman outside. "No, I havena been here. I'm merely visiting from Edinburgh." She produced a card, which she'd carefully inscribed last night. "I'm the barrister to the Duke of Dunscaby."

"Are you staying with His Grace?"

"Aye."

"Did he provide you with a letter of introduction?"

Modesty shifted her weight between her feet. *Would this chap kindly leave well enough alone?* "Not precisely. An acquaintance of mine is one of the contestants in today's match."

The man leaned forward on his podium. "And who might that be?"

"Good God, Findley, this isn't Bow Street," boomed a rather rotund man descending the stairs. He bowed respectfully. "Good afternoon, Mr...?"

"MacFee." Modesty removed her hat and bowed in kind. "Esquire."

"Welcome. I'm Mr. Crockford," he said while the steward took the John Bull from her fingertips.

So this is Crocky the Shark? By the squint of his beady dark eyes, he certainly looked like a crooked gambling hell proprietor. Even his costume was overdone, from his gold satin waistcoat to the gaudy, thick gold chain attached to his pocket watch. He wore rings on all his fingers. All of them! How utterly gauche. Indeed, after reading about his pretentious appearance in the papers, Modesty would have needed no introduction to identify the man. "Verra pleased to make your acquaintance, sir. Might you tell me where to find the chess match?"

"Ah, yes, the gentlemen 'ave assembled in the gaming room. But first, might I give ye a tour of me club? Ye'll find we offer everythin' a gentleman might require." He urged Modesty to follow him up the steps into a smoke-filled hall with men filling nearly every seat from wing-backs to couches, to padded seats situated around card tables. The interior did not exactly fit her imaginings of a den of debauchery. But then again, the debauching most likely didn't occur in the front rooms.

"At Waiter's we take pride in our reputation of 'onest gamblin'," Crocky continued.

Modesty blinked rapidly, but doing so did nothing to ease the smoke irritating her eyes. "Is that so?" she asked, trying to appear as if she believed his deceitful words. Everyone knew this gambling hell was as cut-throat as any in London.

"What is your pleasure? Cards? Dice?" The man waggled his thick eyebrows, looking like a licentious double-chinned hog. "*Women?*"

Drawing back, it was all Modesty could do not to gasp. How dare he insinuate there were women of easy virtue in this establishment to a person who had just arrived? Were there not delicate protocols for addressing such matters?

"I assure you, I'm merely here to watch the gentlemen play chess." She peered around him as a group of men was allowed in, overwhelmingly welcomed by the dratted steward. "Has the tournament begun?"

"Indeed." Crocky continued through the saloon, toward double doors manned by more enormous footmen, through which the group of gentlemen was now passing. He flagged a waiter, removing two glasses of amber liquid from a silver tray. "A brandy? On the house, of course."

Completely flummoxed with the proposition of drinking brandy in public, all she managed was a half-smile as she accepted the drink. She had come to find the fiend who stole her diamond hair comb, not to imbibe in spirits. "My thanks."

Before they reached the gaming room, a woman

approached from the left. "Crockford," she said rather forwardly. "Might I 'ave a word?"

Modesty pretended to sip her brandy while carefully scrutinizing the woman. She reminded herself not to stare, she truly did. Nonetheless, her mouth dropped wide open, her eyes practically popping out of her head. *So this is a Jezabel?* The woman was quite pretty. She was polished with a figure many women of polite society would envy. Except she cheapened her appearance by wearing a scarlet dress with a vulgar abundance of black lace, its neckline revealing far too much of her for this time of day.

Crocky gave Modesty's arm a jab with his elbow.

"Oof," she grunted as the brandy sloshed onto the red carpet.

"Duty calls, Mr. MacFee. Enjoy the chess match," he said, bowing slightly.

The woman winked.

Modesty's mouth fell open. Again. *Holy macaroons! How utterly shameless!*

At least she'd been left alone to fend for herself. She strode directly to the big double doors flanked by the oversized footmen and handed one her glass. "Have a brandy, laddie. You look as if you could use one."

Not waiting for a reply, she marched through the doors as if she'd been born to grace the halls of salacious gambling hells.

The pipe smoke was every bit as thick in the crowded gaming room where spectators gathered around tables of chess players. The conversation consisted of low murmurs. Across the room, a gathering applauded at the conclusion of a game while the two contestants stood and shook hands. Next to them,

Modesty spotted her quarry and she moved toward him.

Of course, she wouldn't make a scene. She needed to wait until he finished his game then she fully intended to calmly and politely ask the fiend to have a word.

Berwick was deep in concentration, his fair eyebrows in a straight line. His hair was rather disheveled as if he'd run his fingers through it and forgot to pat it down afterward. A sunray from the window shone down across his crown, making his hair appear not only coppery, but to be thinning a tad. Modesty folded her arms and imagined him bald. He had a nice shape to his head. Perhaps he might be somewhat attractive without hair? *Aye, if he grew whiskers, he'd be marginally appealing. I wonder if his beard is soft or coarse?*

He drummed his fingers while he waited for his opponent to make a move. Berwick's fingers were extraordinarily long. *Perhaps he is a painter or a musician?*

Physically, he appeared to be in quite good condition. And his neckcloth was perfectly tied. His suit of clothes was well-tailored, yet unpretentious. In all respects most would assume him to be an honorable and trustworthy gentleman.

Except he is a thief. And I cannot abide miscreants— dastards who deign to prey on young ladies. He is a cad and a fiend and a barnacle on the satin sheen of polite society.

He knew her secret? Well, now she knew his and Modesty's certainly did not break the law. She possibly broke an ordinance or two. Definitely broke the riding club's rules. And if Berwick broadcast her riding lessons to the papers, she would most decidedly be humiliated. Possibly ruined. Of course as a viscount, the man could wheedle his way out of anything save murder. Nonetheless, his reputation would be adequately tarnished if she exposed his thievery.

After a few moves had been made, Modesty cleared her throat, the sound serving its purpose to make Berwick look up—straight at her. His eyes grew wide, right before he glanced away and ran a hand over his mouth.

She crossed her arms and tilted up her chin in challenge. *Aye, he kens why I'm here.* In the midst of this crowd, he wouldn't expose her ruse, just as she did not intend to expose his.

Berwick didn't shift his gaze her way again, though his color did take on a rather unseemly, sunburned appearance. Modesty knew all too well how easily red-headed people blushed. She was prone to blushing as well, which was infuriating. Martin always laughed at her—said he could read her like a book. What woman wanted her deepest desires and innermost thoughts broadcast by an internal reaction which she was unable to control?

When finally the steward announced they would break for luncheon to be served upstairs, Modesty strode straight to His Lordship's table. "Might I have a word, m'lord?"

He stood and grasped her upper arm, his fingers roughly digging into her flesh and sure to leave a mark. "What the devil are you doing here?" he growled, his lips not moving, his eyebrows slanted inward as if she were the person at fault.

Before Modesty responded, she allowed him to usher her into a room containing only one round card table and a sideboard with a crystal decanter, which happened to be empty. "I beg your pardon," she seethed, twisting her arm from his grip and rubbing away the burn. "But you are the one who forced me into this situation, you ill-bred, rooting hog!"

"Rooting hog?" He scoffed. "I in no way could be held responsible for your own foolish ruination."

"Oh? Do you not recall the words, 'I ken your secret and you'll soon ken mine?'"

"Good God, woman, you were not supposed to discover it missing so quickly. And when you did, I fully expected you to inform the Duke of Dunscaby forthwith. The missing comb should have been at the forefront of today's news, blast it all!"

"You expected me to upset Mama and Martin when I already kent you were the culprit? How daft do you think I am?"

He took a step away and made an exaggerated show of examining her from head to toe. "Judging by your costume, my *lady*, I have grounds upon which to believe you to be quite mad."

Growling, Modesty made a grandiose gesture at her breeches. "I think not, sir. You are the one who threatened me and—"

"I did no such thing!"

"Och, aye? You made it clear that you kent I'd been taking jockey lessons at Primrose Hill. By that statement alone you led me to believe you would expose my unladylike behavior to all of London. I would have appeared far more a lunatic if I had not devised a plan to recover my stolen comb."

Berwick scowled and sauntered around the table, grabbing the back of one of the chairs, eyeing her. "You could be ruined by coming here."

"Which is why I wore a disguise."

"Which does nothing to mask your true identity. Why, you could face ruination by the very fact you are alone, not only in a card room, but in a gentlemen's club with a man you hardly know."

Not about to allow him to confound her, she crossed her arms and did her best to appear taller. "I kent ye wouldna harm me."

"Oh do you now. How the devil did you arrive at such a decision as to my character?"

"Because of your smile," she said matter-of-factly. With five brothers and all their friends milling about over the years, Modesty had become a rather good judge of smiles and Berwick's was decidedly kind. Though mayhap she had come to her conclusion a wee bit prematurely. After all, he was a thief.

"My lady, you are making no sense whatsoever." The viscount shoved the chair toward the table. "And furthermore, do you, for one tick of the clock, believe any man in all of Christendom would not realize you're a woman?"

"You are wrong. I look verra masculine. I am not wearing a single piece of women's outer clothing and my lady's maid clubbed my hair to ensure there was no mistake as to my gender."

The man's blue eyes slowly traveled downward, stopping at Modesty's hips. "Exactly my point, madam."

She tossed her head. "I even met Mr. Crockford and he didna ken I was a lass."

"That's because the man is either blind or cares more about the coin in your purse than he does about your sex."

As heat burned Modesty's face, she grabbed an opposing chairback and mirrored his stance. "My costume aside, return my comb, and I promise I will never visit this vulgar establishment again."

"I cannot."

"Dunna tell me ye've already sold it?"

"No, but I need it. Only for a few days. A fortnight at most. Then I'll gladly return the gaudy bauble."

Good heavens, this man was insufferable. "So 'tis a loan ye're wanting?"

"Of sorts. Think of it as a favor."

Modestly barely knew the viscount and now he was asking for favors? What would he want next? Her horse? She released the chair and studied him. Why was a diamond comb so important to a man able to buy dozens of them? Or was he penniless? She hadn't read anything indicating the viscountcy was in financial peril—and such news always made the papers. Still, she didn't know his circumstances well enough.

"Tell me." She drummed her fingers against her lips. "Why do you need my diamond comb so badly?"

"It is a personal matter."

"Are you planning to tempt a woman with it? Because if you are, I'll march straight out to the gaming room and tell everyone you are a cheat and a thief and a... a... *dratted liar!*"

"No! No, I beg of you, please, my reasons are quite respectable." He gestured toward the door. "Let us quietly return to the gaming room. I shall finish my game of chess, then take care of the matter for which I came."

"Ah-a, so you are here for a purpose other than to play chess with moderate skill."

"Excuse me, but I am winning."

"You only think you are winning. All your opponent needs to do is move his pawn to d-three and you will be mated. He foxed you."

"But I—" Berwick blinked, looking aside as if envisioning the board. "Damnation."

"Now, unless you want me to immediately turn

around and expose your skullduggery, I insist you tell me exactly why you need my hair comb."

Berwick's shoulders fell as he sighed and straightened. "I have come to suspect my brother was murdered."

Goodness, that was the last thing she expected him to say. "Oh heavens. Do ye ken who did it?"

"I have an ever-growing list of suspects, but as a racing enthusiast, you are most likely aware that Mr. Crockford's horse beat my brother's in the Derby."

"Actually, I attended the race with my kin, and Venom was favored while Red Charlie was an unknown—Crocky's horse was even entered as a last-minute substitution."

"Yes," Berwick said, his eyebrows arching as if he was surprised Modesty knew the name of Crocky's horse. "Furthermore, I wanted the papers to report the diamonds missing because I've learned the man also deals on the black market. I intended to tempt him with the comb after the match."

"But wouldn't he be suspicious of you?"

"That's the point. There could be no way for you to prove I stole your comb because you were not aware of when I took it."

Modesty opened her mouth to argue his point, but he held up his palm. "The thing could have fallen out of your hair for all intents and purposes. Anyway, my ploy was—is to present a business proposition Crockford cannot refuse—one that will allow me to gain access to his underhanded operation and, with luck, expose him as a murderer."

"How exactly? Would you not need a steady supply of diamond combs?"

"Indeed. Where better to find such pieces than in

the ballrooms of the *ton*? Who better to nip them than a peer of the realm?"

"But isna that stealing? How can you return the items if ye're feeding them to the Shark?"

"I'm not planning to become a thief. However to catch a thief who is also a murderer, one has to pretend to be a person of uncouth character."

"I see." Modesty didn't see. His Lordship's plan was full of foibles. Dozens of questions came to the tip of her tongue. "But why did you not take this to Bow Street?"

"I tried. They examined the facts—the coroner pronounced Alfred's death by natural causes, and because he died alone in his bed with no signs of a struggle, they believe there is nothing further to investigate."

"You said you have a list. Aside from Crocky, who else might be on it?"

"A few loose ends mostly. I've been led to believe Alfred might have been courting someone. The day before he died, he purchased a sapphire ring for which I found the box but—"

"No ring." Modesty grinned as the picture began to transform from blurred to murky. "Och, I can help ye."

"I beg your pardon? You need to go home and do whatever it is young ladies of your ilk do."

"Dunna ye see? Just because I'm female doesna mean I'm useless. I *can* help you. Who better to find out who the former viscount was courting than the sister of a duke who happens to be in London for her first Season?"

Berwick studied her. "Are you aware of whom my brother was courting?"

"Nay, but I can find out."

"Thank you for your concern, but no. Alfred's death is a mystery I must solve on my own."

As he straightened and moved around the table, Modesty blocked his path. "I have endured quite enough of men who overlook my value because I am female. Because I have red hair and freckles, men like you assume I'm a flibbertigibbet. But I'll tell you here and now, I have a mind and a strong will, and I am able to access places where you, sir, are not allowed."

"Such as?"

"Such as lady's withdrawing rooms. Such as tea parties for ladies only. Such as chess games in homes where women are actually allowed to play." The last item was merely a reflection of her irritation at being excluded from such games when she was the best chess player in her family. And by the fact that he had no idea he'd already lost his match, she was reasonably confident she was more skilled at chess than Berwick.

He offered his elbow. "My carriage is waiting in the alleyway. I'll have my driver see you home."

"I willna go. Not until you agree."

He huffed, irritation reflected in his eyes. "*If* you believe you can find out who my brother might have been courting without informing everyone in London that I'm looking for Alfred's murderer, I see no harm in allowing you to make a few discrete enquiries."

"Do you honestly believe I would reveal your secret?"

"You have given me no grounds upon which to assume otherwise."

"I disagree. I could have told everyone at last night's ball you stole my comb. And if you are too arrogant to realize that I would be believed even if you tried to disgrace me, then I shall spit in your eye. My brother would believe me and—"

"That is what I was counting on."

"Oh." Modesty brushed an imaginary particle of lint from her jacket. "So, are we agreed?"

With a hard set to his jaw, Berwick took her hand and placed it in the crux of his elbow. "Why do I feel I shall regret this?"

"You willna." She slid her hand away and rubbed her palm on her breeches. "If you escort me out to the gaming room as you would a lady, everyone will ken I'm a woman."

5

———

If only Kenneth could take his leave of Lady Modesty and return to his bloody chess game. Except he had no option but to spirit her out of Waiter's before everyone present realized she was not only a woman, but the sister of the esteemed Duke of Dunscaby. Besides, it was his fault she had come in the first place. He was the reason she'd donned such a ridiculous disguise. If he hadn't taken the blasted comb, she would be happily embroidering seat cushions or engaged in some other appropriate pursuit.

Worse, she wasn't supposed to come after him. Nor was she supposed to know outright it had been he who'd taken the comb. Perhaps he had been too revealing when he said he knew her secret and she would soon know his.

For some mindless reason, at the ball he'd been overwhelmingly tempted to tease her. He was never one to tease, but the woman was so damned adorable —like a puppy one could not resist hugging. Except quite unlike a puppy. Even though her enormous blue eyes did sparkle with a hint of mischief.

What man could resist such a woman when she waltzed as smoothly as a proficient skating on ice?

Wrapping Modesty MacGalloway in his arms could lead to his undoing. Never in all his days had his knees turned boneless as they'd done when he placed his hand on her delicate waist during the waltz last eve. However, an embrace was utterly out of the question. Unthinkable. In fact, Kenneth resolutely determined he must never touch her again.

Perhaps he should have opted for the cotillion or a minuet? Kenneth had only to blame his flapping tongue on the champagne he'd consumed before the damned waltz. Bubbling spirits always managed to go straight to his head. Even beer was more intoxicating to him than a glass of brandy. He sipped brandy—made a glass last for an hour at least. Last night's champagne? Two glasses had slid down his gullet as fast as cool water.

Now it was time to wash his hands of this self-imposed debacle. The issue at hand was Lady Modesty was obviously too clever for her own good. Perhaps she should have been born a man because she certainly handled a horse like one. Dear God, she'd galloped her thoroughbred around the racetrack as if they'd been shot out of a cannon.

Regardless of her skill with the reins, the imp certainly did not fill out a pair of breeches like a man. Her hips were smooth and as round as an hourglass. Her face was far too fetching with delicate arched eyebrows, and a pert little mouth that could not possibly be masculine. Despite her adorable freckles, his fingertips already knew her skin was softer than velvet. The problem was he couldn't stop thinking about how much he wanted to find out for certain.

Damnation! The last thing I need is a woman making a bungle of my investigation.

He cracked his knuckles. "Very well, in order to

avoid a spectacle, not to mention an unmitigated scandal, we shall walk out together and head straight for the rear entry."

"But what about your luncheon? Are you not hungry?" Lady Modesty asked.

Kenneth was famished. "I assure you, I will not be able to eat anything until I am assured you are safely within my carriage and headed for home."

She gave a nod and together they strode through the gaming room, which was empty aside from a handful of oversized footmen guarding the chessboards. Kenneth looked to where he'd been sitting and resisted the urge to examine the board. He had little cause to doubt Her Ladyship's accusation that he was about to lose. Perhaps he'd been distracted by her presence. After all, he wasn't usually one to overlook a pawn about to cause him to be mated.

"This way," he said, leading her through a corridor.

"Oh goodness, I've been so preoccupied about the prospect of solving your mystery I forgot to ask when I can expect you to return my comb. The Ruthland Ball is in a fortnight. It is Almack's most heralded event of—"

"First of all, *you* are not going to solve the mystery of Alfred's death. You are merely to use your network of friends to discover who my brother might have been courting." He opened the door. "And as for your comb, I give you my word it shall be returned before the ball."

"But—" Her expression abruptly changing from curious to astounded, Lady Modesty stopped and clapped her hands to her head. "Oh, my goodness, I forgot my hat."

Hoping no one heard the woman squeaking like a capricious Highland lass, Kenneth glanced down the corridor. Damnation, they were nearly outside. They couldn't waltz back to the entrance hall for a damned hat. "I'll buy you a new one."

"One that fits?" she asked with a saucy toss of her head. "Martin's head is enormous."

Kenneth placed his palm in the small of her back and urged the woman to continue. "Certainly."

"I shall hold you to it." He opened the door and she walked through. "Just so you are aware, on the morrow I will be having tea with my sister the Countess of Brixham and my dear friend Kitty. I will start making inquiries about your brother there."

"Excellent," he replied, not really listening, as he caught his driver's eye. The chap's gaze quickly shifted upward, his expression changing from congenial to alarm.

An immediate sense of foreboding caused the hair on the back of Kenneth's neck to enflame.

Time slowed while the outside air turned deathly still.

Jolted by the sound of shattering glass above, he lunged for the lady, wrapping his arms around her while hurling toward the cobblestones. Twisting as they fell, Kenneth managed to turn enough to absorb most of the impact with his shoulder, protecting Lady Modesty from the jarring fall.

Her high-pitched screech rankled his eardrums.

The sharp cascade of glass clattered around them as Kenneth rolled aside, doing his best to shield the woman in his arms... right before a body landed exactly where they had been standing. The sickening thud chilled Kenneth to the bone as he tightened his grip around Her Ladyship and shifted his gaze to the chilling, vacant eyes of Ward Crockford.

With a startle, Lady Modesty screamed, her body trembling. "He-he-he's deaaaaad!"

Her movement made Kenneth's hand shift across her back. Warm liquid oozed between his fingers. "You're bleeding," he said, pulling a shard of glass from her coat.

"A-a-a man just fell out of a window and you're worried about a wee drop of blood?" She plunged her head atop his chest rather forcibly. "I-I just spoke to him when I arrived!"

"I know," Kenneth replied, looking upward as a shadow moved in the window above. The shadow sent another chill through his blood as if an evil spirit had arrived to make Crockford pay his penance. "Come, I must spirit you away from here before everyone within fifty paces knows a woman was masquerading as a man in Waiter's at the time the proprietor fell to his death."

Appearing to be dazed and befuddled, Lady Modesty started to shift off of him, her legs in a tangle as if she wasn't quite sure what to do next.

"We'll go slowly." In one motion, he sat, holding her in his arms, grunting as his shoulder twinged with pain.

"You're hurt as well," she said, making no move to slide off his lap.

"'Tis nothing," he growled in a low whisper as a line of footmen raced out the door. "Remember you are a man."

His words seemed to ignite a fire in the woman, because she crawled aside, grimacing with pain. "Ouch," she hissed in a deeper voice while Crocky's men surrounded his corpse.

"I saw someone up there!" Kenneth pointed to the window as he tugged Her Ladyship to her feet. "Perhaps you can catch him. Hurry!"

A number of footmen raced back inside while a gathering crowd was so fixated on the dead body they hardly noticed Kenneth and Lady Modesty. He took advantage of their distraction and spirited the trembling woman into his carriage, still waiting a good ten yards away from where Crockford had met his end, thank God.

"Take us home," he said to the driver.

Once inside, Lady Modesty scooted to the far end of the bench. Judging by her ability to move quickly, either her wound wasn't terribly serious or else she was in shock and the pain would come later. "I canna go to your home. It wouldna be proper. In fact, we shouldna be in a carriage together."

The jolt of the wheels starting away made Kenneth drop against the seat—or else he'd just dropped because he was flabbergasted beyond all measure. "Would you prefer to go to your brother's town house looking as if you've been stabbed in the back?"

"Nay." She groaned. "Verra well, if you'll lend me a shirt. But we must enter through the mews. And I am still a man, mind you. If anyone in your household reveals I am the Duke of Dunscaby's sister, I'll be ruined for the rest of my days."

Though the situation was quite dire, Kenneth tried in vain to hold in his laugh while a snort escaped through his nose. This woman who traipsed around London in men's clothing was worried about her reputation?

"Ye're laughing at me."

"No," he fibbed. "Though I do find it somewhat

astonishing that you give a fig about what anyone thinks of you."

"Not true. I care a great deal. 'Tis merely—"

"Hmm?"

"I tire of being the youngest. I tire of everyone telling me what I ought to do and no one believing I can be accomplished at anything."

Kenneth rolled his shoulder, satisfied his joints still seemed to be in working order. "I think you're a very accomplished equestrian."

"Thank you, but I meant to say anything that matters."

"You do not believe the ability to handle a high-spirited racehorse matters?"

"You are insufferable." Modesty arched her back and grimaced. "I'm speaking of all the things society values in a woman. I'm no' terribly graceful, or beautiful, or musically inclined. I find embroidery dull, and I always skim the pages of books so I can speed to the end and find out what happened. Furthermore, my mother thinks I should have been born a lad."

So did Kenneth. "I think you're beautiful," he blurted. Dear God, had he truly uttered such a damnable fallacy? Modesty MacGalloway had too many freckles to be beautiful in the sense of what society believed to be iconic beauty, but she was interesting.

No, that's not it.

Darling?

Cute?

Certainly not pretty?

Multifaceted, definitely.

Oddly alluring and impossible to ignore was more apt, but how does a man express such a sentiment without sounding like an absolute cad?

Rather than gush with grateful appreciation, Her Ladyship eyed him with those intense blues he suspected never missed anything. "I have five brothers and a sister who in her first and only Season was the bonniest lass of the *ton*. I ken my weaknesses as well as my strengths, so dunna go and try to make me feel like a diamond of the first water."

No sooner had she given him the command to close his gob did she curl over and cover her face with her hands. "Och, I canna believe Crocky just fell out of a window not but inches away from where we stood."

By Kenneth's estimation the chap landed exactly where they'd been standing.

"And you were planning to speak with him." She threw out her hands. "He was one of your suspects. Do you still reckon he murdered your brother?"

"I have no idea." Kenneth swiped a hand down his face. Something told him Ward Crockford's death wasn't an accident either. But would anyone be able to prove the man had been murdered? Moreover, Kenneth had no reason whatsoever to assume the death of his brother and that of Crocky were related. The only common denominator he knew of was the fact both men had horses running in the Epsom Derby.

~

THIS WAS AN ABSOLUTELY untenable turn of events. All Modesty had intended to do was retrieve her comb. Once her heartbeat returned to a somewhat normal rhythm, she felt as if she'd truly been dirked in the back. And now she was alone in a carriage with a man she hardly knew who had already stolen from her. What if his character was salacious? What if he harbored torture devices in his town house?

What if he murdered his brother to claim the viscountcy?

Well, I cannot allow my imagination to go that far. After all, it was widespread knowledge Kenneth Davenport was in northern England when his brother met his end. Even the funeral had to be postponed until the new viscount arrived.

She regarded Berwick out of the corner of her eye while the afternoon's catastrophe repeated in her mind. Honestly, if it hadn't been for His Lordship, she would have surely been crushed by Mr. Crockford's immense bulk.

Och, it is still too horrible to think of!

The viscount had reacted before Modesty even knew the windowpane was shattering. She fully expected to land face-first on the cobblestones, but at the very last instant, he had turned, protecting her from harm. Except, since she ended up on top of Berwick, she'd been struck by a shard of glass.

His Lordship shifted the carriage curtain aside. "We've turned into the mews. Do you need assistance alighting, my lady?"

Though he had a captivating deep voice that spilled through her like warm chocolate, she needed to maintain all pretenses of her disguise. "I am perfectly able, thank you."

"As you wish," he replied, opening the door, then hopping down.

"Oof," Modesty grunted, her back searing with a sharp pang as she scooted toward the opening.

"Are you all right?"

She'd been better. "'Tis merely a scratch," she managed to grunt, once again affecting her deepest voice as she lumbered down to the step, which in her estimation was far too low, making her overstretch her leg.

Berwick led the way in through the back door and past the kitchens where a cook hardly gave them a glance.

"There you are, my lord," said a man dressed in a black butler's suit of clothes. "I was expecting you at the front door."

"My friend, Mr. ah... Modistie was struck by a shard of glass, I'm afraid."

"How awful." The butler gave Modesty a concerned once-over. "Shall I fetch some water and rolls of bandages?"

"No," Modesty replied. "Thank you."

"Please do." Berwick led her toward the servant stairs. "And send Mrs. Fielding to my bedchamber with a needle and thread."

"I'm afraid the housekeeper had to urgently leave London for a fortnight or two. Her father is quite ill. Shall I bring up those items as well?"

"Yes, if you please."

Modesty jabbed the viscount with her elbow. "I dunna require stitching."

For heaven's sake, she couldn't go above stairs with a man. Biting her lip, she waited until the butler was out of sight before she stopped midway up the stairs and faced Berwick. Blast it all, he was still taller even though she was standing a step above. "I canna go to your bedchamber," she whispered with sharp emphasis.

"But that is where I keep my shirts." He urged her to keep going. "I give you my word I shall not importune you."

"How can I believe you—a man who stole from me?" she asked over her shoulder.

"I said I would return the comb." As they reached the next floor, he stepped around her, holding out the piece with its gaudily sparkling diamonds. "Here."

"Thank you." she said, taking it and following him into his dratted bedchamber. If her mother ever found out about this, she would convert to Catholicism just to send Modesty to a nunnery and lock her inside for the duration of eternity.

"Would you like me to have a look at your wound?"

She stood in the middle of the floor, her arms crossed over her chest. "You?" she scoffed. "Now I ken you're a wee numpty."

"I beg your pardon?"

"No." She gaped at the huge four-poster bed and took a giant step away from it. "If you would kindly give me a clean shirt and leave me be, I shall be on my way in short order."

He tapped her elbow and urged her to turn her back to him. "By the looks of the hole in your coat, you'll need a replacement as well."

Modesty merely needed to slip into her brother's carriage house where she'd left her pelisse in a dusty old sedan chair—at least it was dusty on the outside. "The coat I'm wearing will be fine."

"At least it is black and doesn't show the blood overmuch."

She waited impatiently while he fetched a shirt and then accepted two rolls of bandages, a bowl of warm water, and a needle with a spool of cotton from the butler. Once the door closed, His Lordship placed the items on the washstand. "Your wound is awfully close to your spine. Are you certain you need no assistance? I could ring for a housemaid."

"And have her ken there's a woman in your bedchamber? I would die of the scandal." Modesty stretched her back and winced. "It isna all that bad. Please go. If I dawdle here much longer, I shall be missed."

"Something tells me a woman who slips out to spend time at a racetrack harbors any number of excuses as to her whereabouts."

She coughed with exasperation. In truth, her lady's maid was a jewel who could never be replaced in that respect. Modesty had never stayed out all night, but if she did Randolph wouldn't allow a soul inside her bedchamber. She just thanked the stars she had no engagements this evening, which was a rare occasion, given this was the height of the Season.

She removed the shirt from his fingertips. "Go. Please."

"Very well." He pointed to an adjoining door. "I shall be in there should you need anything."

"I willna."

As soon as she was alone, Modesty made quick work of removing her ill-fitting coat, waistcoat, neckcloth, and shirt, the back of which was saturated with blood. She turned away from the mirror and regarded her stays over her shoulder and hissed. They were brand new and utterly ruined. Though they most likely prevented the glass from cutting deeper.

She picked up a bandage roll and worked to wrap it around her torso as fast as it would unroll. The fifth time around, she knocked the bowl of water off the washstand, lunged to catch it, the blasted thing slipping just beyond her reach and shattering on the floor as she lost her balance and fell into the puddle.

Before she could manage a shriek, Berwick barreled back through the door and dropped to his knees beside her. "What happened? Are you hurt?"

Modesty curled into a ball, crossing her hands over her chest. "You canna be in here."

"This is my house, my bedchamber, and I can be anywhere I please." He leaned over her and studied her back. "You wore stays?"

"Aye. They're more effective than bindings."

He leaned nearer—far to near in Modesty's estimation. "And by the looks of it, they most likely saved your life."

She tried to twist around to have a wee peek, but her injury was in a most inaccessible spot. "Perhaps if I try with another bandage... "

"I think not. You're still bleeding." He tugged the laces. "This contraption needs to come off."

"What?" she shrieked, clutching her arms across her breasts. "Absolutely not."

"Then I'll have to send for the doctor."

"No!"

"Then who? I'm not jesting, madam. You need care. Someone must see to your wound." He rose and headed for the bell pull. "I'm sending for your brother."

"No, no, no, no!"

Berwick turned and crossed his arms. "Your brother or a doctor. What will it be?"

Groaning, Modesty dropped her head forward. The viscount had already seen her bare shoulders, she may as well avoid having a bevy of other men see her in such a shocking state of undress. "I shall allow you to have a wee glimpse of my wound."

"Thank you."

For the love of Moses, he untied her laces more deftly than Randolph ever did. "You have experience with women's garments?"

"A bit."

"I do not believe you."

"All right. I may have unlaced a set of stays or two in the past."

She didn't push him further, though she imagined the number to be significantly higher than a few.

He hissed as the garment opened.

"Is it bad?" she asked, cringing.

"Nothing a half-dozen stitches won't fix."

"Six? You canna be serious!"

6

Kenneth held up the decanter. "More brandy?" he asked, quite unsure if he was doing the right thing. Obviously, he didn't want to cause her pain but he wasn't keen to see the woman in her cups either.

Lady Modesty swayed on the settee. She still had the bandage wrapped around her ruined stays and a quilt draped over her shoulders. "One more wee dram, I reckon." This was her third, and, with each tot, her Scottish burr became more pronounced like a Highland lass who'd been cloistered away in the Outer Hebrides all her life.

He thought twice before refilling her glass, but stitches hurt when a nimble-fingered physician was sewing them. Kenneth had only sewn up injured animals and they bellowed plenty. Who knew how much the stitches would hurt when he picked up the needle and thread?

She sipped and scrunched her well-freckled nose. "It isna like wine 'cause the taste doesna improve at all after the first few swallows."

"I suppose that is a good thing, otherwise there would be a great many more men wandering about in their cups."

"And women," she mumbled, taking another drink. She sat for a moment, then dropped her chin to her chest. "Och, what you must think of me. I am a disheveled mess."

"Not at all," he said, replacing the decanter on the sideboard, returning with his glass.

"I dunna want you to think I'm a loose glove, ye ken. Ye canna ever utter a word about this. After all, if you hadna stolen my diamonds, I wouldna be in this position."

If he regretted pinching the damned comb before, he did so doubly now. Kenneth needed time to think. The person at the top of his list of suspected murderers had just fallen out of a window, yet there he was, playing healer to a young lady who should be sitting in her drawing room, enjoying a cup of tea. *Tea, dammit!* Not swilling brandy in his bedchamber.

Kenneth moved to sit beside her on the settee, but halted, deciding Her Ladyship might be more comfortable if he opted for the chair opposite. "You have my word, none of what has transpired this day will be remembered."

She slumped a bit farther. "I kent I wasna fetching enough for the likes of you."

"I beg your pardon?" he asked, completely flummoxed. No, Lady Modesty MacGalloway wasn't beautiful by polite society's standards, but she did have a unique allure, exemplified by the mere fact he'd been unable to ignore her since setting foot in the Duke of York's damned ballroom. He thought to reach for her hand but stopped himself and curled his fingers into a fist. "You misunderstood me. I simply meant to say I will not betray your confidence."

"Oh." She smiled, quickly hiding her grin behind her hand. The lady had a lovely smile. Her bottom lip a tad fuller than the top and her eyes sparkled as if she alone possessed the key to happiness.

He sipped. She did as well. "Tell me about the horse you were riding at the racetrack," he said.

This time her smile brightened the entire room like a sunbeam radiating through a windowpane. "Poseidon. He's retired from the track, of course, because Marty wouldna allow me to buy a horse who was still racing. My brother insists racing horses in their prime are far too spirited for the likes of me."

The duke appeared to be a reasonable man. Though Kenneth had seen Dunscaby a time or two, he was still too new to the title to come to know the duke. "Well, Poseidon certainly is no nag."

Her expression changed yet again to that of a satiated cat. Unlike most Englishwomen who had a reputation for their stoicism, Modesty was quite expressive. "He's faster than Marty kens."

"Hmm. That surprises me. I'd think His Grace would be an excellent judge of horse flesh."

"Mayhap, but I'm better. Take Venom for instance."

Kenneth sat straighter. "You are familiar with my brother's horse?"

"I wagered on him."

"You?"

"Well, Kitty and I wagered between us."

He recalled Brixham's sister, she was rather fetching, and more like a typical darling of the *ton*. But Kenneth wasn't interested in darlings even redheaded ones wrapped in quits sitting on his bedchamber's settee. Still, he did want to know more about his brother's champion. "How well-acquainted are you with Venom?"

"I've admired him from a distance," she replied,

sighing as if the horse was an untouchable beau with whom she had fallen hopelessly in love. Either that or she was well and truly falling into her cups. "Since he's housed in the same stable as Poseidon, I've slipped him the odd piece of li-*erp*-corice." She placed her glass on the low table, then patted her lips. "Pardon me. I'd best no' finish that wee dram, else I willna find my way home."

Though there was no chance he would allow the young lady to leave his house unescorted, Kenneth agreed and reached for the needle, which he'd already threaded. "Are you ready?"

Her brow furrowed. "Must I be?"

"I think it is time we take care of your injury. Will there not be someone searching for you soon?"

She glanced at the mantle clock and Kenneth followed her gaze. It was nearly half past three in the afternoon. "No' right away. Fortunately, Mama is has gone to Bath to take the waters with some of her friends." She snorted with a hiccup. "Kitty and I have dubbed them the Wayward Widows."

"Truly? How did you arrive at such a name?"

"Well, Wicked Widows didna fit, and meddlesome didna start with a W. So, since they annually gather in London and leave their families to go on a wee jaunt about the countryside, we settled for wayward."

Kenneth chuckled. He and Alfred had dubbed a number of people with bynames, though most of them were far more insulting than *wayward*. He shifted to the settee and lightly touched the quilt covering Modesty's shoulder. "May I?"

"I'll do it," she said, turning her back to him and allowing the quilt to slip down to her hips.

She slowly unrolled the bandages as if she was aware of how much doing so tortured him. With heavy-lidded eyes, she glanced over her shoulder, stirring a fire within him. But she was an innocent. A woman who knew little to nothing about seducing men.

God save him, her skin was the color of fresh cream and appeared to be softer than the downy coat on a newborn lamb. If only he could press his lips to her nape and allow himself a small sample of such succulence. But he'd promised to behave. Kenneth might have raised his share of skirts over the years, but he was still a man of his word.

Instead, he waited for her to finish and then she clutched the blanket over her chest as if she were inordinately self-conscious. Her shyness he could believe.

Forcing himself to revert his attention to the task at hand, Kenneth inspected the wound. "The bleeding has stopped for the most part."

"Do I still need stitches?"

He gently placed his fingers on either side of the scarlet and jagged wound. Pressing, the cut opened and a stream of blood trickled downward. Kenneth was not a doctor, but he did tend to the wounds of his sheep, and past experience had taught him it was best to err on the side of caution. "Perhaps only a couple."

"Two?"

"Or three." Cringing, he applied the needle.

With a gasp, Modesty jolted and arched away, making the needle drop from his fingertips. "*Screaming banshees*, ye said if I drank a wee tot or two of brandy, it wouldna hurt!"

Kenneth fished the needle out of the pile of bandages. "I said it wouldn't hurt as *badly*."

"Dunna lie to me. That hurt."

"I didn't even draw a drop of blood," he said,

though on closer inspection, he'd drawn more than a drop.

She arched and looked over her shoulder as if she could see anything in the middle of her back, let alone a pinprick. "Are ye certain ye ken how to wield a needle and thread?"

"I've sewn up many wounds in my past," he replied, conveniently leaving out the fact that his ministrations had all been on animals. Sheep, mostly, but he had set a dog's broken leg once. "Try drawing in a deep breath and releasing it slowly."

Lady Modesty did as he asked twice after which, the tension in her shoulders visibly eased. Before Kenneth tried again, he placed one of his palms onto her cool flesh. His hands were always warm, and his action was rewarded by the slightest of sighs.

"Tell me about Kitty," he said to distract her.

"She's my dearest friend."

"How did you meet?"

"Och, 'tis quite a story."

"I have time," he replied, carefully pushing the needle through the two open halves of skin.

Lady Modesty hissed and shifted a little but didn't come unglued like before. "Well, after Marty married Julia, he purchased the Brixham estate for his wife because it was where she grew up—her da was the former earl, ye ken...

"Julia wanted to turn it into a home for young ladies who had fallen upon difficult times. I traveled there with my eldest sister, Charity." Modesty turned her ear over her shoulder. "Charity was given the opportunity to run the household for the summer."

"Was she?" Kenneth asked.

"Aye, and shortly after we arrived the barn's roof caved in—nearly killing me, mind you—and the butcher came to repair it. He also was a carpenter of sorts, not to mention a boxer. Anyway, he brought his sister along with him, who happened to be Kitty."

After tying off the first stitch, Kenneth made another. "But I thought she was the Earl of Brixham's sister."

"I wasna finished with the story yet, was I?"

"Continue," he said, tying a knot flush with Her Ladyship's skin.

"Well, I reckon Charity fell in love with Harry afore he found out he was next in line for the earldom. I even stumbled upon them kissing behind the woodshed. Och, afterward, Mama was ready to lock my sister into one of the towers at Stack Castle... until the Regent's man came to tell Harry his third great grandfather happened to be the twelfth Earl of Brixham. It took the royal offices months and months to track the line back five generations, but once they had, they named Harry the seventeenth earl."

"A butcher, did you say?"

"Aye, and a boxer. The man is as strong as an ox."

Alfred's death had come as enough of a shock. But Kenneth had been raised as a second son in the viscountcy. He was the spare. And as such, he generally had received the same schooling as Alfred. At least until Kenneth opted to study biological inheritance at university. "Goodness, the change from commoner to a peer must have been a difficult transition," he said, unable to fathom how hard it must have been for a butcher to take up his mantle in the House of Lords.

As he snipped the thread, Modesty actually yawned. "Mayhap at first but he had my sister to help him. And my brother, of course."

"What happened to the home for young ladies?"

"Chairty and Brixham still run it. Though once

Hyacinth was born they added a wing to the manor to keep the family and the boarders somewhat separate."

"I'm glad to hear it," Kenneth said, resting the shears and the needle on the low table.

"Why?"

"I suppose it is easy to turn one's back on philanthropy, especially once a person is faced with the rigors of raising a family."

"Charity would never think of such a thing. She's the kindest, most gentle woman I ken." Modesty looked to the table and yawned. "Why did you stop?"

"Because I'm finished." Kenneth raised the quilt and gently placed it over her shoulders, ever so sad to see such loveliness once again hidden from him. "Tell me, if your sister is so congenial, might I send for her? Something tells me if the countess is the matron of a home for young ladies who've fallen on difficult times, she would be likely to keep your confidence."

"Charity?" Lady Modesty tugged the blanket closed. "I think not. If Charity kens I've been masquerading about as a man, then Kitty will find out, and though I love Kitty as much as my own sisters, she canna keep a secret for more than a day or two."

"But Lady Brixham keeps confidences?" he asked.

"Och aye. If it werena for Kitty living in their town house, I most likely would tell Charity everything, even about learning to be a jockey."

Perhaps he could summon the countess and speak to her about Modesty's concerns. "How long do you intend to visit the racetrack without His Grace finding out about it?"

"At least through the duration of the Season." Sitting a bit taller, Lady Modesty chuckled. "Mr. Willett says I'm better that most of the jockeys he kens."

"From what I've seen, I'm not surprised, but truly

you do not expect to jockey in a sanctioned horse race? Women are forbidden."

"Och, tell me something I dunna ken. But I love horses. I love the feel of the wind in my hair, galloping faster than most lassies ever dared. Aye, more than anything, I want to prove myself on a real racetrack in a real race, but I ken my place."

"I see," he said, though he wasn't quite sure he understood. Was she referring to her gender or her role as sister to a duke?

"Mama reminds me at her every opportunity," Her Ladyship continued, while the quilt slipped off one shoulder. Perhaps she was still a bit affected by the brandy. "I'm to make a good match. I'm to act the proper lady and marry well. I'm no' to travel and see the world. I'm no' to go anywhere without an escort, and I'm most definitely no' supposed to be traipsing about London in men's breeches."

Kenneth plucked the edge of the blanket to shift it back over her bare shoulder. However, he hesitated for a moment. He'd never really thought much about highborn women's lives. But everything Her Ladyship had said was the absolute truth. She had no freedom to move about, especially not on her own. True, he'd assumed most young ladies were content with their lives, having tea, embroidering linens, and attending soirees. But certainly not everyone was suited for such a life. Perhaps that's why they invented the term bluestocking.

Yes, Lady Modesty's shoulder was as beautiful as a calla lily, but this woman was as faceted as the dandelions her sister had pegged her with. Before Kenneth thought better of it, his lips caressed her lovely shoulder—not a ravishing kiss, but an expression of reverence, of understanding, of recognition of her worth.

A tiny gasp sounded beside his ear. "Sir," she whispered, the sound far womanlier than he might have expected.

"Forgive me," he uttered, meeting her half-lidded gaze. Her lips were parted and moist and if Kenneth didn't know better, he'd think she was inviting him to impart a passionate kiss.

Instead, he stood and cleared his throat, pretending he'd never had a single yearning for the red-headed lass whom he watched ride a horse like wildfire. "I'll go fetch another roll of bandages."

7

Berwick's delicious lips brushed her shoulder time and time again. And with each press of those warm, masculine lips, she yearned to turn her head and capture his mouth—to kiss him fully and wrap her arms around his neck, and—

"Modesty?"

"G'way," she garbled, groggy and suddenly sore-headed, rather than besotted by feathery kisses. Dreaming during the day was always so much more vivid than it was at night, but being roused in the middle of a fanciful dream was miserable.

"Good heavens, if you dunna wake now, I'll have to toss a glass of water in your face!"

Modesty's eyes snapped open. "Charity?" she asked, wondering why her sister was there and... Good glory, she was still in Berwick's bedchamber. Aside from her loose stays, which barely concealed anything, she was naked from the waist up, merely covered by a blanket. "W-what are you doing here?"

"I beg your pardon? The question is what are you doing here of all places? Merciful fairies, I thought you had better sense than to traipse around London dressed as a man. Do you have any care whatsoever for your reputation?"

"Berwick told you?" she asked, clutching the blanket under her chin and sitting up, reminding herself to kick him in the shins regardless of whether or not if he'd kissed her shoulder with more passion than she'd ever imagined possible.

"He said you were at Waiter's when Mr. Crockford was stricken by asphyxiation and fell to his death."

"Ye ken about Crocky?" Modesty rubbed her temples, willing her megrim to clear. "But he fell out of a window. Are you certain he died of asphyxiation?"

"Aye, the news is all over London. Everyone kens."

Modesty glanced at the mantel clock. Two entire hours had passed since she'd last looked at it at half three. Why did His Lordship allow her to fall asleep? And in his bedchamber of all places? If anyone aside from Charity had come, her life would be over.

"Now let me have a look at your wound."

Modesty turned her back enough for her sister to pull away the bandages and take a wee peek at the viscount's needlework. "'Tis angry red, but I daresay the stitching is sound. Does it hurt overmuch?"

"Not anymore."

Charity gave the bandage a gentle pat. "Berwick said he had to make three stitches himself because you refused to let any of the maids in the house see you."

"Aye, because I'd be ruined for certain."

"Ruined?" Charity threw her arms wide, casting her gaze from one wall to the other. "You are presently in a state of undress in a viscount's bedchamber. Your clothing is bloodstained and your hair clubbed back as if you were planning to smoke cigars and swill whisky at a dratted gentleman's club." Charity fumbled with the buttons on her blue woolen redingote. "'Tis a verra good thing Mama isna here to see how close you came to serious injury, else you'd be locked in your bedchamber for the rest of your days—either that or she'd arrange a hasty marriage with some odiferous, elderly baron who canna see beyond his nose."

"Did Berwick tell you why I had no choice but to dress as a man and make wee appearance at Waiter's?"

"Why does the reason matter?"

"Because he nicked my diamond hair comb when we waltzed last eve."

Charity shrugged out of the redingote. "Stolen by a viscount? *Pshaw*. How could you be certain he was the culprit who stole it?"

Modesty retrieved her bloodied jacket from where it was draped over the settee's arm, reached into the pocket, and pulled out the comb. "I kent as soon as the waltz was over and I kent Marty would make a fuss, so I took it upon myself to retrieve the bauble. Ye ken the *Gazette* reported Berwick as one of the contestants in the chess match at Waiter's?"

Sighing, Charity lowered herself onto the settee. "So, you dressed in breeches and went to confront him?"

"Aye." Modesty rushed ahead. "That's when I discovered His Lordship is trying to find out who murdered his brother. Since Crocky was at the top of his list of suspects, he was planning to entice the fiend with the stolen comb—then I upset his ploy because rather than complain to Marty who Berwick assumed would have reported the piece missing to the magistrate, had I not kent who stole it. But it seems Berwick underestimated me in every way. I went to Waiter's to face the thief myself."

"I still canna believe you did such a thing. What

were you thinking? Your disguise might have been revealed and you never would have been able to show your face in polite society again."

"Aye? Just like you could have been ruined when you were out in the barn taking boxing lessons afore you married Harry? What about Julia when she dressed as a man and took the position of steward to our brother?"

Charity picked up Modesty's half-full glass of brandy and swirled the liquid. "Good heavens, it seems we MacGalloway women are an adventuresome lot." She returned the glass, then slid an arm around Modesty's shoulders. "But you could have been killed, and I'd never forgive you for being so careless with your sweet self."

Modesty reached back and ran her fingers across her newly bandaged wound. "I didna ken Crocky would fall out a window."

Charity took Modesty's coat and held it up, hissing when she spotted the slash made by the shard of glass. "There's more you're not telling me, is there not?"

"Och, nay. I kent Berwick took my diamonds and I went to confront him. I didna expect to end up here."

"I understand, but what I meant to say is this isna the first time you've dressed as a man is it?"

Modesty's face burned. Blast it all, why did she have to turn as red as an apple whenever anyone asked her to be honest about something she'd rather sidestep? She had kept her secret from Kitty but the lass must have found out all the same. "What has Kitty told you?"

Tossing the coat onto the low table, Charity sighed. "She merely said you're always away at the same time every Sunday and she's beginning to think you're having secret rendezvous. Please tell me you're not taking boxing lessons."

"I'm not."

"But you are doing something unladylike. I ken you, Modesty Alice MacGalloway and you've never been one to stand on convention."

"Aye, well just try to be me for a day. Freckles and flaming red hair—pair me up with Kitty and her lovely complexion and her blonde locks. Ye ken what the gossips are whispering behind my back."

"They wouldna dare!"

"Och, ye have been away from ballrooms for too long. They all say Kitty should be sister to a duke, and I should be a dratted scullery maid."

"What an awful thing to say. I canna believe it."

"Well, I overheard those verra words at the Theater Royal Thursday last."

"Some things never change. Forget the gossips and their nasty backbiting. I cannot abide snobbery." Charity held up her finger a gesture far too reminiscent of their mother. "Now, tell me true, what has you occupied on Sundays?"

Modesty glanced toward the door. If only she could slip away and conveniently forget to tell the truth. But lying would only make things worse. "Och, ye must promise not to tell a soul, especially, Mama, Kitty, Martin, Harry, or—"

"If you dunna tell me this instant, I will report to everyone what I *think* you are doing."

After being nearly crushed to death by Crocky out the back of Waiter's, then found in a disgraceful state of undress in a viscount's boudoir, Modesty could only imagine what her sister was thinking. "I'm taking horseback riding lessons."

Charity's lips parted, her eyes widened... and then

they narrowed. Of their vast family members, Charity knew Modesty best, which was rather unfortunate at the moment. "What kind of riding lessons, exactly?"

She bit down on her lip. "Fast ones?"

"Do you mean to say ye're learning to be a jockey?"

"No' exactly. After all, they'll never allow a woman on the back of a horse during a race."

"Oh my word. I wondered why you talked Marty into purchasing Poseidon. But I should have known. Mama always said you behaved as if you were born in the saddle." Charity clapped both hands over her heart. "Do you have any idea how dangerous horse racing is?"

"Aye... but I'm good at it."

"Being talented at an endeavor and being fool-hardy quite often court each other. Now quickly, put on my redingote and let us haste away. We've imposed on Viscount Berwick's kindness long enough."

"Kindness?" Modesty asked, pushing to her feet. "The man stole my diamonds and I ended up stabbed in the back by a shard of glass for my trouble."

"I'm verra sorry you were injured, but at least he intended to return your comb all along."

"So says he." Modesty hissed at the sting from her stitches as she shrugged into the over garment. "You found me in his bedchamber of all places. How do you ken the viscount hasna ravished me?"

"Oh, please." Charity batted a dismissive hand through the air. "A man who comes to me worried half out of his wits, telling me what happened with Crocky, and how he stole your comb as well as the reason—"

"He told you all that?"

"Aye."

"Well, why did ye let me repeat it?"

"Because I wanted to be certain he *didna* ravish

you, sweeting." Charity stood and started for the door. "Come now, you need to have Randolph tend your wound. Your lady's maid is certain to have a salve to keep it from festering."

Modesty followed. "Verra well, but you must promise never to utter a word of this to Kitty."

Laughing, Charity led the way through the corridor. "You are fortunate Kitty was at tea with Miss Pinter when Berwick arrived at the town house."

"Felicity? Why wasna I invited?"

"Most likely because you were masquerading as a man at Waiter's."

In London, if the coroner determined a death was from natural causes, then there was no need for a case to be brought before the courts, and thus the magistrate. Which was why Kenneth was presently sitting upon a very uncomfortable bench in the coroner's office, staring at a door from which all manner of unpleasant odors oozed.

He had waited at least three quarters of an hour before the door opened and an older gentleman emerged, wearing a waistcoat and rolled up shirt sleeves, his face drawn. Kenneth stood and held out his calling card. "Mr. Clark, might I have a word?"

The man took the card with a filthy hand, covered with blood and Lord knew what else. "Ah yes, you're the new Viscount Berwick. Please accept my condolences for the untimely loss of your brother. How may I help you?"

"I've come to enquire about Alfred. I understand you are the coroner who determined the cause of death."

The man scratched the day-old stubble on his chin. "There's not much to say, really. In my estimation there could have been only one possible cause of death and that was asphyxia."

"As it was for Mr. Crockford?" Kenneth's clenched his fists. "You also performed his autopsy I'm told."

"I did." Mr. Clark returned to the examination room, Kenneth following before the coroner could shut the door. "Though Mr. Crockford's death posed more of a challenge since he also suffered from falling out a second-floor window."

Kenneth had thought the same. Actually, the fact that Crockford's death was caused by asphyxia was the reason he'd decided to speak to the coroner directly. "What made you arrive at your conclusion?"

"The lack of bruising that would normally be seen if the fall had killed him. The swollen tongue. And the fact that the dog didn't die."

"Dog?" Kenneth asked as the sound of dogs barking resounded from beyond the examination room.

Mr. Clark moved to a washstand and poured water into a bowl. "Indeed. I always perform a dog test in cases of asphyxia to rule out poisoning."

"Which is effective how, exactly?"

"I feed the mutt the contents of the decedent's stomach," replied the coroner, washing his hands. "If the dog lives, then I can safely rule out poisoning, and thus murder as the cause of death."

Beside Kenneth was a table piled with freshly laundered cloths, and he handed one to the coroner. "Did you perform the dog test on my brother?"

"I just said so, did I not?" Mr. Clark replied, drying his hands, then tossing the cloth into a barrel full of dirties.

Kenneth opted to rephrase. "Tell me, is there any poison you know of that would not cause a dog to die?"

"Do you not have anything better to do with your time, sir?" asked Mr. Clark, rolling down his sleeves. "You may be a man of leisure, but I assure you I must work to feed my wife and children."

There was no use explaining that less than a month ago, Kenneth had been running a farm to earn his keep and was quite content to do so. "I assume your answer is no?"

"Correct. Otherwise what would be the point of making a dog suffer?"

"I know you are busy but this business has me flummoxed. My brother was a pillar of health. And I happened to be in the alley when Crockford met his end. I saw a shadow move across the window from which he fell."

"Shadows and hunches?" Mr. Clark retrieved his coat from a peg behind the door. "Next they'll be saying Mr. Crockford's ghost is haunting Waiter's. Do me a favor and leave the medical examination to the men who have studied to make decisions based on scientific fact."

Enough was enough. Kenneth planted his fists on his hips. "I'll have you know I studied biological inheritance at Cambridge and am a scientist in my own right."

"Excellent." Mr. Clark escorted him to the door before ushering him out to the footpath. "Then you ought to readily accept my findings. I am terribly sorry you lost your brother, but I assure you His Lordship did die of natural causes. I hope this brings you some peace of mind. Good day, sir."

Kenneth watched the man toddle off into the mass

of traffic, pedestrians, all manner of carriages and carts, sedan cars, and wheelbarrows of all things. London was a hub of activity not unlike a beehive in summer, which was in a constant state of commotion.

How many other murders were overlooked by that man and his hounds? Well, this particular peer isn't going to sit idly by and think nothing more of it. There is a murderer on the loose and I will not rest until I expose the bastard.

8

———

Bless Randolph, she applied a bit of padding to protect Modesty's wound and laced her stays much looser than usual. Duty called, and she didn't dare miss her social engagements, less Mama become suspicious. With the padding, the pain was bearable.

"Where were you yesterday?" Kitty asked as she met Modesty in the entry of Lady Warwick's elaborate town house for her annual end-of-spring luncheon. The entry alone was festooned with five Grecian marbles. Five!

Modesty pretended to admire a statue of Aphrodite, thus hiding any expression she might unintentionally reveal since everyone believed her face always exposed her very soul. "I went to the library to return a book. Where I happened to encounter Charity and we spent the afternoon browsing the shops at the Piccadilly Arcade." Fortunately, Modesty and Charity had agreed on the wee fib during their carriage ride back to Mayfair last evening.

"Well," Kitty replied, following a footman though the corridor leading to the enormous banqueting room where luncheon was to be served. Today, rather than one long table, there were a number of small tables set with pink coverings and four to six chairs around each one. She cupped her hand over her mouth and lowered her voice. "I, for one, am glad you weren't home because after I had tea with Felicity, Lord Richter stopped his phaeton whilst I was on the footpath."

"Lord Richter? Is he another of your suitors?"

Beaming radiantly, Kitty executed a pirouette. "He hasn't written any poetry or sent flowers, but he did ask me to accompany him on a ride along Rotten Row."

"Truly? And at the proper time when everyone in Hyde Park would see you," Modesty mused.

"Mm hmm." Kitty tapped the tips of her fingers together. "Moreover, he asked me if I would be attending the Ruthland Ball at Almack's."

"Which you will be, of course."

"I wouldn't miss it for a hundred sovereigns."

I would. I'd miss it for a wee farthing. The only good thing about the Ruthland Ball was it marked the beginning of the last fortnight of the Season, which was to end with Lady Northampton's masquerade.

Felicity waved from a table set for four and the two ladies made their way through the maze of tables to join her.

After they were seated and Modesty made a quick apology for missing tea yesterday, their party was joined by Lady Philomina who had recently become a fast ally. Not only did she have a very handsome brother, she was acquainted with nearly every member of the *ton* and if anyone might know who Alfred Davenport was courting it would be she. Of course, Modesty had been introduced to most everyone as well, but after a half-dozen comments about her hair and freckles, she opted to pretend to be a wallflower. After all, she was certain this would be her one and only Season, after which she fully intended to establish a horse-breeding venture and enjoy a life in Scotland as far away from London as she possibly could be.

She just hadn't sorted out the details of how she might finance such a venture. But if anything, Modesty MacGalloway was tenacious. Today, however, her future aspirations had nothing to do with solving not one, but perhaps two murders. And she intended to commence her investigation this very day.

Felicity leaned forward and cupped her hand to her mouth as if she harbored a secret. "Did you hear that Lord Bottesford was caught slipping out of Miss Trent's window?"

"Oh, my heavens." Kitty drew her fingers over her mouth while a footman placed a glass of cordial in front of her. "How could she have allowed that scoundrel to seduce her?"

Felicity selected a baguette from a basket in the table's center. "If only I knew. He might be a baron, but his reputation is abominable."

"Dear, oh dear." Philomina shifted her gaze to her lap, shaking her head as if she personally might have been able to prevent the scandal.

Felicity continued, wide-eyed, her lips pursed, "I understand her father confronted Bottesford and all of them are already on the North Road heading to Gretna Green for a hasty marriage."

A footman placed a plate with roast chicken breast and braised potatoes in front of Modesty. "Miss Trent should have been more careful."

"Modesty!" all three ladies said in unison.

"All I'm saying is it appears as if they wanted to be caught. After all Miss Trent's bedchamber overlooks Oxford Street—one of the busiest roads in London. I imagine Lord Bottesford would have been spotted even after the witching hour."

"Perhaps Miss Trent wanted Lord Bottesford to be seen so he'd have no choice but to marry her or, heaven forbid, duel with her father," said Kitty.

"I think not." Modesty picked up her knife and fork. "I wouldna be surprised if His Lordship staged the whole thing. After all, Miss Trent has a sizeable dowery, and the papers have indicated Bottesford is all but penniless. Moreover, if he werena a peer, he would have already been taken to debtor's court."

"The papers are renowned for reporting misinformation." Felicity dabbed her lips. "My father says so. He forbids me to read anything but the ladies' fashion pages."

"Which are full of gossip. They are filled with more ruinous falsifications than any other column," Modesty mumbled behind her glass. After sipping, she said more loudly, "I'm sorry your father is so prudish. However do you keep yourself informed about what is happening in the Kingdom, let alone Town?"

"Papa tells me what I need to know."

"My father as well," Philomina agreed.

"Well, I rather like forming my own opinions." Modesty raised a finger as if she had an important tidbit of news. "Do you not find it strange that both Mr. Crockford and Lord Berwick died of asphyxia within a few weeks of each other?"

Philomina gasped, her hand clapping over her mouth as her eyes brimmed with tears.

Before Modesty had a chance to enquire as to why

the lass had such a violent reaction to her statement, Philomina dashed for the ladies withdrawing room.

Kitty thwacked her shoulder. "Goodness, sometimes you have the sensitivity of a goat."

"Me? Why? I simply was stating fact. Both men did perish from asphyxia."

"But the former Lord Berwick was courting Philomina," said Felicity. "Did she not tell you?"

Holy hedgehogs, both of her closest friends already knew what she was there to find out. "Obviously I didna. How many others kent? All of polite society?"

Kitty and Felicity exchanged glances before Kitty shrugged. "She told us in confidence."

"Made us swear not to tell a soul," Felicity added.

Well, if that was the case, then perhaps Modesty was sitting with the only people who actually knew upon whom the former viscount had turned his attentions. And since when did Kitty start harboring secrets for more than two days?

Modesty pushed her chair back. "If you'll excuse me. I must apologize, forthwith."

She found Philomina sitting on an ottoman in the center of the ladies withdrawing room, sniffling and dabbing her eyes with an embroidered handkerchief. Rather than speak, Modesty sat beside the young lady for a time, thinking about what words she might use to help ease her burden. "I'm verra sorry," she finally said. "I didna ken you were fond of His Lordship."

"Not many did." She sniffed, dabbing a tear, which had leaked from the corner of her eye. "He was sh-sh-shy."

"I recall." Modesty had seen him at the stables a time or two on days when she visited Poseidon without riding him. Alfred Davenport had always been reserved yet imparting an unmistakable sense of nobility. "You loved him, did you not?"

Philomina glanced over, her eyes red and swollen. "I did. I thought he was going to propose."

"Oh my."

"He rescued me in my family's theater box when..."

"When?" Modesty encouraged, taking the lady's hand between her palms.

"Well, I was attending the opera with my mother when she stepped out of the box for a moment. The next thing I knew, Lord Bottesford found me alone and threatened to ruin me by climbing into my bedchamber window. Alfred charged in from the neighboring box and told the baron to apologize. He said if he ever heard him threaten a woman again, he'd thrash him."

"Oh, my heavens, how heroic," Modesty replied, her mind racing. Was Bottesford the murderer?

Philomina sighed, dabbing her eyes with a pink handkerchief. "Berwick was a hero, and the very next morning he sent me two dozen white roses."

"He was a hero and a romantic." Modesty wondered if Alfred's brother was a wee bit romantic. He certainly seemed romantically inclined when it came to kissing shoulders. "How long did he court you?"

"Thirty-seven glorious days."

Modesty smiled, though her mind was racing. She not only had found the object of Alfred's affection, Bottesford's financial difficulties were no secret. Furthermore, Waiter's was the type of gentlemen's club a man like Baron Bottesford would frequent. The scoundrel more than likely owed a great deal of money to Crocky the Shark.

"If only I'd exposed Bottesford, I might have prevented Miss Trent from being forced to marry him."

"But by doing so, you would have put your verra own reputation at risk."

"I hate all the stupid rules governing our sex. Why can a woman not come forward and accuse a man—a peer—of inappropriate behavior without being ruined herself?"

"Because men make the rules and not a one of them kens what it is like to be a woman, though they certainly believe they have every right to do with us what they please. They're prigs, the lot of them."

"Perhaps everyone aside from Lord Berwick the former."

"Aye? I shall have to accept your opinion on that count."

~

KENNETH LEAFED through the *Gazette* while breaking his fast in the east-facing breakfast room. With yellow and white striped wallpaper, it was a brilliant if not happy place to begin one's day. And no room was brighter or better for catching up on the morning's news, which happened to be rather lackluster compared to the day prior when a sketch of Ward Crockford's face appeared on the front page. Fortunately, Kenneth had spirited Lady Modesty away from Waiter's before the newsmongers had arrived in the alleyway.

"Good morning, my lord," said Brown, stepping inside.

Kenneth lowered his paper and studied the butler. "Have you contacted anyone about finding a cottage in Surrey?"

"Not as yet, sir."

Honestly, in the past three-and-a-half weeks Brown had carried out his duties quietly and efficiently. He always answered questions honestly (which Kenneth knew because he'd questioned the butler on a few topics for which Kenneth already had the answer). Of course the man had been the butler to the viscountcy since Kenneth's childhood and had always seemed to be staunchly loyal. In his observation, Brown was about as likely to have murdered Alfred as the mousy scullery maid below stairs who'd blushed and hastened away when he'd made an unannounced visit to the kitchens.

Brown presented a silver tray with a calling card. "There is a Mr. Modistie here to see you. Shall I have him wait in the parlor?"

Kenneth removed the card and rubbed his thumb over the expert, yet feminine calligraphy. Good God, did the woman ever rest? "No. Bring her—ah—*him* to me forthwith."

"In here, sir?"

"Yes," Kenneth replied, offering nothing further. Not only had he not finished reading the *Gazette*, he was quite certain an encounter with the redheaded imp wouldn't take long.

Of course, as a well-bred gentleman, he stood when Lady Modesty MacGalloway followed Brown into the breakfast room and was subsequently introduced as Mr. Modistie. And she still looked like a bloody female. Why the devil everyone went along with her ridiculous disguise, Kenneth couldn't fathom.

As Brown took his leave, Kenneth eyed his manservant who presently was stepping in as footman. "Welch, please allow us a moment."

"Of course, my lord."

Once they were alone, he grasped the woman by the shoulders. "What the devil are you doing here? And at this hour? And with stitches in your back, no less. Aren't you in pain?"

"My lady's maid has made your needlework bearable, m'lord." Her face instantly coloring, she shrugged out from under his fingertips. "And this isna a social call."

"Stop trying to deepen your voice. You sound hideous."

"I beg your pardon," she replied, dropping the ruse. "I am not hideous!"

"Well, you certainly sound unnatural."

"And you are too judgmental." She swiped a sticky bun from a plate on the table. "Besides, after yesterday's luncheon, I couldna wait another moment to tell you all I have found."

"I do not want to know what you found. I want you to stop dressing as a man and putting yourself in precarious situations that could ultimately lead to your ruination."

The bun delicately balanced between her fingertips, Her Ladyship gestured to herself. "But I'm wearing these clothes to *avoid* ruination."

"So say you."

She took a bite. "Verra well, if you dunna want me to wear trousers, then where shall we meet?"

"*We* shall not meet."

"But how am I to help you solve the murder without speaking with you? Would you prefer it if I were to send you a missive?"

Honestly he would prefer it if he never set eyes on her again. The woman was too confounding. Even her honeysuckle scent sent his mind in a bloody whirr. "I do not require your help."

"Why, because I am a female?" she asked, stuffing the remainder of the sticky bun into her mouth, then wiping her fingers on a serviette.

"Because this business requires visiting some unsafe parts of Town as well as speaking to the odd unsavory sort, and doing so is dangerous for a man let alone a woman."

"You are verra short sighted for a lad who attended university." She shoved his shoulder. "Now sit down and allow me to have my say. For the love of Moses, I suffered a shard of glass in the back for you, the least ye can do is be hospitable."

Kenneth dropped into his chair, his mouth agape while Lady Modesty took a cup from the sideboard and set to pouring herself a spot of tea, adding milk and a pinch of sugar. Judging by her bitter frown, she ought to have taken two spoons rather than a pinch. She sipped before looking at him over the rim of her cup and emitting a satiated sigh. Did her moods always shift from hot to cold as quickly as the swing of a pendulum?

"So," she began. "Lord Berwick the former—"

"Please refer to my brother as Alfred. I cannot bear to hear him announced as 'the former.'"

"Verra well, *Alfred* was courting Lady Philomina Carmichael. She was certain he was about to propose when..." She set her cup down and frowned. "You are well aware of what happened."

"Lady Philomina?"

"Aye, and furthermore, their courtship began when your brother interceded on Her Ladyships behalf."

"Interceded?"

Modesty went on to explain how Alfred had stopped Baron Bottesford from tricking the Lady Philomina so she would have no choice but to marry the reprobate. Kenneth was ready to confront the bastard with a pistol by the time Modesty assured him the baron was presently on the way to Gretna Green to marry poor Miss Trent.

Kenneth ground his knuckles into his palm. "He should be stopped."

"Perhaps, but in my opinion, Miss Trent is a far better match for Bottesford than Lady Philomina would have been."

"How so?"

"Miss Trent's father is a merchant. Wealthy for certain, but his family are social climbers, so to speak. If their daughter marries into a barony, their grandchildren will be unquestionably accepted into the *ton*. Furthermore, I know Miss Trent, and if any debutante in London has the mettle to bring that miscreant to heel, it is she."

Kenneth vaguely remembered Miss Trent from the ball. She was tall and broad-shouldered with a hard edge to her jaw. "Do you believe she wanted to hasten to Gretna Green with a penniless baron?"

"All I am saying is that the marriage will suit both of them."

"Very well, if you believe so," he replied, his mind trying to fit mismatched pieces together.

"But we've veered from the topic at hand. Philomina professed to loving your brother, but I am quite certain Baron Bottesford must have been unduly slighted by Alfred's meddling."

Kenneth had thought the same as soon as Modesty exposed the man's character. And it wasn't beyond the realm of possibility for a man like the baron to be indebted to Ward Crockford.

"So, ye'd best move His Lordship to the top of your list of suspects." Of course, Kenneth agreed, though admitting it to the unpredictable Lady Modesty MacGalloway might very well end up causing him heartburn. "And now ye ken why I can be of assistance to you."

Kenneth shifted his gaze to the *Gazette*. He needed to dissuade her. "Indeed, I am thankful to learn who my brother was courting and that there had been a bit of a rift between him and Baron Bottesford, however—"

"I promise to wear a dress at all times..." Modesty said, hastily continuing and leaving Kenneth unable to get a word in. "Except for Sundays at the racetrack. And I promise to keep my lips firmly closed when you believe I ought to. However, you *do* need me. I insist upon it. So... what is on the agenda for today? Will you be visiting Lord Bottesford's residence? Call on Lady Philomina? What about the Theater Royal where Alfred had his box, which is now your box, of course? You ken your brother rarely missed a production."

"My box?" Kenneth mused.

"Aye. 'Tis adjacent to the Carmichael's, which is where he overheard the baron threatening Philomina."

Kenneth tapped his lips with his pointer finger. Alfred had always loved theatricals, and it didn't surprise him to hear his brother never missed a theater production.

Lady Modesty stood and tugged on his coat sleeve. "Come, there are places to go and things to do."

Standing, Kenneth realized how petite Her Ladyship was. She had to be at least nine inches shorter.

But, by the saints, the diminutive woman could twist his arm. "Do you know any apothecaries outside of Mayfair?"

Modesty's crystal blue eyes twinkled with mischief. "I ken a chemist from the Highlands who mixes all the old remedies... and he's in Southwark."

Perhaps she could be useful from time to time? "What might his name be?"

Modesty looped her arm through his. "Let us discretely hire a hack and I shall introduce you."

9

"Lady Modesty MacGalloway, is that you?" asked the bespectacled, stooped Mr. MacDougall from behind the counter of the apothecary shop.

For a moment, she stood stunned, her face burning, but she'd known this man since the first time she'd visited London—at least the first time she remembered visiting. At the time she'd been a wee lass with her nanny, collecting a tincture for a cough that was spreading through the family. "Och, I'm wearing a disguise. Ye are nae supposed to recognize me."

"I'd ken ye anywhere, lassie." Mr. MacDougall shot a disapproving glance at Lord Berwick. "But why are ye wearing breeches?"

Modesty moved in front of the viscount. "'Tis for an upcoming masquerade," she fibbed, deeming it necessary, of course. "The modiste must have misunderstood my meaning when I said I wanted a Samhain costume. Ye ken how the English never understand our wee Scottish brogues."

Mr. MacDougall's lips twisted along with the knit of his brow. To allay any further questions, she stepped aside and gestured toward His Lordship. "Please allow me to introduce Viscount Berwick. I brought him here today because he has questions of an apothecarial nature, and I kent this was the best shop in all of Britain for such an inquiry."

"Aye, that it is," replied Mr. MacDougall, bowing. "Pleased to make your acquaintance, m'lord."

"Mr. MacDougall." Berwick bowed in kind. "How is it a Scottish apothecary came to London to peddle his trade?"

"Och, I fell in love with an English rose. Still in love with the bonny woman. Gave me six children, she did." The man winked at Modesty as he placed his palms atop the glass counter. "What can I help ye with?"

His Lordship explained about his visit with the coroner and the fact that he'd left the man's offices feeling as if he'd been played for a fool. "After all, I am a scientist in my own right. Furthermore, I will not accept natural causes as the reason for my brother's death until I have exhausted all possibilities. I know right down to my bones skullduggery is afoot. I know it."

Mr. MacDougall scratched beneath his plaid cap. "The dog didna die, aye?"

"No. Neither did they find any signs of struggle."

"Well, I'm no' a physician, but I do ken more about herbal lore than most everyone. What I find most interesting about my profession is that doctors often stand exactly where you are at the moment, but I've met verra few who would admit to consulting with me, especially a coroner."

"Did Mr. Clark consult with you regarding my brother?"

"Nay, I dunna reckon Mr. Clark has ever come to Southwark to ask me a single question."

"But it is common practice to feed the contents of a

deceased person's stomach to a dog to determine if he has been poisoned?" Modesty asked.

"Aye, has been for centuries." The old apothecary narrowed his gaze as if thinking. "What about suffocation? Was it ruled out?"

Berwick nodded. "Ruled out because Alfred was quite fit and there was no sign of struggle—moreover, nary a soul saw anyone enter the house."

"Hmm." Mr. MacDougall moved to a large volume on a podium and flipped through the worn pages. "There is one other option aside from smothering that wouldna turn up in a dog test."

Modesty leaned nearer, reading the word at the top of the page. "Wolfsbane?"

"Aye."

"But that's been around since the beginning of time," said the viscount, sounding flabbergasted. "I know myself wolfsbane would have killed a dog. Would have killed a bloody horse."

Mr. MacDougall blinked, peering over his spectacles. "Not if it was used as a salve."

While Modesty and Berwick stood side-by-side pondering the apothecary's words, the man clapped his hands together. "Allow me to give you an example: Say His Lordship had a cold and someone gave him a salve with a wee bit of mint oil to clear his congestion. The poor fellow would have been dead within hours of application. Furthermore, the only postmortem sign of such a death is asphyxia." Mr. MacDougall closed the book and eyed the viscount. "I dunna ken if your brother was poisoned or nay, but if someone wanted him dead, I'm guessing the murderer was a person he knew well."

Berwick gave a single nod. "I agree since there was no sign of a struggle."

"What about Ward Crockford's murder?" Modesty asked, looking between the two men.

"What does the viscount's death have to do with Crocky the Shark?" asked the apothecary.

Modesty opened her mouth to explain, but Kenneth silenced her with a shift of his hand. "We thought the gaming hell proprietor might have been involved because of the questionable way in which Crockford's horse won the Epsom Derby."

"And Lord Berwi—I mean *Alfred's* horse was favored to win," Modesty added.

"I see." Mr. MacDougall returned to his book, opened it to wolfsbane and skimmed the page. "Did the fall kill Mr. Crockford?" asked the apothecary.

"I think so," Modesty replied. "He certainly looked dead."

"What if was already dead? What if he had been poisoned by a salve of wolfsbane?" Kenneth asked.

"Then I reckon the dose must have been verra high to cause him to react so violently he fell out a window. However, since the fall didn't kill him, then between the time he fell and the time the coroner had a chance to examine him, no signs of poisoning would have been present."

"He could have been pushed," Berwick mused. "The whole incident might have been staged."

A chill ran up the back of Modesty's neck. "The shadow you saw. Do you think it was the murderer?"

"Possibly. But the papers did not indicate anyone was seen fleeing Waiter's."

"The culprit mightn't have fled," said Mr. MacDougall.

Modesty's gaze connected with Berwick's falcon-like stare. If both victims were killed with a wolfsbane salve, they must have had a close acquaintance in common. "Perhaps I ought to have a word with Mr. Willett. Mayhap Alfred and Crocky used the same horse trainer?"

Berwick's lips thinned. Why was it whenever she suggested she help in some way, he acted as though he didn't need her assistance? And why did men always act as if they were the only ones who could solve problems?

~

AFTER HAILING a hack to ferry them home, Kenneth sat on the opposing bench, facing Lady Modesty. He'd made the mistake of sitting beside her on the way to Southwark and it had taken an enormous act of self-control not to touch the exquisitely lithe thigh pressing against his. In no way should he entertain any amorous pursuits with this woman. Every man in England knew one did not dally with highborn females. Besides, he was on a quest to uncover the mystery of Alfred's death and mustn't allow himself to get sidetracked by a debutante who paraded about Town wearing breeches.

He chose to continue to the subject at hand, asking, "Were Venom and Mr. Crockford's Red Charlie both stabled at the London training track?"

"I ken Red Charlie wasna there after the race. I didna start lessons with Mr. Willett until after, but Crocky's horse might have been there before the derby." Her Ladyship tucked a ringlet of hair behind her ear—a very feminine-looking gesture and one she ought never do when attempting to impersonate a man. "At least I'll be able to find out on Sunday."

Kenneth's stomach clenched. "I do not consider it safe for you to make any further enquiries."

"I beg your pardon? I already have a lesson scheduled with Mr. Willett. There is absolutely nothing dangerous about asking him if Mr. Crockford's horse has ever been stabled there. 'Tis a perfectly innocent question."

Must she always be so reasonable? And with her reason, must she stare at him with huge, piercing blue eyes? Kenneth glanced away. Lady Modesty was right, of course. Even if she were overheard by some nefarious scoundrel, no one would think she was asking because she wasn't convinced Crockford had died of natural causes.

Who was the person in the window? Had Kenneth imagined seeing the movement? The incident was such a jumble in his mind, a cloud could have sailed past and made it look as if there had been a shadow behind the pane.

Suddenly full of exuberance, Modesty clapped, making her hat tip to one side. Did she borrow from her brother again? He hadn't purchased a new one for her as of yet, not that he approved of any woman wearing a John Bull. "I have a wonderful idea."

Groaning, Kenneth rolled his eyes to the carriage ceiling. "Please, not another."

Her ladyship coughed an ahem. "You truly can be a curmudgeon, even though I ken you are not. You remind me of my brother Philip. He always acts like a sore-headed grouch, but he ties better bows than any lady's maid in my brother's household."

"Philip?"

"Third son—first born of the twins."

Kenneth knew the MacGalloway family was large, but in truth, he had no idea how large. Moreover, he was quite certain he didn't need to know. "Oh."

"Anyway, Mr. Willett said I am ready to race—"

Slicing his hand through the air, Kenneth vehemently shook his head. "No, no, no, no. You would be utterly ruined if you took up the reins at a sanctioned race. Mind you, I knew you were a woman from fifty paces, and you were riding around the track like hellfire at the time."

"I didna say in a *sanctioned* race—I'm ready to pit Poseidon against another jockey on Sunday... *if* Mr. Willett can find someone who will keep mum. And—"

"I forbid it! You cannot trust some jockey to hold his tongue about racing against a duke's sister. Besides, you have three stitches in your back!"

"Wheesht!" A fire ignited in Her Ladyship's eyes as she vehemently shook her finger beneath his nose. "First of all, you have absolutely no right to tell me what I can and canna do. My back is healing, thanks to Randolph. I'll be set to rights by Sunday. And furthermore, afore you rudely interrupted me, I was going to suggest we pit Poseidon against Venom. That way ye'll be there when we talk about Crocky, and since Venom was bested by Crocky's horse, it is perfectly logical for *you* to pose such a question."

Kenneth blinked. How the blazes could he argue with the imp? True, it was logical for him to give Venom a run. However... "It makes no sense whatsoever for a viscount to agree to a race with a young lady."

"No one kens I'm a woman."

"Mr. Willett certainly does."

"Aye, but he doesna care."

"I assure you he will care if we tell him we've agreed to race. He'll assume I've taken advantage of you."

"Balderdash!" She removed one of her gloves and thwacked his knee with it. "We can tell the truth, ye numpty. We'll say ye recognized me at the ball, and I suggested you pit Venom against Poseidon and we agreed to meet at the track—easy peasy."

Had the lady been a man, Kenneth would have taken offence to being struck by her glove, but it was all he could do not to laugh aloud. Good heavens, Lady Modesty had a backbone.

"Whoa!" hollered the driver from his perch while the brake engaged, unseating Her Ladyship. She shrieked as she hurled across the gap, landing awkwardly onto Kenneth's lap.

His arms flew around the woman, protecting her from harm. "Are you hurt? Is your back awfully sore?" he asked.

The driver cued the team to walk on. "Sorry, my lord. We nearly went head-on with a phaeton that lost its driver."

"Carry on," Kenneth replied before looking downward and rephrasing his question, "Are you unharmed, my lady? Are your stitches still intact?"

Not replying, Modesty met his gaze and then those blessed blues trailed to his mouth. "Hmm?" she asked, running her teeth over her bottom lip.

Ye gods, the woman was magnificent. How did he ever think her merely cute? Simply her heavy-lidded blink stole the breath from his lungs. Lady Modesty was intelligent and caring and ever so eager to help when everyone else had told him he was a fool for thinking Alfred's death was not from natural causes. The woman had no fear of danger and faced it like a warrior-woman dressed in rose-gold armor. But she was too cavalier in her fearlessness with no idea of how vulnerable she actually was.

She smiled, endearingly, the freckles across the bridge of her nose further captivating him. He brushed an errant curl away from her face as he slowly inclined his lips toward hers. His eyes closed as he lingered, kissing her gently, only intending to give a small peck. Yes, that was it, a peck to show her his concern for being flung across the carriage and landing sprawled atop his lap.

He kept his arms tightly around her, his hand caressing her lower back where there were no stitches.

Then the lady slid her hands around his neck, emitting a womanly moan.

Utterly undone, Kenneth asked permission to enter her mouth by stroking the parting of her lips with his tongue. As she yielded to him, the sweet remnants of a sticky bun rendered him mindless. All concept of time vanished as he indulged in her softness, her sensuality, her unignorable allure.

When finally their kiss ended, Lady Modesty seemed to sway on his lap. Or did Kenneth sway? Or was the swaying sensation from the rocking of the carriage? His fingers brushed the nankeen fabric of her breeches, reminding him of why they were together, reminding him that she was a lady presently dressed in men's clothing. He looked to the window, the curtain thankfully closed. "Forgive me. I had no right to take liberties."

"I ken. It was a mistake." Modesty removed her arms from around his neck, slid off his lap, and resumed her proper seat. She folded her hands and stared down at them. "I'm not bonny like Kitty, or my sister Grace, or even my sister Charity."

Had the warrior woman receded into her shell? Kenneth didn't understand why at one moment they were locked in a passionate embrace and with his apology, which was certainly called for, she suddenly became meek and demure—very unlike her. "I beg your pardon?"

"Och, ye dunna have to pretend I'm otherwise. I'm not deaf to the gossips."

He studied her for a moment, recalling her words from the day Crocky had met his end and they were riding away from the scene in his carriage: "*dunna go and try to make me feel like a diamond of the first water.*" At the time they were embroiled in a crisis, giving Kenneth no time to ponder what she'd said. But now, as a man who grew up as a ginger, he understood all too well.

She thinks she's plain.

"You have no idea how lovely you are, do you?"

"Me? Lovely? Did Mr. MacDougall slip you a love potion afore we left his shop?"

She was also quite adept at deflecting any conversation that centered upon her looks. "He did not." But Kenneth was well-aware of the deprecating comments directed at redheaded individuals. "I take it you have been teased mercilessly because of the color of your hair."

"Have you not been? You're nearly as red as I."

"I attended Eton—the foremost boys' school for privileged aristocrats who loved to laugh at my expense."

"Oh." Her gaze fell again. "How awful."

"It made me stronger. Also gave me a distaste for mingling with polite society."

"You as well? Och, when I finish with this horrid Season, I'm going to find a way to start a racehorse training and breeding operation."

That was Alfred's passion. "Horse breeding? What does your mother have to say about such a venture?"

"I havena told her as of yet. I havena told anyone aside from you and Mr. Willett."

"Are you aware that I breed sheep?"

"I thought you kept bees."

"I do, but I've also undertaken work to scientifically produce a more robust breed of sheep that produces more wool, more meat, and more milk."

"Truly? How are you progressing? What will you call your breed?"

"Honestly, progress is slow. One lot of lambs might appear more robust and the next might digress a bit. However, after the last two lambings, I believe I am on to something." With her nod of encouragement, he continued, "I thought I might name the breed the Northumberland Longwool."

"I like it. The name sounds quite genuine." Lady Modesty slid her hand back into her glove. "I think I might like to observe your sheep husbandry. Would there be any land nearby suitable for horses?"

"I reckon horses thrive just about anywhere on the Isle of Great Britain."

"Hmm." Her expression changed from one of wonder to one more resembling the temptress who'd only recently been in his arms. "Why... um... ?"

Kenneth leaned forward, his heart beating as if he would die if she did not ask her question. "Why?" he encouraged.

"Why did you kiss me?"

He rubbed the back of his neck. How could he have not kissed her? She was on his lap, looking more tempting than a warm cherry tart. "Because I was unable to stop myself. Can you possibly forgive me?"

She touched her fingers to her lips. "I believe it was quite an adequate experience for my first kiss. No, I do not forgive you."

Oh, dear, he'd really overstepped his bounds this time.

"I do believe your actions have entitled me to a redeemable token."

Blast it all, she was scheming, and he'd fallen straight into her snare. "I beg your pardon?"

"Well, you did indulge in a wee slip of the tongue, as it were… " She presented him with a wily grin akin to the imp he'd come to know. "'Tis settled. And I shall redeem my token when Venom races against Poseidon on Sunday."

Kenneth's mouth grew dry. How was it this woman could manage to obtain her every whim? He had but one more argument, though it held little water. "If I ride Venom, you will be on an older horse. I will be favored by lengths."

"Aye?" She snorted. "I reckon you're afraid of being bested by a lass."

He scoffed. "How preposterous."

"Verra well, then I shall ride Venom and you shall ride Poseidon."

10

The wounded sailor liked the view from his window. At least he would have liked it if he weren't blind. He'd lost his sight in the Battle of Trafalgar—lost his wits, too. It was the fire that took his sight but it had been the endless blasting of cannon that had sent him to the asylum. At first they'd put him in the Bethlem Hospital in London—the miserable, smelly prison known to those captive within her walls as the Bedlam Insane Asylum. There the old sailor had been shoved into a room with dozens of other beds along with as many tars who had been driven mad from the rigors of the sea.

The girl never visited him there. He thought she had forgotten him. After all, everyone else forgot him, why shouldn't she?

But after he'd been transferred to Hasler across the harbor from Portsmouth, she came. Just once, but she came.

He couldn't recall how long ago. It could have been a few weeks or a few months, but certainly not longer than a year.

The wounded sailor liked Hasler. He shared his room with only three other men. And when the nurse opened the window, the breeze brought in the re-freshing scent of the sea. He had always enjoyed the surf even though the wars had robbed him of his life as a sailor.

When he inhaled, he caught the scent of a new fragrance—decidedly female, strange but familiar at the same time.

Footsteps approached the bed where he was propped against a pillow. They were a woman's steps. They weren't the heavy steps of a man, or the thick-soled shoes of a nurse. These were delicate taps. Most likely those made by slippers with a bit of a heel.

"Good afternoon, old man," she said.

It was her! The girl the sailor loved but couldn't remember from where.

If only his vision were to clear so he might see her, he'd remember for certain. Inside his body, the rhythm of his heart sped. He wanted to smile and tell her how happy he was to see her. Mayhap he actually was smiling?

Soft, warm lips caressed his forehead as lithe fingers wrapped around his hand. "I've missed you," she said.

Oh, Lord how much he had missed her. Where had she been? Why had she stayed away so long?

"I finished the work I told you about. Do you remember?"

She waited for him to answer. Damn, it was frustrating not to be able to do so. She'd told him about some sort of labor. He hated that she had no one to take care of her. A woman with such a silken voice ought not to callous her hands with hard labor.

An image of a woman with her sleeves rolled up washing the laundry in a bowl in a dank cellar came to mind. Who was she? Not this woman. But the cellar was familiar. He'd spent a great deal of time there.

"I suppose not," she said.

What is your name?

"Anyway," she continued, "I've found a cottage to let in Portsmouth and now have enough coin to live comfortably."

A cottage? How nice. I wish I could stay with you there.

"And that means I shall be able to visit you more often. I'll be able to start anew as well."

Yes, a fresh start was what the wounded sailor longed for.

"You must know you are the only person I care about in all of Christendom," she whispered, her breath warm and gentle on his ear.

He willed himself to smile broadly, not knowing if his efforts were successful. *I love you as well. Thank you for coming to see me.*

"Would you like me to tell you a story?"

Oh yes, I could listen to you speak for the rest of my days.

"Very well," she said. "There once was a little girl who lived with 'er mother in a cellar beneath an old gin distillery..."

11

A bell rang as Kenneth entered the jewelry shop on Bond Street. The singular positive thing about accepting Lady Modesty's challenge was it afforded Kenneth time to accomplish a number of things on his list without glancing over his shoulder to see if she was following.

"Welcome to Phillip's," said a well-dressed clerk, coming out from behind a counter. "How might I assist you today?"

Kenneth produced the bill of sale, which he'd taken from the top of his "of interest" pile. "My brother purchased this ring from this shop the day before he passed away."

The man covered his heart as he slipped the document from Kenneth's fingers. "Oh dear, such a tragedy."

"Indeed it was."

"You are the succeeding Viscount Berwick, I presume?"

"I am," Kenneth grimly admitted. "And I was wondering if you might be able to provide some information about this piece."

"Certainly. But can you not see the ring for your-self? The sapphire is nearly flawless."

"If I were able to look at it, I wouldn't be here."

"I see." The clerk returned the bill of sale. "Then may I safely assume the ring is missing?"

"Affirmative." The corners of Kenneth's mouth tightened. "I found the empty box beneath the bed where Alfred took his last breath."

"My word."

"Did he perchance tell you for whom he pur-chased the ring?" Yes, from Modesty's sleuthing he was aware that Alfred had been courting Lady Philomina, but he wanted more proof.

"Oh, yes. His Lordship informed me that he'd fi-nally found his viscountess."

"Hmm." Kenneth stroked his chin. If only Alfred would have written to him about the young lady, but his brother's correspondence was infrequent and short. "Please tell me true—have you seen this ring since it was sold?"

"No. Why—?" The man gasped. "Oh my. Have you asked his intended?"

"Not yet, but do I have it on good authority the young lady merely thought Alfred was going to propose. Evidently he had not done so at the time of his passing."

"Stolen only a day after it was purchased—of course, I can attest there was no mention of His Lord-ship's acquisition in the papers because he wanted his proposal to come as a surprise."

Kenneth had already perused the back issues of the *Gazette*. "May I confide in you, sir?"

"Certainly. Phillip's is the foremost jeweler in Lon-don. Trusted by the royal family, no less."

"I believe my brother was murdered and..." Kenneth shook the bill of sale. "This ring has something to do with it."

"Murdered?" the man whispered, his eyes growing nearly as large as the glass in his monocle.

"If you please, I would like to obtain a description of the ring, the stone, and its setting so I might be able to better understand what it looks like."

"I shall give you that, but would you not rather have a drawing of the piece?"

"Do you have one?"

"Phillip's keeps drawings of everything we create. Doing so helps markedly for insurance purposes, or if an issue goes before a court of law."

By the time the clerk copied the original drawing for Kenneth, he'd learned stolen jewelry often made its way to the markets at Covent Garden, if not the Continent. He also had been given a quick tutorial on how to identify paste jewels. Of course, nearly everyone could spot a fake if it was old and faded or chipped, but there were a good amount of reproductions available from some very clever counterfeits.

After Kenneth left Philip's, he opted to walk the mile or so to Covent Garden. A breeze blew, reminding him of how Lady Modesty's curls often escaped her various hats and flailed on the wind. The woman's hair was as adventuresome as she.

Dear God, he'd nearly come undone when she'd landed upon his lap with those soft, heart-shaped buttocks. In truth, he had completely lost his mind when he'd plied her lips with a kiss. Worse, he'd wanted to do a great deal more than kiss her.

I should have stopped myself, no matter how tempting her lips.

How would the events of their trip to Southwark have played out had the carriage not been forced to brake, thus keeping Lady Modesty's backside firmly on her bench? Regardless, no matter what might have otherwise happened, he knew Her Ladyship would have found a way to challenge Venom to a race. Something told him that, though the woman might appear to be spontaneous, she did not do anything without at least a moment of forethought.

The only positive thing about agreeing to her suggestion was he now had two days to himself without the chit poking into his affairs. This morning, he was most relieved to discover she did not present herself upon his stoop wearing breeches and claiming to be *Mr. Modistie.* Fortunately, she did not even inquire as to his next steps in his investigation, else she might have insisted on accompanying him today, and if she'd batted those damned beguiling eyes at him, he never would have been able to refuse her.

As he strolled along the footpaths, the building fronts grew shabbier, fine carriages were replaced by hackneys and wagons laden with all manner of goods. Men labored with shovels and wheelbarrows to clean up after horses, and women lifted their skirts ankle high as they crossed the filthy cobbled roads.

As Kenneth approached the entrance of the markets, a woman wrapped her fingers around his arm, her lips and cheeks brightly rouged. "'ow 'bout a tup, luv? 'Tis only two bob."

He extricated his arm from her grasp. "No, thank you."

"C'on, Two bob's nothin' to a dandy the likes of you."

Aside from being repulsed by this woman's brash advances, Kenneth made a rule of staying away from whores, especially pox-ridden women who prowled the streets of London. "Take your business elsewhere."

"Ach, ye're a lecherous back door usher," she replied, her voice loud. Evidently she didn't give a rat's arse who she insulted.

Kenneth hastened into the crowd as her taunts rose. "Too good for me? Ye ruddy 'ighbrow!"

He passed through the arched entrance into the markets without breaking into a run, ever so grateful not to have Modesty on his arm—wearing a dress, of course. Then again, if she had come along, the prostitute most likely would have set her sights on some other poor soul.

The markets were bustling with activity beneath a myriad of umbrellas and awnings. Wagons were haphazardly strewn about, selling everything from burlap to apples to garden herbs. Shoppers comprised every walk of humanity from the wealthy to shabbily-dressed children who appeared to be running errands for their masters.

A barefoot lad dashed in front of him and held up a pitifully small fish. "'addock, guvnor. Caught this morn."

Generally, Kenneth would decline and continue on his way, but this child was too thin, his face dirty, and his sandy brown locks were matted as if his living conditions were no better than a hound's.

"I don't have a taste for haddock today, lad." Kenneth tossed the boy a sovereign—a coin worth several shillings more than the fish's value. "But no self-respecting merchant ought to be peddling his wares without proper footwear. Go on and buy yourself a pair of boots."

"Cor... " the boy said, his voice filled with awe as he bit the coin. "No, sir. Me ma thrashes me if I don't give 'er all me blunt."

Kenneth kneeled down and looked the lad in the

eyes. He smelled worse than the fish. "Do you own a pair of shoes?"

"No, sir."

"What do you wear on your feet in winter?"

He dropped his gaze to his toes. "I wrap them."

Kenneth didn't have the heart to ask what the lad wrapped them with. "Did you catch that fish?"

The boy shook his head.

"If you tell me where it came from, I promise I won't tell a soul."

"Nipped it from the fish monger down on the embankment."

"You stole it?"

"Me ma says it's just nippin' a bit so we don't starve."

Through his questioning, Kenneth discovered the boy's name was Freddie, he was eleven years of age, or near enough. His mother was a woman who took him in from the streets—she'd actually taken in a number of children and trained them as pickpockets. Freddie didn't know who his parents were.

"Tell you what." Kenneth stood. "I am in need of an errand boy—one who can also clean horse stalls. The job pays seven guineas per year. Do you know how many shillings are in a guinea?"

"No, sir."

"One and twenty, which means you will earn one hundred forty-seven shillings per year, or two shillings and ten pennies per week."

Freddie eyes grew round and hopeful. "That much? Every week?"

"You will have a bed of your own as well as three warm meals a day and no more nicking. Would you like to come live with me?"

The boy's toes turned inward, overlapping the big ones. "Me ma will whip me if I'm not 'ome by dark."

"Oh, no. If you take me up on my offer, I'll see to it the woman you refer to as Ma never sets eyes on you again."

Freddie opened his palm and looked at the shilling. "Ye mean I can keep this?"

"Yes. You can keep it and everything you earn. But I do have one rule, to which I will not bend."

"What is that?" he asked, his fingers tightly closing around the coin.

"Honest labor only. No more nicking fish. No more pickpocketing. Can you promise me that?"

Nodding excitedly, Freddie agreed. "Yes, sir."

"Very well. Can you point me in the direction of the jewelers?"

"Jewelers? Cor. Ye must have a purse full of shillings."

Kenneth gave the lad a dour frown. "The number of shillings in my possession is no concern of yours."

Freddie shrugged. "Follow me, then. But my week's pay starts today, aye sir?"

"We shall see."

The melodic street cries from the hawkers filled the air as he proceeded through the throng, the clouds thick, spitting a few drops of water here and there, though posing little threat of a downpour. The vendors of the Garden hardly noticed as they carried on with the labor of trying to sell their wares from flowers to thimbles to snuff boxes to barrels of pickled cabbage. And the farther into the market they ventured, the finer the quality of wares. Burlap had given way to Holland cloth, apples to tea, and snuff boxes had shifted from hewn of crude wood to porcelain.

Freddie tugged on Kenneth's coat and pointed. "There. That's where all the fancy baubles are."

Beneath the eaves of a small brick shop, an object glittered in the window. And upon further inspection, there were a half dozen jewelers all nestled together.

Kenneth patted the lad's cap. "Go and give the fish to someone who needs it, then meet me back here in ten minutes."

The boy skittered backward. "Give it away? I could get good blunt for this fella."

"The fish is stolen, therefore it is not yours to sell. Do as I say and I'll buy you a pair of shoes myself."

As Freddie skipped away, Kenneth watched for a moment. What a bloody fool he was. First letting Lady Modesty trick him into the horserace, and now hiring an admitted thief. He sighed and headed beneath the awning. At least Freddie would be off the streets and given the opportunity to make an honest living without being whipped by the shrew who had taken him in, and then used him for her own devices.

Kenneth resolutely went into each shop, the vendors rubbing their palms and eager to show him their wares. There were no actual sapphire rings. Because of his encounter with the clerk at Phillip's, he was able to spot paste—the rounded facet edges, gas bubbles, some very difficult to see, the lack of crystal structure, and colors that were far too brilliant to be real. He did find one sapphire ring that appeared to be real— priced accordingly as well. The only problem was the size and setting were nothing like the drawing the clerk had given him.

It nearly surprised him to see Freddie watching from behind a wagon, his gaze shifting, his expression anything but confident as if he expected Kenneth to renege on his word.

"Come, Frederick," he said with a stiff incline of his head. "We have a great deal of work to do."

~

"Modesty, dear?" Mama entered her daughter's bedchamber without knocking.

Modesty gasped and crossed her arms over her stays. "Mother?" she said, trying not to sound as panicked as she felt.

Randolph curtsied deeply. "Your Grace."

Mama shut the door and tipped up her chin. "Why, exactly, are you wearing a pair of men's breeches?"

Because I'm going to beat Lord Berwick in a horse race today.

Affecting her most innocent expression, Modesty twisted her long braid around her hand. "I was thinking of wearing a jockey's costume to Lady Northampton's masquerade."

"Dress as a man? That is completely out of the question. There are plenty of proper costumes for you to wear." Mama plucked the red satin shirt from the back of the settee and examined it. "These seams are horrendous. Wherever did you find such a poorly made garment?"

Mr. Willett gave it to me.

"Forgive me, madam," said Randolph, bowing her head. "I found it among… ah… along with some cast-offs in the servant's quarters."

"My heavens you are a lady's maid. It is your duty to recognize good workmanship. I am astounded that you would permit my daughter to wear such a garment."

"Aye, madam."

"Mama, 'tis only a costume, and as you said, I canna wear it anyway."

"Then why are you whiling away the day with such frivolousness?"

So many things came to the tip of Modesty's tongue. If only she'd been born a lad, she'd be free to win horse races because she was the most naturally talented horsewoman Mr. Willett had ever seen. Moreover, in her opinion, London was the foulest, most unpleasant place to spend any season, let alone "the" Season. She didn't want to marry any of the pompous self-serving aristocrats she had met, and she fully intended to become a spinster and find a way to own a stud farm of her own.

Instead, she shrugged. "A lassie can dream, I reckon."

"Well, your dreaming can wait until you are asleep. And if you want to dream about masquerade costumes, you'd do far better to conjure up images of Queen Elizabeth or Eleanor of Aquitaine—she was quite well-loved by her subjects."

"Aye, Mama."

"Goodness, how you always manage to make me lose my train of thought—far more than any of the seven children before you." Patting her chest, Mama cleared her throat. "George Hamilton, the Earl of Roxburgh came to call and asked me if I might act as chaperone whilst you serve tea."

Modesty snorted. "Given his age, wouldna it be more apt if I chaperoned you?"

"Good heavens, you oft say the most preposterous things. Besides, he is only forty."

"Over twice my age, mind you."

"This is the way of things, dearest. Your father was sixteen years my senior. And Roxburgh is wealthy. He owns lands on both sides of the Scottish border, and he is rather fond of red hair."

And he still wears powdered wigs. Modesty glanced at the mantle clock. It was already half past eleven. She needed to convince her mother to leave and hasten to the racetrack. For heaven's sake, it was only tea. Perhaps if she simply agreed to appease the old coot, her mother would leave her be. "Did you tell Lord Roxburgh I'd be delighted to serve tea?" she droned, sounding about as excited as a dying cat.

"I did." Mama snapped her fingers in Randolph's direction. "You must make haste to don a proper frock, my dear. I shall tell him you will be down directly."

"The earl is *here*?" Modesty asked, her voice all but screeching. "But what about your Sunday luncheon with the Wayward Widows?"

"I loathe your referring to my friends thus." Mama opened the door. "And I have sent them my regrets. It is far more important for me to play chaperone than it is to visit with my widowed companions today. I shall see you in the front parlor within a quarter of an hour."

As her mother's footsteps faded, Modesty shot a panicked glance toward her lady's maid. "Good glory, she never misses a Sunday luncheon. Why today?"

Randolph had already selected a blue muslin day gown. She cringed as she held it up. "Lord Roxburgh sounds like an affable chap."

"Laughable is more apt. I swear he wears calf improvers to make his legs look more robust. He's a codfish."

"But a wealthy codfish."

"I doubt he'd be the type of husband who'd be content with a wife who spends more time in the stables than she does in the house." Still wearing her breeches, Modesty stepped into the dress and shoved her arms through the sleeves. "It is nigh time for me to tell Mama that I do not intend to marry anyone."

"Yes, m'lady," Randolph said, tugging on the back laces of the dress. "Dunna forget to remove your trousers."

"They're similar enough to pantaloons. I shall keep them on."

"Ye're no' thinking of going to the racetrack after serving tea?"

"Aye, I am. I challenged Berwick to a race and I am not one to ever go back on my word."

"But you'll no' make it in time."

Modesty dashed to her writing table, opened the drawer where she kept her pin money, and removed a handful of shillings. "Hail a hackney. Go to the track and tell Mr. Willett I have been detained and will be there forthwith."

"Me?"

"Aye, you. And haste. Oh... and tell the driver to return to our mews and wait for me."

"But what about your hair?"

"Once I slip out of my pelisse, I'll stuff my braid down the back of my shirt. No one will ken the difference." Modesty pulled a lace cap over her hair. "Go on, haste away. Ye must inform Mr. Willett afore Berwick arrives, else he'll say he didna intend to race at all. Besides, 'tis verra important to ask Mr. Willett about Red Charlie."

12

Modesty paid the driver handsomely and hastened into the stables with her satchel tucked snugly under her arm. The dratted codfish had insisted on three cups of tea. Three! By the time Lord Roxburgh said his goodbyes it was already ten minutes past twelve. And then she had to listen to her mother's five-minute lecture on what a good catch the earl was. Thank heavens she'd had the forethought to ask Randolph to tell the driver to wait.

"Mr. Willett," she called as she pushed through the door, unbuttoning the pelisse covering her "masquerade" costume. "I'm so sorry I'm late."

The stablemaster appeared, leading Venom who was outfitted with Modesty's saddle. "There ye are. I was about to give up on ye."

"But I sent Randolph to let you know I was running behind."

"Aye, and if you 'adn't, I would have assumed you were not comin'."

Modesty moved to the mounting block while Mr. Willett stopped the horse beside it. "Have you seen Lord Berwick?"

"'e's puttin' Poseidon through 'is paces, 'e is."

"Oh, thank goodness. I was afraid he mightn't wait."

"'e nearly didn't until I said 'es as good as beaten if 'e doesn't give your 'orse a go. Why the devil did ye agree to swap mounts in the first place? Venom is only a two-year-old. If the duke finds out I let ye ride 'im, 'e'll skewer me."

"Wheesht. Lord Berwick considers himself a better rider and I aim to prove him wrong."

"Are ye certain about that? Berwick 'as seen ye ride!"

Modesty smiled to herself. The viscount mightn't underestimate her riding skills, but he underestimated everything else about her. She greeted the racehorse by letting him sniff her palm, then rubbed his neck. "Och, ye are a bonny lad." She leaned toward his ear and whispered, "Are ye ready to ride with a lassie? Prove who's the king of this wee racetrack?"

To that Venom snorted and shook his head.

"Aye, there's a good lad," she said, taking the reins and making herself comfortable on the small saddle.

Mr. Willett kept pace alongside her as she cued the horse to walk on. "Venom isn't exactly the 'orse I would 'ave picked for your first race."

"Why not?"

"'e's skittish and a might younger—very young and still a colt. Poseidon is eight years of age."

"Well, you said I was ready to race, and at a ball Lord Berwick recognized me, so I thought it was only fair to challenge him."

"Just don't try to push too 'ard, else ye might break your bloody neck."

"I'll be fine. My seat is sure." Modesty grinned down at her trainer. "Besides, Berwick weighs a great deal more than I do."

Before Mr. Willett had a chance to utter another word, Modesty spotted His Lordship riding Poseidon, and she trotted toward them. "Are ye ready for a wee hiding?"

"Oh?" Looking as dapper as any gentleman riding through Hyde Park, the viscount tugged on his reins and grinned as if he were pleased to see her—either that or his smile appeared to be exceptionally bright in today's sunlight. "So, you decided to make an appearance, did you, my lady?"

"You kent I would, m'lord."

He squinted. "I thought you were rather anxious to best me in a race."

"Aye, but my mother intervened."

"A dress fitting perchance?"

"Worse. The Earl of Roxburgh invited himself for tea—but only if I poured."

Berwick scowled as if a dark cloud were passing overhead. "I didn't know His Lordship was courting you."

Modesty scowled right back. "Och, he is most definitely not courting me because I am not courting him. In fact Roxburgh ought to be courting my mother."

Berwick threw back his head and laughed, making his mount skitter aside. "My, you are a fiery vixen."

She reached back and grasped her club of shiny red. "Did you not ken? Fieriness comes with the hair color."

"Really? I would have thought your temperament had more to do with being Scottish."

"Aye?" she asked, slapping her crop through the air and making it hiss. "What about your wee temperament?"

The viscount ran his reins through his fingertips. "I have no idea to what you are referring, madam."

"You forget my mother is English. I ken all about the wars at work within the breasts of your countrymen. At least the Scots are honest with their emotions."

The dark scowl returned. "Shall we race or shall we continue to argue on the virtues of being raised either side of the border?"

Modesty cued Venom to trot toward the starting line. "This is a race for the ages—Scotland versus England."

Berwick trotted alongside her. "Shall we wager?"

"Sir, I am but my brother's sister. I have little with which to wager, whereby you are a viscount in possession of a vast estate."

"There you go, being overly literal again."

As she reined her horse to a stop, she glanced at the viscount. His eyes were sparkling with mischief. Her gaze trailed to his lips, bringing with it a distracting memory. One that made her insides feel as if they were dancing with fairy dust. "What sort of wager did you have in mind if not a literal one?"

He stopped beside her, near enough to finger her billowing satin sleeve. "If I win, I should like to reserve the waltz at the Ruthland Ball."

Hmm. Within the blink of her eyes, Modesty suddenly visualized dozens of things upon which to wager. Licking her lips, she admired Venom's sleek, shiny coat. The horse was truly a prized stallion, chestnut in color without a spot of white on his pasterns or his nose. "Verra well," she said, again leveling her gaze at the presumptuous viscount. "If I win, I should like to be Venom's jockey at the race at Primrose Hill."

Berwick gaped. He shook his head. He scoffed. "Have you heard nothing I have said in the past fortnight? If I were to agree, you would be ruined."

"Not if no one kens it is me."

"But I will ken... er... know it is you."

"That's because you are something of an anomaly."

"What, exactly, do you mean?"

"Well, I reckon 'tis on account of your red hair. Mayhap because we are gingers, we are drawn to notice each other far more than others are drawn to notice us."

He glanced her way, his eyes a wee bit dark. "I assure you, everything about you is noticeable, my lady."

Well, there was a perfectly good reason for him to notice her, of course. "That's because you are drawn to me. I have to say, I've been awfully preoccupied with thoughts about you since you kissed me. Twice, mind you. And I havena even been trying to think about you."

"Oh, well, if that is what you consider a compliment, then might I suggest you—"

"What the blazes are the pair of ye doin', holding a session of Parliament?" shouted Mr. Willett from his place at the finish line. "'Tis almost one o'clock. The lads will be returning soon."

Modesty immediately cued Venom to sidestep, then assumed the racing crouch with her backside high in the air and her nose out over her mount's withers. With her eyes on the track she gave a single nod.

Mr. Willett fired the pistol and Venom shot ahead faster than Poseidon ever started before. But Berwick was nearly as fast, his horse's nostrils flaring as if he recognized the challenge and harbored one single desire—to win.

Well, Modesty MacGalloway wasn't going to allow her tried and true eight-year-old to beat a two-year-old, especially not when she was riding the younger horse. Wielding her crop, she demanded more speed, slapping the reins and projecting her weight as far forward as her thighs could bear.

Venom nosed ahead. "That's right faster, lad, faster!"

"Oh no you don't!" Berwick hollered, thrashing with his crop, urging Poseidon forward until the two were again nose-and-nose. Good heaven's she hadn't been wrong when she insisted that Poseidon was faster than her brother realized.

Around the bend the two champion horses battled as if they were born for this very moment. As if their entire lives had been spent training for this single event.

"Go, laddie, go, go, go!" Modesty shouted as she and Venom galloped into the straight and took the lead.

Mr. Willett hollered something imperceptible, one arm flailing while his other hand gripped his pocket watch.

Modesty didn't dare look back even though the thundering beat of Poseidon's hooves was too close.

"Give him some rein!" shouted Willett.

Modesty obeyed. So did Berwick, gaining, Poseidon snorting, now even with her stirrup. Was her horse actually insulted that she opted to race another?

Drat!

With one furlong to go, she gnashed her teeth and leaned out farther over her horse's neck than she'd ever dared in her life. But her dear "retired" horse continued to squeeze the distance.

As they neared the finish line, Venom was ahead by a nose. "Faster, faster!" Modesty shrieked, urging the younger horse to surge forward.

"Oh, oh, oh!" Willett shouted, running after them while they worked to slow their mounts. "'Twas too close to call! I've never seen anything like it. I didn't think Poseidon 'ad that kind of speed in 'im. 'e's a competitor 'e is. And Venom. He wasn't about to lose even when carrying a jockey who 'adn't the time to take 'im through 'is paces!"

Modesty turned her horse and trotted toward her trainer with Berwick at her side. "What do you mean it was too close to call? Venom won fair and square."

"Ye crossed the line at the same time, milady. Might I say at record pace. If you managed that in a sanctioned six-furlong, no one in Britain would be able to come close."

"Aside from me," said Berwick rather dryly.

"Aye, milord, can ye imagine how fast Venom would run if 'er ladyship 'ad a chance to work with 'im a bit?"

Modesty smiled. "So, it was a tie?" she asked, barely able to believe it.

"I reckon so," Willett agreed.

"Then congratulations, Lord Berwick, we shall waltz at the Ruthland Ball." Grinning from ear-to-ear, she let her statement hang in the air for a moment. "And I shall be Venom's Jockey in the six-furlong race at Primrose Hill."

Mr. Willett's pocket watch slipped from his fingers. "You?" he asked, stooping to retrieve it.

Berwick frowned. "I didn't agree to your terms."

"Oh? I didna think it was like you to renege on your word, m'lord."

"I—ah." His Lordship thrust his finger at the trainer. "He will not allow it."

Modesty glared at Mr. Willett. "You said I was ready."

The man cleaned his watch on his trousers' leg. "Aye, but..." He glanced toward the barn. "What if we cut your 'air?"

"Absolutely not," said Berwick as Modesty simultaneously replied, "What a brilliant idea!"

13

As his manservant slowly scraped the sharp straight-edge against the grain of the stubble on Kenneth's neck, he didn't dare swallow.

"Might I speak freely, sir?" asked Welch, wiping the blade on a cloth.

"Yes, of course." Out of the corner of his eye, Kenneth watched the shiny razor return to his neck. "Don't you always?"

"I suppose." Welch swiped ever so carefully. "Though since you've risen to the lofty post of viscount, I feel as though it is now best to ask beforehand."

"What's on your mind?"

Welch used his pointer finger to raise Kenneth's nose as he shaved above his lip. "Well, the lad you brought in to serve as an errand boy... "

"What about Freddie?"

"He seems to be a good-hearted chap, though I daresay Brown is not convinced—grumbles like a sore-headed oaf below stairs—says the child doesn't belong in a peer's household and whatnot."

In Kenneth's opinion as viscount he was the person who decided who remained in his employ and who did not. "Why? Has the boy tried to steal the silver?"

Using the cloth to clean the remainder of the shaving cream away from Kenneth's face, Welch shook his head. "Not that I am aware of."

"Then what is it? I've noticed Frederick has cleaned up quite nicely. Were you the one who cut his hair?"

The manservant stepped back. "I was, sir."

Kenneth stood and stretched. "Well, you did a fine job of it. He looks as if he'll make a respectable footman someday."

"If only he acted accordingly."

"Does Freddie need a lesson or two in propriety?"

Welch set to returning the shaving equipment to the velvet-lined box kept beneath the washstand. "Yes, very much so. He needs to learn proper manners and how to address people according to rank. He also could learn to read."

Kenneth hadn't thought about the boy's illiteracy. But what did he expect from a street urchin who picked pockets for the benefit of a woman who whipped him? "Whom should I set to the task of teaching the lad his trade?"

"Most definitely not Brown, sir. The butler is quite intolerant of errors."

Of course, Kenneth knew something of Brown's rigid scruples since the man had always been the driving force who'd kept the Berwick servants in line. He also doubted Brown had ever encountered a child as uncultured as Freddie. "How about you?"

With the shaving kit stowed away, Welch tugged down his cuffs. "Me, sir?"

"You read quite well. Your manners are impeccable, and yet you have no problem speaking your mind when warranted."

Welch huffed a sigh, rolling his eyes to the ceiling as if taming a lad far exceeded his abilities. "Freddie is quite *worldly* for his age, though I believe he's far more intelligent than Brown gives the child credit for."

If Kenneth didn't go for the kill now, the manservant would be allowed too much time to conjure up dozens of excuses as to why he wasn't a good candidate to take the boy under his wing. "So, what say you?"

The man rubbed the back of his neck. "I could *offer* to help him?"

"No. As of today, I am promoting you to head butler and Freddie to footman. It is your responsibility to bring the lad up to snuff."

"Why the blazes did I bring up the lad in the first place," Welch mumbled, reaching for a newly starched neckcloth. "But what of Brown, sir?"

Kenneth stood with his shoulders back and chin held high. "Brown is retiring."

The manservant set to tying a gordian knot. "I thought his retirement date had not yet been set."

"I've just decided it is time to make a formal announcement."

Once Kenneth was fully dressed, he found Brown polishing the silver in the butler's chamber below stairs. "Might I have a word?"

The old man shot to his feet. "My Lord? Is something amiss?"

"Not at all," Kenneth replied. He'd ruled out Brown as a possible suspect ages ago and it was nigh time to let the fellow enjoy the quiet solitude of Surrey. "I have decided it is time for you to begin your retirement. I shall grant you an additional two months wages, which ought to suffice to set you up in a boarding house whilst you find the cottage of your dreams."

Brown gaped, his expression bewildered. "Have you found my replacement?"

"Indeed I have." Because of his scientific nature, Kenneth wasn't accustomed to beating around the bush, but in this instance, it wasn't entirely unreasonable to apply a bit of mollification. "You have served my family extremely well and I shall always look upon you with fondness."

The man still looked lost as he glanced from one wall to another. "So soon?"

"Go on, Brown. You have earned the right to enjoy your retirement in comfort."

"Thank you, sir. However—"

"Hmm?"

"Well, might I be permitted leave to speak frankly?"

The butler was nothing like Welch. Kenneth couldn't ever remember the man voicing his opinion, at least not with any conviction. "Yes, please do."

Brow riffled his fingers through his grey hair. "Well, I've wondered if I might be on that list of yours... the one with the suspects."

"You were initially, as was everyone."

"And what changed your mind?"

"I didn't believe you capable of..."

"No, I most definitely am not," Brown agreed. "You must know Alfred was always my favorite."

"Truly?" Alfred was everyone's favorite. Nonetheless, Kenneth feigned shock. "You wound me."

"Of course, you were a good lad as well, but Alfred used to come down to my rooms and play checkers. He'd sit here for hours. Sometimes I..."

"Hmm?"

Brown rubbed his temples as he shook his head. "You'll think I'm but a silly old man."

"No, quite the contrary. I loved Alfred as well. He was... well, to tell you true, he was a better man than I."

"I'm not certain *better* is correct, but he was gentler."

Kenneth couldn't agree more. Alfred would have gone about this whole business with a fair bit more tact. "What were you going to say? Sometimes you...?"

"Well, when we'd play checkers, he would tell me about whatever happened to be on his mind at the time. And there were moments when I felt as though he were as dear to me as a son. I grieved his death— am still grieving. Furthermore, I am more astonished than anyone at his bequest."

"If you are the one who taught him to give me a hiding at checkers, then I believe he was quite genuine in singling you out in his will." Kenneth smiled as he gripped the old man's upper arm. "Go on to Surrey with my blessing."

"Thank you, sir, and if Alfred did perish at the hands of another, I truly hope you find the culprit and bring him to justice."

~

IT WASN'T but a few days later when Kenneth found a very small entry at the bottom of the social page of the *Gazette* reporting Baron Bottesford had returned to London with his new Baroness. Kenneth put a checkmark by the baron's name on his list of possible suspects. Though every avenue he had pursued thus far had turned out to lead nowhere, he still was not convinced his brother had died of natural causes.

Though he had never met Bottesford, as the senior peer, it was Kenneth's place to call upon the chap. He donned his hat and gloves and headed out on foot, arriving at the baron's door approximately ten minutes later. He promptly presented his card to the butler and was asked to wait in the entrance hall.

And though he didn't stand on ceremony, as a viscount he ought to have at least been shown to the parlor. Except when the butler slid open the slot doors to said room, the glimmer of red hair caught Kenneth's eye.

"Lord Berwick," Lady Modesty exclaimed, rising from her perch.

Kenneth frowned at the imp. How had she known he'd be there? Of course, she couldn't have. But why was it Her Ladyship managed to be everywhere he went? Did she not have a recital or something requiring her attendance today?

As the butler stood aside, the baron, baroness, and Lady Modesty filed into the entrance hall. "My lord, how fortuitous it is to receive you," muttered Bottesford obsequiously as he read the card still on the butler's silver tray.

"My thanks," Kenneth replied, bowing, of course.

"I was just about to serve tea," said the baroness. "Won't you join us?"

"Actually, I was wondering if I might have a word with you, my lord?" Kenneth gave Lady Modesty a pointed stare before he cleared his throat and returned his gaze to Bottesford. "In *private.*"

Thankfully, the baron led the way into his library and headed for the sideboard. "I'm ever so glad not to have to drink tea. Will you join me in a tot of brandy?"

"I think not."

Bottesford turned, the hint of alarm reflected in his expression. "By your tone, I sense this is not a social call."

"Quite right." Kenneth removed the pistol from his pocket and slid a finger along the sleek barrel. "I have a few questions to which I require truthful answers."

Bottesford dropped the crystal decanter stopper onto the carpet. "How dare you come into my house and threaten me."

"How dare you take advantage of inexperienced young ladies with the intention of coercing them into agreeing to marry you in order to steal their fortunes."

"I assure you, Lady Bottesford is quite happy with our arrangement."

"Is she?" Kenneth stepped forward. "What about Lady Philomina Carmichael?"

At the mention of the woman he had unsuccessfully tried to woo, the baron blanched, a bead of sweat rolling from his temple. "I may have misjudged her intentions."

"You tried to ruin the poor woman—"

"I may have been a tad forward, but I assure you once I discovered she was being courted by your brother, I stepped aside—I *willingly* stepped aside."

"I think not."

"What are you saying?"

"I believe you entered my brother's home, stole the ring he purchased for his future bride, and murdered him with a salve of wolfsbane."

Kenneth had seen any number of baffled expressions in his life, but the baron's face was utterly bamboozled. The man didn't blink for several ticks of the clock.

"You are mad! I've never had the occasion to be

inside your brother's town house. Furthermore, my pockets might have been a bit light of coin, but never in all my days have I contemplated murder, let alone have I killed someone." Bottesford stumbled to a chair, pulling a handkerchief out of his breast pocket, and wiping the perspiration from brow. "I haven't the stomach for blood of any kind. Not even my own. Now please put that vile weapon away before you actually shoot something!"

Kenneth stood stunned. Damnation, he'd chased after yet another red herring. He should have known by the man's past behavior that the baron was a milk-livered fiend. He shoved the pistol back into his pocket. "We shall see," he grumbled, marching out of the library and hastening to the parlor.

The ladies looked up, Modesty stopping her cup halfway to her mouth.

After hesitating for a most awkward moment, Kenneth turned to the baroness. "Forgive my impertinence, but might you be so kind as to show me your wedding ring, my lady?"

Her Ladyship beamed as she held out her hand, presenting a gold band set with five small garnets. "This belonged Bottesford's mother."

Obviously there was not a bedamned sapphire in sight.

14

"Why the blazes were you having tea with the baron and baroness?" Berwick demanded as he strode along Culross Street, the wind so fierce it blew Modesty's bonnet off.

She grasped the ribbons and adjusted her hat, endeavoring to tie it tighter while struggling to keep pace with the viscount's long strides. "I didna ken I wasna allowed, ye sore-heided oaf!"

"You should have realized I would seek out the baron as soon as he returned to London."

"Is that so? And am I also supposed to have a wee Druid's crystal ball so I may watch your every move?"

"Don't be ridiculous," he said, crossing the street into Hyde Park.

Modesty dodged a barrow full of hay as she hastened after the ogre. "I'm the one being ridiculous? I beg your pardon, but we are supposed to be partners and solve this mystery together."

Berwick proceeded onto one of the lesser used pathways and threw out his arms. "We are not bloody partners."

Modesty marched alongside him. Either the man

was daft or he'd been in a trance over the past weeks. "Did I not find out who Alfred was courting?"

He pursed his lips, giving her one of those glares that was supposed to scare her into keeping mum. Except Modesty was the youngest of eight children and over the years she had grown impervious to such unuttered threats.

She stopped and thrust her fists onto her hips. "Answer me!"

Turning on his heel, Berwick sauntered toward her. "You proved somewhat helpful in that matter."

"Aye, and did I not take you to the apothecary, and did I not convince ye to talk to Mr. Willett about Red Charlie? And didna ye receive the information ye were seeking without causing a wee stir?"

"Yes, I suppose that was fairly helpful, however, you have now put me in a most precarious situation."

"Why?"

"Because you cajoled your way into being Venom's jockey for the six-furlong race at Primrose Hill."

"Cajoled? We had a *wager*, which happened to be your idea, sir!" Modesty had been practicing with Venom and Mr. Willet had uttered nothing but praise. "Do you have another jockey for your horse? Didna Alfred sack the last fella after the Epsom Derby?"

Berwick didn't answer.

Modesty shoved his shoulder. "No you dunna have a jockey. And just because I'm female doesna mean I'm as fragile as a glass windowpane. I'm utterly sick of men who believe they are the superior race and I'll not tolerate—"

Within a heartbeat, she was in his arms, his warm lips claiming hers. Before her mind had a chance to think, she melted into his kisses as if her life would be smote if she did not. His body pressed flush against hers. Without words, his delicious mouth soothed Modesty's pent-up ire and replaced it with swirling, blissful, unimaginable desire.

As the kiss ended, she gazed into his eyes—darker now. She reached up, her fingers brushing the pulsing vein at his temple. The softness of his skin made her lips part with a tiny gasp. "This is the third time you've kissed me, m'lord."

He tilted his lips lower and nibbled her neck. "Mm hmm."

"But this time there is more passion in it," she whispered, not wanting him to hear, but wanting him to understand all the same. What was it about Kenneth Davenport that confused her so? One moment she was certain she was winning an argument, and the next, he claimed her mouth, sabotaging her advantage and sending her capacity for reason into retreat.

He captured her mouth once more, plying her lips until she went completely limp in his arms. Was this what the other debutants meant by going weak at the knees?

Modesty's voice quivered as she sighed. "I still believe I am the best jockey for Venom."

"Agreed," he whispered, the single word also barely audible.

Lightning flashed above as she tipped her head back enough to stare into his eyes. "Truly?"

"It seems where you are concerned I am utterly helpless to deny you."

Evidently her argument hadn't retreated very far.

She rose and brushed her lips over his, impervious to the downpour's onset. "I do believe I quite enjoy kissing."

～

M ODESTY STOOD on the platform in front of the modiste's three full-length mirrors. Though she was staring at herself, in truth she could have been staring into an abyss and wouldn't have noticed. She did indeed enjoy kissing Lord Berwick but doing so utterly complicated their arrangement.

First of all, the viscount hadn't done one thing to properly court her. Didn't that make him a rake of the worst sort? In truth, every time his lips met hers, she should have protested quite vehemently.

Except his kisses are too divine to think about protesting anything.

"Modesty, you haven't listened to a word I've said." Mama's voice meandered into her thoughts.

Blinking, she returned to the present, first looking at the modiste's assistant on her knees, pinning the lace of the azure-blue gown she was to wear to the Ruthland Ball. "Please forgive me, I was daydreaming again."

"My heavens, no wonder you haven't found a husband as of yet." Mama cooled her face with her fan. "I said the satin bodice brings out the color of your eyes. It is quite flattering."

"It truly does," said Kitty, sitting beside Mama, her blonde curls bobbing in agreement.

Modesty regarded her reflection, imagining jockey silks—in blue since the color suited her so well. "I do like it."

"Merely like?" asked the modiste. "The lace I used for the skirt is from France, it is of the best quality."

"I think you'll be the belle of the ball," said Kitty, bless her. She was ever so supportive, even though with her flawless complexion, Kitty was always the belle. "How are your horseracing lessons coming?"

Mama shot straighter. "Horseracing?"

"Riding lessons, Mama," Modesty corrected while shooting Kitty dagger eyes. The dratted lass had promised to keep mum, but there she sat beside Modesty's mother, talking about horse racing. "You know I've been taking riding lessons on Sunday afternoons."

"Ah yes, but why you need lessons when you have the most natural seat of any of my children is beyond me."

"Mayhap it is because I dearly love to ride." Modesty plucked a rogue thread from her bodice. "Doing so makes me happy."

"Well then, by all means, I would not want to impinge on your happiness." Mama snapped her fan closed with a *thwack*. "However, I would be far more pleased if your lessons were provided by Lord Roxburgh. I wonder why he hasn't come to call again?" she asked, her voice trailing.

Modesty had no intention of encouraging the earl's affections. Not ever in her life could she see herself married to that pompous windbag. "Perhaps he has found another redheaded lass upon whom to shower his attentions."

"Perish the thought!" Mama said wielding her fan in the direction of Modesty's behind.

"I'll wager Roxburgh will be at the ball." Kitty clapped, bouncing like an excited bairn. "Everyone will be there."

Modesty leveled her gaze at the imp. "Even Lord Richter."

"Richter?" Mama asked while Kitty turned the color of the scarlet settee upon which they were perched. "Is there something I do not know?"

"Not at all, Auntie Patience." Though not officially her aunt, years ago, Mama had suggested Kitty call her thus, because she had become such an important part of the family. Kitty winked Modesty's way. "Though I daresay His Lordship is quite skilled at handling the ribbons."

Mama's lips stretched into a sly grin. "I do believe all of London admires Richter's shiny black phaeton."

"There we are," said the assistant standing. "How is the length now?"

Modesty stepped off the dais and walked a few paces. "I think it will be fine."

"The gown is lovely," Mama said, turning toward the modiste. "Of course it will be ready by Wednesday, yes?"

The seamstress fluffed Modesty's puff sleeves, the style this Season a bit fuller than last. "I shall have it delivered to the duke's town house in plenty of time to dress for the ball."

While the assistant unlaced her, Modesty glanced at the mirror out of the corner of her eye. Would Berwick like the gown as much as Mama and Kitty had? What would she do if the viscount actually did decide to court her rather than merely steal kisses?

She touched her lips with her fingertips. *Perhaps I shouldna allow him to kiss me again. After all, I cannot lose sight of the fact that I am merely helping him solve the mystery of his brother's death. Once Berwick uncovers the answers he is seeking, he'll head home to his bees and his fleecy sheep whilst I will quietly slip into spinsterhood.*

~

As the sister of a duke, Modesty had been invited to and attended the weekly Wednesday balls at Almack's, but the Ruthland Ball was touted as the most extravagant of the Season. As she stood beside Kitty and Felicity, she wondered why. The rooms at Almack's, though elegantly appointed, were the same as always —brightly lit crystal chandeliers with mirrors reflecting the light from the hundreds of wax candles, chairs covered in gold velvet, cream chiffon draperies. Of course, everyone who entered presented their voucher—the coveted, stamped document indicating the bearer was an esteemed member of the *ton* and had earned the right to enter through her aristocratic doors.

Men wore knee breeches, pristine neckcloths, and cutaway coats. Women always donned their finest gowns, though never the same twice. And there Modesty stood between Kitty and Felicity, in their usual positions near the entry, watching people arrive while Mama came past frequently and introduced gentlemen who signed their dance cards.

"Oh, oh!" Felicity grabbed Kitty's elbow. "There's Lord Richter!"

Kitty leaned away, patting her hand over her heart. "He does look rather dashing in black."

"Shall I wave?" asked Modesty, her question earning her a jab in the ribs.

"You know better than to do something so utterly gauche," Kitty scolded.

"Aye." Modesty scanned the room for any sign of Lord Berwick who, she was quite certain, had not yet been announced. "But I couldna resist. Goodness, you do seem smitten."

"So? What if I am? We're mulling about the marriage mart to find husbands, all three of us."

"Actually," said Felicity. "Since the Season is nearly over, I've decided to accept a position as governess for my aunt over the summer."

"And then what?" asked Kitty.

"And come back to London for a second Season."

Felicity patted Modesty's elbow. "You'll be here as well, won't you?"

"I'm not certain."

"Oh?" asked Kitty, her gaze finally shifting from Lord Richter. "Do tell. I knew you were hiding something from me."

True, Modesty had become far more secretive ever since starting jockey lessons, and more so after agreeing to help Berwick, but Kitty had assumed incorrectly. "When we commenced the Season, I was full of excitement, but nothing is akin to what I envisioned."

"Are you jesting?" Kitty asked, throwing out her arms and gesturing to the ballroom. "All of polite society is here—at least those who have not done something to create a horrendous scandal. Men come to Almack's in search of well-bred young ladies whom they can wed."

"Then it should be called a breeder's mart," Modesty mumbled. In all intents and purposes, she ought to be stained by scandal by now. She had ridden in a carriage with a single man more than once. She had passed herself off as a man and attended a chess match at Waiter's. And every Sunday she donned jockey silks and galloped around the racetrack at full tilt.

Lord Richter averted the ensuing debate of marriage versus breeder's mart when he bowed to the ladies and signed all three dance cards. Of course, he opted to waltz with Kitty. He returned Modesty's card, having selected a quadrille. As she slipped it from his fingertips, she spotted her mother weaving her way through the crowd with Lord Roxburgh in tow. Turning, Modesty quickly penciled in Berwick's name for the waltz.

"Ladies," said Mama, clearing her throat. "Have you had the pleasure of meeting George Hamilton, the Earl of Roxburgh?" she asked, introducing Felicity and Kitty. "Of course you already know my daughter."

Felicity was the first to curtsy. "My lord, it is a pleasure, truly."

Good heavens, the lass had stars in her eyes. Modesty sighed. "M'lord, I hope you have been well."

He slipped the dance card from her fingertips and frowned. "Berwick has reserved the waltz?"

"Aye, though no one has added their name to the Grand March as of yet, and I'll reckon it will start soon."

While Roxburgh complied and signed his name to the march, Felicity stepped forward. "The waltz on my dance card has not yet been claimed, my lord."

The earl gave Felicity a once over. "Your father is Baron Drummond, is he not?"

The lass blushed, looking to her toes. "Yes, sir."

It was all Modesty could do not to roll her eyes. Felicity was about as demure as a goat. Though she was a kind goat, and if she wanted to flirt with Lord Roxburgh, then she was more than welcome to do so.

Mama didn't arrive at the same conclusion because she managed to bump His Lordship's arm and made it appear as though she had been pushed from the crush of the crowd. "Oh, my heavens, I do believe the hall will be close to bursting by the time all the guests have filed in. I do hope you will see fit to visit us again. My daughter so enjoyed serving you tea."

"You may have misunderstood, Mama," Modesty said. "But I did enjoy *drinking* the tea for certain."

Roxburgh threw back his head and laughed. "I do like the Scottish spirit."

Drat, drat, drat! Could she say nothing to adequately express her disinterest in the wig-wearing arse?

A fanfare alerted the dancers to take their places for the grand march. Roxburgh offered his elbow and led her to the floor.

"I'll wager you have had dozens of proposals this Season," he said, staring ahead as if his question had been about the weather or if the Thames flowed east.

The orchestra began Mozart's Turkish March and Modesty proceeded to promenade like an obedient lady. However, she had no intention of encouraging the earl's pursuit. "I intend to remain a spinster."

Again the man laughed, though this time his expression was puzzled. "I realize by your nature you Scots tend toward being sardonic—"

"Och, I dunna tend toward anythin'," she replied, emphasizing her brogue. "Marriage is no' for me. I just havena told my mother as of yet."

"I see." Roxburgh sniffed. "I am sure once you have discussed your stance with Her Grace, she will impart the matronly advice a young woman such as yourself needs."

Ye overstuffed codfish.

"Now tell me." Roxburgh surveyed the room. "I haven't seen hide nor hair of Lord Berwick. How is it he came to sign your dance card?"

"'Twas an agreement."

"Oh?" the earl asked, leaning too close, his eyebrows arched.

"Which is none of your concern, sir."

"I should like to make it my concern."

Dear Father Christmas, will this man not leave well enough alone? If Modesty told him Berwick was courting her, it not only would be a lie, the earl was likely to go forth and accuse Mama of lying, which would be like telling a housecat there's a mouse under the bed. The poor mouse wouldn't stand a chance.

"Is he courting you?" Roxburgh persisted.

"My heavens, you overstep, sir," Modesty said, throwing her shoulders back to express utmost indignation.

"I am quite curious as to why your mother invited me to visit again."

She offered a half-smile, unmistakably expressing her "sardonic nature." "Mama is verra accomplished at pouring tea." Thank heavens the march came to an end. Modesty curtseyed. "The Dowager is much closer to your age as well."

Seemingly at a loss for words, Lord Roxburgh escorted her off the floor. He bowed. "Since you insist on continuing with this charade of churlishness, I shall find out what is going on between you and Berwick, mark me."

"But—"

Modesty groaned as the earl turned on his heel and disappeared into the crowd.

"There you are, my dearest," said Mama materializing from the surrounding mass of humanity. "I was thrilled to see you having a grand conversation with Lord Roxburgh."

"Who is a boor-heided numpty. I willna serve that old man tea. Not ever again in all my days!"

Modesty hastened away to the lady's withdrawing room. At least that's where she thought she was going until her mother grabbed her by the wrist and pulled her into one of the side rooms, which was lit only by a wall sconce.

The whites of Mama's eyes shone fiercely, reflecting the candlelight. "I knew on the day you were

born you were going to be obstinate and dis-
agreeable."

"I thought you had dubbed me incorrigible."

"Yes, well, that was before you were out. Now you
have nearly completed your first Season and you
haven't even had one proposal."

"But Charity didn't find her match in her first
Season."

"That's because she was the eldest daughter and I
was still in mourning when she had her come out."

Mama paced the floor, wringing her hands. "At
least she had suitors. I have introduced you to every
available bachelor worth his salt and you act like a
curmudgeon. My word, you were born into a dukedom. You have had a fine education. Most of the time
you actually are charming in your own *unconventional*
way. Yet, as soon as we arrived in London, it was clear
you chose to turn into a prickly shrew." Mama pressed
her palm to her forehead. "I am at my wits' end. Kitty
is going to receive a proposal before you do, even
though you outrank her in every way imaginable."

"Kitty can have the *ton*. She's bonny and doesna
have a single freckle on her face."

"Is her beauty the reason you're so out of sorts?"

Aye, Modesty had grown apart from Kitty since
they had arrived in London, but there were too many
things that had brought on her bitterness to list them
all in this dimly lit room in the midst of one of the
most heralded balls of the Season. So, reaching down
to the core of the problem, she decided to be completely honest. "I hate trying to be something I'm not."

"What are you saying? You are your father's daughter. I should know. You resemble him quite significantly—in a feminine way, of course."

"I'm not referring to my parentage. I'm not referring to the *ton* or to all the superfluous things we do to fill our days. I dunna want to be a wife to some wealthy buffoon who doesna love me. I dunna want to marry at all."

"Of course you want to marry. You have been preparing to be a wife since you took your first steps. It is your duty."

"Is it? Truly?"

"Yes," Mama said emphatically.

Feeling a megrim coming on, Modesty pressed the heels of her hands against her temples. "Bless it, Mother, I want to breed racehorses. I want to rise every morning, don my boots, and spend my days in the stables."

Seemingly undaunted, her mother held up her pointer finger. "Horses?"

"Aye."

"Everyone has horses, but there are only a handful of successful racehorse breeders." Mama resumed her pacing, shaking her finger as if she were reciting lessons from *The Mirror of the Graces*. "Some are peers, of course."

"So, is that the lot of it? Now I have shared my deepest desire, you'll set to finding a suitable husband who owns a prized stallion?"

"Whyever not? If that is what you wish, perhaps I ought to have a word with Martin. I'm sure your brother knows a number of nobly born, wealthy horse breeders."

Modesty curled her fingers into fists to keep herself from groaning. "Why not have Marty post an advertisement in the *Gazette*?" Not caring if she sounded sarcastic or not, she threw out her arms and held forth, "*Duke in search of stud farm owner for his rather plain sister. All offers will be considered. Sizeable Dowry.*"

"How dare you patronize me!" Mama thwacked Modesty's shoulder with her fan. "I have done everything for you this Season—I've scheduled your appointments with the modiste. I've responded to every worthwhile invitation. I've introduced you to one perfectly acceptable gentleman after another, and what thanks have I received from you? Your words are so bitter they cut me deeply."

Modesty's skin burned. She hated the *ton* and all it represented. She hated London. But she definitely did not want to hurt her mother or anyone in the family. "You're right. Forgive me. I—I—I just dunna like it here."

"You may not care for London, but there are many peers with seats in the country. Once you find your match, you'll most likely spend the majority of your time on a vast estate with rolling hills and as many horses as you desire."

Modesty nodded, utterly unable to accept her future, heavy with child so frequently she'd never have a chance to ride Poseidon, let alone any other racehorse. Mama was right. All the MacGalloway daughters had been born to marry well—to strengthen the power of the Dunscaby Dukedom. *I shouldna have pressed Berwick to let me ride Venom. He ought to hire a proper jockey. Lord kens I'll never be one.*

Mama slid her hand up and down Modesty's arm. "There's my girl. Two years from now you'll be so happy, you'll wonder why you suffered so much trepidation during your first Season. It isn't easy for women, and stepping out into polite society causes a great deal of consternation for all young ladies of your ilk."

"Aside from Kitty."

"Well, your brother-in-law's sister is an unusual

case. She's like Cinderella in a way—born in a one-room flat above a butcher shop. Until Harry became an earl, Kitty was destined for a life of poverty. You, on the other hand, have always been destined to marry well. That is, *if* you will deign to take the advice of your mother."

15

Kenneth slipped into Almack's surreptitiously, nabbing a flute of watered lemonade from a passing footman. This was the sort of event he loathed. Not only where there dozens of giggling young ladies mulling about, their mothers were all searching the crowd for gullible new viscounts.

Mothers and debutantes weren't the only reason for his tardiness. Though there was one particular debutante who he wanted to avoid—yet did *not want* to avoid. Kissing her had been a mistake.

Three bloody times.

Yet, for his life all he managed to think about since attending the Duke of York's ball was the redheaded Scottish woman who'd vexed him. Perhaps it was merely every-other thought. But he couldn't fathom why the woman constantly popped into his mind. Lady Modesty galloping around a racetrack with wisps of lustrous red hair flowing away from a perfectly chiseled feminine behind. Lady Modesty appearing in his breakfast room, claiming to be Mr. Modistie and looking utterly female no matter how hard she tried to appear otherwise. Lady Modesty demurely sitting in Baron Bottesford's parlor. Lady Modesty finding out who Alfred was courting. Lady Modesty in his carriage, on his lap, her lips slightly parted, her eyes half cast.

God's stones, I owe it to Alfred to find his murderer, yet for the first time in my life I cannot manage to focus my thoughts on anything except a disgustingly darling female!

Kenneth almost hadn't come here tonight. Except he had won a wager for a dance with the lady. And she had seemed so genuinely appreciative as if she had no idea of the strength of the hold she had on him.

"Viscount Berwick!" cooed a mother, whom he could have sworn he'd never seen in his life. "I was afraid you weren't coming to the Ruthland Ball. You are aware it is the most prestigious event at Almack's this Season."

"No. I was not." His back muscles clenched as his gaze darted to numerous unfamiliar faces, until he saw someone he recognized. He gave the mother a nod. "If you'll excuse me, madam, there is something of import I must discuss with Her Grace."

In a half-dozen strides, he was standing beside Lady Modesty's mother.

The dowager duchess glanced his way and offered a cool smile, her fan wielded by lithe fingers. "Ah, Berwick, how good of you to make an appearance."

"I did so only because I promised Lady Modesty a waltz."

Her Grace's delicate eyebrows arched ever so slightly. "You have been conversing with my daughter?"

Good Lord, had he overstepped? "Our paths happened to cross at... ah... the stables. Where I understand she is taking riding lessons."

"Indeed she is." The dowager duchess's smile broadened. "My dear viscount, please tell me you did inherit your late brother's stallion. What is his name? Something like Viper or—"

"Venom. And yes, the horse is boarded at the same stable where Her Ladyship keeps Poseidon."

Amusement glistened in the dowager's keen eyes. "Modesty and her love of horses. She can make even the most skittish nag look like a champion."

"Indeed she has an impressive seat. I say, I've never seen a woman with such a natural predilection for riding."

"Yes, well, if only she were better suited to flirting." The corners of the dowager's lips turned up ever so slightly, clearly playing the part of a debutante's mother yet doing so ever so stealthily.

If Kenneth hadn't been in London at a ball, he might have assumed the lady was making idle conversation. But mothers of the *ton* attended these events for one reason only. "Where is Lady Modesty, perchance?"

With her fan, Her Grace pointed to the floor where the dancers were performing a cotillion. Nearly all the way on the far side of the hall, it was still impossible to miss Modesty—her hair glowed like fire, her gown was the color of Northumberland bluebells, and the bodice fit her as if it had been painted on. She drew in a breath, making her breasts strain against the scooped neckline.

Kenneth stared, his lips parted, his breath arrested.

Modesty looked his way and stumbled.

Her mother gasped, swiftly recovering her composure by tapping her lips. "My Lord Berwick, I would be honored if you would come to tea at your earliest convenience."

Damnation, Kenneth had fallen straight into the woman's snare. "Tea?" he croaked.

"Of course. And I shall see to it Modesty pours for you."

"I would love to come to tea, but I must preface my acceptance by letting you know I am presently not looking for a wife."

"No?" Her Grace asked with an air of amusement. "I sincerely hope you do not perish before you sire an heir as..." She glanced aside while her pause lingered in the air. "Well, we all know you wouldn't want that, now would you?"

Kenneth gulped down his lemonade as the cotillion ended. "I believe it is time for the waltz," he replied, purposely avoiding the duchess' question.

The duchess beamed quite radiantly. "Indeed it is."

He met Lady Modesty as her partner was leading her off the floor. "I believe the next dance is mine." Kenneth relieved the man from his escorting duties.

She gave him a rather panicked grimace and examined the dance card hanging from her wrist. "I was beginning to think you werena coming."

He leaned in, the word *"waltz"* catching his eye. "You added my name."

"Aye, because you promised me the final dance of the eve."

"No, if you recall I asked for the waltz and you promised to reserve it for me."

"Verra well, but one way or another I didna want anyone else to claim that space so I wrote in your name since ye werena here to do it yourself."

"Well, since I did ask, we could skip the set if you would prefer."

"Have you lost your mind? My mother will be

thrilled to see you waltzing with me. She might even invite you to tea."

He grinned, squeezing Modesty's arm and giving her a gentle nudge. "She already has."

"Is that what the two of you were talking about?"

"Yes," he said. "She also mentioned how proud she is of your skill in the saddle."

They assumed their positions as the orchestra played an introduction. "Ye ken she was referring to a sidesaddle."

"Mm hmm," Kenneth replied, his fingers molding into the arc of her waist, his heart suddenly thumping faster than the three-beat tempo. However, at least this time he started on the correct foot.

Lady Modesty's movement was fluid as she smiled up at him. "Ye've been practicing."

"I haven't had the time but thank you nonetheless."

Those blue eyes sparkled as she met his gaze. "Have you been working on solving the mystery?"

He liked how she opted to say mystery rather than murder. Mystery sounded so much more civilized. "Some."

"Aaaaaand?" she asked as he led her into a turn beneath his raised arm.

"There's nothing new."

"Havena found the ring?"

"No, but I did hire a young pickpocket and have decided to train him as a footman."

Lady Modesty stopped, making him pull her along with the music. "Why do you need a pickpocket? Are you planning to continue pilfering jewelry from unsuspecting ladies?"

"Not at all. The chap was—"

"Hmm?"

"Freddie is his name. He's an orphan and he wasn't stealing for himself and I—" The music ended, demanding he bow to Lady Modesty's curtsey.

"Berwick," said Lord Roxburgh, meeting them at the edge of the dance floor. "Might I have a word?"

Kenneth had heard the earl speak in the House of Lords. He hadn't been impressed then and thus far, he believed his first conclusion had been sound.

Lady Modesty squeezed Kenneth's arm. "Ahem."

It took but a glance at her eyes, and her proclaimed distaste for the man came flooding back. Roxburgh was the fop who was attempting to court her and, now that Kenneth saw the man up close, he realized the earl must be twice her age. He kissed her hand, taking his time, making certain their gazes met in a heated stare before he returned his attention to Roxburgh. "I won't be but a moment, my lady."

Scowling, the earl led the way to the opposite side of the ballroom and slipped into an empty window embrasure.

Roxburgh's nostrils flared as he drew in a breath, stretching himself to his full height, which was still a good five inches shorter than Kenneth. "I'll have you know," he said, his breath decidedly pickled by an overindulgence in brandy. "That I've been carefully cultivating an alliance with Lady Modesty and I'll not have a young viscount who has barely entered the peerage ruining all the work I have done to earn the favor of the young lady and her family."

Resisting the urge the issue a direct slap, Kenneth crossed his arms. "Lady Modesty serves you tea once and that constitutes courtship overexertion?"

"That is none of your concern. I saw your name claiming the waltz on Her Ladyship's dance card yet you were nowhere to be seen. Exactly what are your intentions?"

Perhaps a slap is in order? "It appears you wrongfully believe you have earned some sort of entitlement where Lady Modesty is concerned."

"Indeed I have and I'll not idly stand by and allow you to woo her away from me. I'll wager you are unscrupulous, exactly like your brother and I'll not have you importing Dunscaby's sister."

Trying to avoid turning this tête-à-tête into a violent interchange, Kenneth stepped back, clapping a hand over his heart. "How dare you speak ill of the dead! Alfred would never importune a lady. He was a better man than I'll ever be."

Roxburgh snorted, his sneer menacing. "That is as I feared."

A spike of fiery heat seared the back of Kenneth's neck. "You, sir, are very close to being called out. Explain yourself. What grounds have you to accuse my brother of any impropriety whatsoever?"

"Most everyone knows the rumors. After the Derby, I was convinced he was in collusion with Ward Crockford. The three of them teamed up to throw the race. And I lost a thousand pounds, mind you. Crockford and the late Berwick stole my coin. He and that crafty mistress of his."

Three of them? Mistress? Kenneth didn't know what to do first, wring the earl's neck or demand some damned answers. "I assure you my brother was as upset about the results of the Derby as you were." Dammit, if he were to wring Roxburgh's neck now, he wouldn't receive a single reply to his questions. "But what of Alfred's mistress? She was at the race?"

"I wouldn't be surprised if she was."

"Did you see her there?"

"No."

"What is her name?" Kenneth probed, realizing the earl was full of wind and completely lacking in veracity.

"She's a moll. Why should I care what her name is?"

Still, by the way Kenneth's gut quickened, he needed to probe further. "But you are certain my brother was entertaining a mistress?"

The earl's wig shifted with his nod. "Saw him with her—at Waiter's. She was one of Crockford's girls, of that I'm certain."

Kenneth squinted, tipping up his chin. "Why are you so bloody sure?"

"Because the only women allowed inside the gentleman's club are his hired wenches."

And Lady Modesty when she's impersonating a dandy. "Who else knew of this woman's involvement with Alfred?"

"Plenty."

"I think not. My servants certainly were not. Furthermore, Alfred was courting a lady, to whom he was planning to propose."

"Is that so? Come, Berwick, can you honestly say courtship precludes a man from a jaunt with a saucy mistress?" Roxburgh tugged his wig back into place. "Over half the gentlemen at this ball have mistresses."

Kenneth highly doubted the number amounted to half, but arguing the point would do nothing to help him find answers. "Very well, if you do not know the name of my brother's mistress, what did the woman look like?"

"Dunno." The earl scratched beneath his damned wig. "Tall for a woman. Dark hair. Of course, she had a pair of apple dumplings no man could ignore."

"Anything else?" Kenneth asked, since the earl had described at least a quarter of the women in London.

Roxburgh's brow furrowed. "Dammit, man, I did not bring you over here to talk about your brother's improprieties I—"

"I beg your pardon," Kenneth sniped, leaning forward. "But that is exactly why you brought me over here. Without having met me, you formed an erroneous opinion as to my character."

The earl moved away, his back now flush with the wall. "I want you to stay away from Lady Modesty."

"Why? So you can hear it from her own lips that she will never condescend to marry you? Are you aware she believes you are better suited to court her mother?"

"I—"

"Furthermore," Kenneth jammed his finger into Roxburgh's sternum. "She considers you to be a boor and told me herself she would rather remain a spinster than marry you."

The earl batted Kenneth's hand away. "You lie."

"Oh? Somewhere beneath that hideous wig of yours you know you are not the sort of man with whom a vivacious young lady such as Modesty Mac-Galloway would want to share the rest of her life. You're only pursuing her because we are approaching the end of the Season and you have not yet found a bride." Kenneth jabbed his finger into Roxburgh's shoulder. "Tell me, how many other young ladies have refused you this year?"

"How dare—"

"I'll wager you spotted Her Ladyship across the floor of a ballroom. Her fiery hair aglow—a color which is not favored by the *ton* at the moment. I can see it now. The lady was acting the wallflower while other 'prettier' girls were dancing. You knew she had a sizeable dowery, and you knew her to have excellent breeding. You must have decided you could tolerate her hair color along with her freckles—possibly even make them the reason for your attraction."

"I did not—"

"You did. I can see it in your eyes. And let me tell you this very instant, Lady Modesty is intelligent and talented and full of life. If she were to marry you, it would take but a year or two and you would suck all the goodness out of her."

Sweat streamed from beneath Roxburgh's wig. "You are a fiend."

Kenneth took a step back, tugging down his coat. "Coming from you, I shall consider your words a compliment."

"Not only are you a fiend, you are in love with her. And I'll wager she'll not have you either."

"Since I am a score of years younger, I would deign to disagree." *If I were in love with the woman, which I am not.*

Roxburgh leaned forward, his face apple red. "You are a pig."

Kenneth barely heard the insult. *She has merely vexed me. As soon as we solve the murd—*Kenneth stopped mid-thought, another more pressing question wedging itself into his consciousness. "Tell me, my lord, is Lady Philomina Carmichael one of the debutants who refused your suit of marriage?"

Roxburgh's eyes popped wide at the mention of the woman, but he quickly schooled them into an accusing squint. "I beg your pardon? How dare you insinuate that I have been refused by anyone? I am a widower. I was happily married for fifteen years. Furthermore, I am an earl—and outrank you, ye undeserving whelp."

"I may be undeserving, but I can outmaneuver you in a duel of fists." Kenneth slammed his knuckles into his palm. "Stay away from Lady Modesty. She is mine!"

Before he shamed himself and threw the first strike, Kenneth marched away, ire raging through his breast. Had he just faced Alfred's killer? He damned well intended to find out. Roxburgh was a pompous bastard of the highest order. No, Kenneth wasn't looking for a wife, but Modesty hated the cur and there was no way he would stand idly by and watch the fop woo her. She deserved better. She deserved a man who admired her for all of her virtues. She was no wallflower and Kenneth intended to see to it that the hypocrites of the *ton* stopped treating her as such.

16

___

"You are a lady's maid. You're supposed to know all of the latest hairstyles. Have you not heard of hair *à la Titus*? The *Lady's Magazine* reported the cut is ever so fashionable in Paris," Modesty said, sitting on the silk-upholstered stool in front of her toilette.

Randolph ran the brush down Modesty's inordinately long tresses. "But I feel as if it is a sacrilege to shear off all this bonny red hair."

Modesty pushed the hair away from her face with a groan of disgust. "It is a bane to me."

"That is because the English envy such color." Randolph brushed again. "And your mother will string me up by my toenails when she discovers I've cut it all off."

"I will not allow anyone to lay a finger upon you. This is my decision." Modesty snatched the shears from the toilette. "Do it now, else I'll be late to the track."

The lady's maid heaved a sigh as she took the shears and made the first cut. "I canna believe Berwick is letting you ride his champion."

At the Ruthland Ball, Modesty had considered suggesting he find another jockey, but after Roxburgh pulled the viscount aside, Mama had ushered her out the door because their carriage was first in line. She hadn't even been able to bid Berwick a goodnight.

Perhaps it was for the best she didn't offer to bow out because Modesty truly did want to compete. And in order to do so, she couldn't club her hair back as if it were the 1790s. All the other jockeys cropped their hair and if she wanted to fit in, she needed to look the part.

"Have you thought about what you'll tell your mother?" Randolph asked, chopping her way around to the back.

Deciding not to look in the mirror, Modesty caught a fallen lock and watched the strands slip through her fingers. "I'll simply say I wanted to try the Paris style and if it doesna work, I shall grow my tresses back over the summer."

"How do you reckon she'll respond."

"She willna be happy."

"Agreed. But I suppose it is best to cut it afore ye ask permission."

"I dunna need permission to cut my own hair. I'm nineteen years of age. My tresses are my own, not Mama's."

"Well said, m'lady." Randolph cut a few snips over the crown, then set the shears down and riffled her fingers through what remained. "It pains me to chop away such beauty, but it is done. What do ye think?"

Rubbing strands of hair between her fingers, Modesty drew in a deep breath and allowed her gaze to drift up to the mirror. Sitting across was a completely different person. Well, it was her, but it wasn't. She fingered the cap of curls. "I didna ken my tresses were so curly."

Randolph leaned sideways and made a wee snip.

"Now they're no' weighed down, the curls just bounced into place." She straightened, biting the corner of her mouth. "If I werena so afeard of losing my post, I'd say this cut looks utterly bonny cute on you."

Modesty cringed. "Would you say *cute*?"

"Most definitely!"

Holy hedgehogs, now she'd gone from being cute to being most definitely cute? Modesty wasn't completely certain she liked being cuter. Nonetheless, she did quite like the new style. She stood and squeezed Randolph's shoulders. "Thank you. And if anyone asks, it was I who insisted you cut it."

"Well, I say you're so bonny, once the dowager recovers from her initial shock, she'll love it as much as I do."

"Aye, miracles do happen." Modesty headed for the settee where her silks were waiting. "Now I'd best make haste."

It only took a moment to slip into the breeches and button falls, then she stepped into her riding boots.

Randolph held up two hats. "Do you want the poke bonnet or the straw?"

"I think the poke will do nicely." Modesty selected the bonnet and tugged it over her head. "It will be easier to conceal once I transform myself into Mr. Modistie."

No sooner had the words left her lips when the door burst open, making Modesty nearly jump out of her boots. "Whaaaaaat?" Kitty asked, looking from one woman to the other. "It is not Sunday!"

"Wheesht!" Modesty pulled the lass inside and shut the door, ever so glad to have a bonnet covering her hair. "You're supposed to be dressing to attend the races with Charity and your brother."

"Yes, well, since you're not going, Martin sent a missive to Harry, suggesting we all ride to the track in the Dunscaby carriage."

"Ugh."

"And why are you not abed? Auntie Patience said you had an unbearable megrim."

"Before I utter another word, ye must swear to me ye found me asleep and tiptoed back down the stairs."

"But—"

Modesty stamped her foot. "Swear it!"

"Very well, you are asleep." Kitty smiled at Randolph. "With your eyes open."

"Wheesht. My eyes are closed."

"Since they're supposed to be closed, then you'd best tell me what you're up to. Ye're not doing something to investigate Lord Berwick the former's murder, are you?"

Modesty's mouth dropped open. Her breath caught in her throat. "I'll bloody murder Charity!"

"It wasna her," said Randolph.

Completely betrayed, utterly flabbergasted, Modesty whipped around and faced her lady's maid. "You? You are sworn to utmost secrecy. Whyever would you tell anyone about the investigation?"

"Don't blame her. After I spotted you riding with Berwick in Hyde Park, I insisted Randolph inform me as to what you were doing, on threat of telling Auntie Patience what I'd seen."

Modesty covered her face in her palms. "Och, this is an unmitigated disaster."

"Of course, I wouldn't have gone to Auntie Patience, but it was the only way I could get Randolph to tell me anything." Kitty rubbed her hand down Modesty's back. "Come, sweeting. You've always been able to confide in me."

"But sometimes you blurt things out—secrets not meant to be uttered."

"I never mean to." Kitty took Modesty by the wrists and tugged her arms around her neck. "You are my dearest friend. I want only for your happiness. You know that."

"Aye, and I love you like a sister."

"So, then, tell me why you're not abed."

Modesty held Kitty at arm's length and looked at her sternly. "If anyone, anyone at all, including your brother or Chairty or Martin or my mother find out about this, I will be flayed and locked in the medieval tower at Stack Castle for the rest of my days."

Kitty drew a line across her lips. "I promise I'll not tell a soul. You know me."

That was the problem, Modesty knew all too well the lass could blurt out a confidence at exactly the worst moment. Kitty never meant to, but she was such a flibbertigibbet, the secret was out of her mouth before she realized she had promised to keep mum. "Well, this time I am counting on you." Modesty slipped her arms into the pelisse Randolph was holding. "You came up, I was sleeping, and that is all."

"Yes, you're sleeping, but you still haven't told me why you're dressed like a jockey." Kitty tied the ribbons of Modesty's poke bonnet, making a perfect bow. "Do not tell me you are going to try to ride Poseidon in a race today?"

"Nay, I definitely will not be riding Poseidon."

Kitty narrowed her gaze, her lips twisting. "I know you too well, Modesty MacGalloway. You dream of horses. Furthermore, you've been training as a jockey. You would never miss a horse race if you had the opportunity to go, which you most definitely do today. Tell me what's going on this instant or I will shout at the top of my lungs and call for your mother!"

Modesty waved her hands in front of Kitty's face. "No, no, no, dunna do that. Viscount Berwick didna have a rider for Venom—a-a-nd when he saw me on Poseidon, he thought I was a lad and asked Mr. Willett if I might be Venom's jockey." At least her explanation was close to being factual.

"Berwick? But didn't he recognize you?"

"Not at first." Modesty shot a panicked glance at Randolph. "Once he realized who I was, he tried to retract his offer but when I rode Venom and proved to him I could handle his stallion, he agreed."

"But he could be fined for allowing a woman to race, couldn't he?"

"I dunna intend for anyone to find out." Modesty removed the bonnet. "That's why I had Randolph cut my tresses."

Kitty gaped. "Oh, good glorious celestial heavens, your hair!"

"I rather like it. It feels... airy."

Playacting a swoon, the lass dramatically wielded her fan. "Your mother will have one of her spells for certain."

Modesty slid the bonnet back over her head and then retied the ribbons. "She'll love it, I'm certain." *In time.* "Now go and tell them I'm sleeping. And not one word of anything you've seen, promise?"

Kitty locked pinky fingers with Modesty, her grin reminiscent of their days of mischief. "Promise."

~

HIDDEN INSIDE A HACKNEY, Modesty removed her pelisse and bonnet and stowed them in her satchel as the carriage jostled through the London streets on its way north to Primrose Hill. By the time she arrived, she'd transformed into Mr. Modistie, careful to pay the driver for his silence.

"Thank the stars ye're 'ere!" said Mr. Willett, grabbing her by the hand and tugging her through the busy stables.

"Am I late?"

"Aye. Ye've almost missed takin' 'im though 'is paces." The trainer leaned in. "And do not forget to lower your voice, sir."

"But ye said the races start at one," she replied in her deepest brogue, catching a glimpse of the stands through one of the barred stall windows and noting they were still empty of spectators.

"Ye're supposed to be here two hours afore the gates open," he growled.

"Why didna ye tell me that in the first place?"

Not responding, Mr. Willett quickened his pace, nearly making her run.

She'd never seen such a whirlwind of activity in this barn. Little men hardly larger than she wore brightly colored silks. Stableboys with their shirtsleeves rolled up picked hooves, pushed barrows to and fro or carried bales of hay on their broad shoulders. Important men in their finery stood by, smiling and talking loudly as if they were quite assured their thoroughbreds would win.

Lord Berwick leaned against the door of Venom's stall, straightening as he saw her. "Here at last."

"Aye? No one told me to come sooner," she replied, finding Venom already outfitted with her saddle. "If there's no time to lose, I'd best be off."

Berwick removed her bridle from the hook, opened the door, and put it on himself.

"Where's your groom?" Modesty asked.

"I felt it was safest to involve as few people as possible." With an incline of his head he led the horse to the mounting block. "Your reputation is at grave risk."

"Good thinking," she replied, climbing up the steps, then sliding a leg over the horse. "I apologize for not bidding you goodnight last eve. Our carriage was first in line, and you ken how the patronesses hate it if a laggard holds everyone up."

Berwick handed her the reins. "Not to worry. The hour was late."

"What did Roxburgh have to say?" she asked.

"Plenty."

Venom sidestepped beneath her. "Tell me else I willna be able to concentrate on the race."

"The man is as you described. First he accused Alfred of impropriety and then tried to insist that I leave you alone."

I kent Roxburgh was a fiend. 'Tis just as well he didna try to court Mama. "And how did you respond?"

"I may have mentioned that you have a mind of your own." Berwick patted Venom's hip. "Now go on. You're slated for the first race."

"Wait, what did you say first about Alfred's—"

Mr. Willett came up with one of the stewards from the Jockey Club. "This is the new fella I've been training, Stephen Modistie."

Stephen? Good Lord, if this ruse grew much more, she'd have to keep a journal in order to remember everything.

She shook the man's hand and kept her mouth shut, letting Mr. Willett respond to the steward's questions. "He'd best hasten to the track, sir."

"Well, good luck. New jockeys always encounter a barrel of nerves the day of their first race."

"My thanks," she replied in her manly voice, cueing Venom to walk on. In no time she was out on the familiar track, except the dirt had been grated and groomed. She put Venom through his paces much the same as she did with Poseidon, except the younger horse was far more spirited. He smelled the excitement on the air and fought the tug of the reins, clearly yearning to run.

By the time she was finished, the stands were nearly full of the well-dressed upper crust, while folks from all walks of life crowded into the foreground. Primrose Hill was nowhere near as fancy as Ascot, but it was closer to London and was renowned for bringing in the largest crowds—especially since Ascot only allowed members of polite society to attend her races.

After Modesty was confident Venom was ready, she headed back to the stables with a few other jockeys who had been exercising their mounts as well. Mr. Willet met her outside the door. "'ow does he feel?"

"As jumpy as a finch." She was feeling about the same. Here she was, a woman on the back of a glorious racehorse, about to prove her worth. "I reckon he kens there's a whole parcel of people here to watch him. It took a great deal of effort to keep him from tiring himself out."

"Good. Are ye ready?" he asked, leading her toward the pen where the horses walked in a circle, until their race was called.

"Now?" she asked, her stomach falling into an abyss.

"Venom is in the first race, ye silly ferret." Mr. Willett consulted his pocket watch. "They'll announce when the 'orses are to move to the starting line."

He opened the gate and she cued Venom to a trot, joining the other seven horses and their riders.

"Ye're new," said a jockey, falling into a trot beside her.

Venom seemed to not care for this horse, because he threw his head, attempting to pull forward.

"Aye," Modesty replied, trying to use as few words as possible lest someone become suspicious of her gender.

"How's the new viscount?" the jockey continued. "As ornery as the last chap?"

"Ornery?" she asked. "What do you mean?"

"He sacked Venom's last jockey right in front of all of us, mind you. Accused him of throwing the race."

Though Modesty was aware Alfred had sacked Venom's jockey, she puzzled. *Wasn't it Ward Crockford who threw the race? Had Crocky colluded with the Venom's jockey? Besides, I'm certain Alfred demanded the stewards conduct an investigation. And they refused!*

"Did ye ken Viscount Berwick afore he perished?" she asked, trying to assemble the pieces of the conundrum.

"A Scot are ye?"

"Aye." She arched her eyebrows at the fellow. "Well? Did ye?"

"Saw the chap about I suppose." The man tugged down the brim of his cap. "The 'ighbrow was always around the stables. He and 'is wench."

"Wench?" Modesty asked. "But he wasna married."

The jockey roared with laughter. "What are ye, still attached to yer ma's apron strings? All the fops take a bit 'o pleasure from convenient missies on the side."

Good Lord, Modesty had never heard such crudity.

"He had a mistress?" she asked, trying to sound worldly.

"Aye, 'e did."

"Do ye ken her name?"

"Somethin' Eve, or Evelyn." The jockey patted his horse's neck. "That's it, Evelyn."

"Is that why—?"

"Six-furlong horses to the starting line!" boomed a steward, opening the gate to the track.

17

As Kenneth made his way to the owner's box, he was detained by the densely packed crowd in the vestibule.

The man in front of him turned. "Berwick!" This was not simply a man but the Duke of Dunscaby, Lady Modesty's brother.

"Your Grace," Kenneth said, bowing his head and noting the gathering of MacGalloways around the duke, including Modesty's mother as well as the Earl of Brixham along with his wife and sister, Kitty. "I see you've brought the whole family for today's excitement."

"Indeed. I rarely miss a race."

"I say, it is a pity my dear Modesty is suffering a megrim," said the dowager duchess. "My youngest is most enthusiastic about horse racing."

Dunscaby examined his program while his duchess looked over his shoulder. "I see Venom is racing first."

"Indeed, he is."

"Are you nervous, my lord?" asked Lady Brixham, who had come to Modesty's rescue after Kenneth had stitched her wound. The fact that she kept the secret spoke volumes about the sincerity of her character.

"Perhaps I am," he admitted. "And rather anxious to find my seat."

Dunscaby pointed to a side staircase, which was blocked by a steward wearing a red sash emblazoned with the Jockey Club's seal. "Well, lad, that wee passage there will take you to the owner's box much faster than using the main stairs."

"Thank you." He tipped his hat to the ladies. "I hope you enjoy the day."

As he departed, someone tugged his sleeve, making him stop. "I beg your pardon, my lord," whispered Miss Kitty.

He bowed to the young lady. "Yes?"

She drilled her finger into his arm. "You had best know what you're doing with my dearest friend. She might be a spitfire, but she is as innocent as a rosebud."

She knows.

He eyed her dryly, trying to show absolutely no emotion. "I believe the person to whom you are referring has become quite accomplished at winning her own way."

"Perhaps. But I do fret over her ever so." Kitty patted his arm. "I wish you well."

He bowed. "And you, my lady."

The owner's box had padded chairs, though they were all vacant while the eager gathering of owners and their wives crowded along the balustrade overlooking the finish line.

"I see Venom is up first with a new jockey," said one of the well-dressed owners. "Not a one of us have heard the name Modistie. Where did the fellow come from? The Continent?"

"France," Kenneth replied. After all, the word modiste had French origins.

"Ah, yes, I should have guessed. But whatever happened to Venom's jockey—the one who lost the Epsom Derby?"

"I understand my brother sacked him immediately after the race."

"I suppose I might have done the same. But now you're starting all over with an unproven man."

Kenneth shrugged. Who gave a whit if the jockey was actually an unproven woman?

The chap leaned nearer. "Or has your fellow made a name for himself in France?"

A dandy Kenneth didn't recognize turned from his place at the balustrade. "I was in Paris buying horses one year past and I do not recall any mention of Mr. Modistie."

"Well, I suppose that isn't surprising," Kenneth said, offering nothing further and pointing to the starting line. "If you gentlemen would excuse me, I'd like to watch my horse win this race."

Dark clouds loomed above, swirling as they passed over the green interior of the racetrack. Though it hadn't rained this morning, Kenneth was glad Venom was racing first, else he might have to do so in a quagmire of mud soup.

His stallion queued up in the middle of the line of starters, held at bay by ropes pulled taut by men who reminded him of the overlarge footmen at Waiters. Impatiently pawing his right front hoof on the turf, Venom was very difficult to miss with Her Ladyship perched upon his saddle, wearing scarlet. She didn't sit quite as tall and her shoulders weren't quite as broad as the other jockeys'. But other than that, if he didn't know she was a woman, he wouldn't have been able to guess her sex from his vantage point.

Nonetheless, he shouldn't have let her talk him into allowing her to ride. Hell, he hadn't put up much of an argument. Why was it that woman could render him unable to deny her? He glanced across the stands to Dunscaby's box. If the duke ever found out Kenneth had allowed His Grace's sister to enter a sanctioned race, he would be within his rights to demand a duel. Either that or insist Kenneth marry the sprite.

Oddly, the idea, though not particularly appealing, did not make him shudder.

As the ropes fell away and the flag dropped, his heart flew to his throat, his fists clenched, and he managed to draw in a shallow breath as Modesty and Venom surged forward. Their first strides stretched ahead, the horse's nose leading the seven others. Modesty jolted sideways as the nearest jockey struck her with his crop.

"You bloody bastard!" Kenneth bellowed as the crowd gasped. Damnation, he should have thought about the underhanded competitiveness of jockeys when there were high stakes in the offing.

Venom dropped back to second place as Modesty regained her grip, her face determined, her eyes straight ahead, crouching over the stallion's withers, her hips high. Dear God, she was a glorious sight to behold. She was the epitome of Boudica, leading her Druid army into battle against the Roman scourge. If only her waist-length red hair were free to lick the wind like fire...

Oh, fie, fie, damnation, and fie!

He hadn't noticed when she'd come into the barn in a flustered flurry. He'd been too busy trying to outfit

Venom with his bridle, helping her into the saddle. But she'd gone and cut her hair!

Blast the ever-living stars, even though he'd forbidden it, Modesty had ruined her mane of fiery red locks. How the hell was the imp going to explain the shearing to her mother and brother?

Thundering past the owner's box, Venom surged forward, his nose inching closer to the leader's. Modesty wielded her crop demanding more speed while the horse beneath her opened up on the home stretch, his stride wide and long and glorious as they took the lead.

But they hadn't won yet. The third-place horse, Wild Ben, made a play for the lead. He thundered past the colt in second place, now inching up on Modesty, his nose nearly even with Venom's withers.

Modesty glanced back, slapping her crop while Venom held his place. With a vicious crack of his whip, Wild Ben's jockey struck Modesty's shoulder so forcefully, she flew from her saddle, soaring over the rail, her high-pitched shriek audible above the gasps from the crowd. She landed with a *thud*, her body unmoving.

Venom finished the race riderless while Wild Ben's jockey held up his fist in victory.

As Kenneth leaped over the balustrade of the box into the stands below, the gentleman's taunt rattled his eardrums. "It seems Mr. Modistie's voice hasn't gone through the change as of yet."

Damnation!

He pushed his way downward through the press of humanity, not giving a fig if everyone at Primrose Hill discovered Modesty's gender, he only cared she was unharmed. Not once did he take his eyes off her as he reached the bottom of the stands and catapulted down to the ground into the mob of bystanders. Not bothering to slow his pace as he approached the fence, he hurdled the rail, and dashed across the dirt track toward Modesty. Her silk cap fell off as she slowly pushed herself onto her haunches

Kenneth arrived first, dropping to his knees, and tugging her into his arms. "Are you hurt? Is anything broken?"

"I thought I was going to win," she cried no louder than a whisper, closing her eyes and leaning into him.

For the love of God, the woman was a fighter. She could have been killed and her first care is the outcome of the race?

Mr. Willett hastened beside them. "That was a nasty fall. But everyone is watchin' and we need to move off the track straightaway. Can ye walk, Modes— er—*Modistie*?"

She nodded, braver than most men.

Kenneth gripped her hand. "Allow me to help."

"I dunna want anyone to think I'm weak."

"Dammit all," Kenneth swore. "Not only were you struck twice, you flew through the air at least twenty paces before you collided with the ground—a fall that could have killed you!"

"I reckon it was a good thing she was thrown so far," said Mr. Willett. "Else she—er—'e would have been trampled."

Modesty allowed Kenneth to pull her up, then tested her weight, crying out when she tried to step forward on her right foot.

"Your ankle?" he asked.

"My knee."

Mr. Willett bent down and examined the injury, pressing his fingertips around the hem of her breeches. "I mightn't be a doctor, but I reckon we'll 'ave to 'elp ye off the track."

Kenneth stooped, meaning to pick her up. "I'll carry you."

"Nay, ye wouldna carry a man!" She gave him a quick thwack. "I'll put one arm around your shoulders and the other around Mr. Willett's."

Given their differences in height, Kenneth basically carried her off the track as a bolt of lightning flashed overhead, bringing with it booming thunder and pouring rain. But the weather wasn't what gave him pause.

The Duke of Dunscaby stood in front of the entrance to the stables, his arms folded across his broad chest, the expression on his face nothing short of enraged.

18

Modesty sat sandwiched between Mama and Kitty in the cramped carriage while Martin and his wife Julia perched on the bench opposite. In concert with the pelting rain, her megrim thundered in her skull, growing worse every minute due to the coach jerking and joggling over the cobblestone streets.

"I believe we are the only people who are aware Modesty happened to be the jockey who lost her mount," said Kitty, her arm through Modesty's elbow —that hurt too. "I promise I didn't tell a soul she had agreed to be the jockey for Lord Berwick's horse."

"Well, you should have told me," said Mama. "I would have put an end to this nonsense before it began. Now we have a horrendous scandal to deflect from which Modesty may never recover."

"I dunna care about a scandal. Mayhap it is better if I'm ruined because I'm not about to marry one of those snobbish English dandies."

"Of all the impertinent things to say!" Mama thwacked Modesty's elbow, causing a shock of pain to run up her arm and all the way to the top of her pounding head. "You forget your mother is the daughter of one of those highborn Englishmen whom you despise so awfully."

"Ruination aside, how, exactly did you come to convince Lord Berwick and the Jockey Club to allow you on the back of a racehorse?" Martin demanded, his tone harsher than Modesty had ever heard her brother sound before.

"She's been taking jockey lessons on Sundays," Kitty volunteered as easily as one spoke of sunshine in July.

Drop-mouthed, Modesty regarded her dearest friend—possibly not so dearest, and not so friend-like. "You promised to keep mum about it *all!*"

"Perhaps we ought to wait until our sister has been seen by the doctor before we start digging into the cause of the incident," said Julia who, in Modesty's opinion, was always level-headed and kind. She was the perfect duchess. And the only person in the carriage who spoke a lick of sense.

Prior to their departure from the racetrack, on threat of death, Martin had sent Lord Berwick to fetch the family physician. Of course, Marty wouldn't kill His Lordship... at least Modesty prayed he wouldn't.

"It was my idea," she said as the carriage negotiated a turn, she clapped her hands to her cheeks to keep her head from falling off. "Mr. Willett said I was ready to race and Berwick happened to be at the track during one of my lessons. And I had the astounding idea to ride Venom while His Lordship rode Poseidon and we tied—the verra first time I rode the stallion, mind you. Moreover, since Venom was entered into the race and had no jockey, I convinced Mr. Willett and Lord Berwick to let me have a go."

"Of course you did," said Julia leaning forward and

patting Modesty's unharmed knee—which did not hurt in the slightest. "How are you feeling, dearest?"

"Thank you for asking." Modesty leveled a heated gaze at her brother. "To be honest, I feel as though I've been thrown from a rogue carriage careening down a steep mountain slope."

"Not verra original," Martin replied. "Our sister, Grace, already did that."

"Have you a megrim?" asked Kitty.

"Aye."

Mama wielded her lacy fan. "Well, I say this whole debacle has gone much too far. As soon as we arrive home, I shall have a word with Randolph about your hair. How dare she take the shears to it without informing me first!"

Martin shook his fist. "And I'll skewer Berwick as soon as he shows his face at the town house with the doctor."

Modesty raked her fingers through her shorn locks, the length feeling oddly liberating. "None of this was His Lordship's fault."

"All of this was his fault. He owns the goddamned horse!" Martin boomed.

"But, Marty, dear, he is a *viscount*." With her fan, Mama smacked Modesty's inflamed knee, commanding a jolt and a grunt from her daughter. "Do not overlook the fact that he is worth eight-thousand a year. And, though he told me he is not presently on the marriage mart, the chap *is* single."

"A proposal would solve a great deal of consternation," Julia agreed.

Modesty was about to reach across her mother, open the door, and leap from the carriage. Except given the fact that just about every fiber of her body was in pain, she most likely had done enough hurtling from moving conveyances today. "Would you all stop trying to run my life? Lord Berwick is a verra nice gentleman who keeps bees and has bred a line of sheep capable of yielding more wool and milk than any other variety. He's only staying in London at the moment because he thinks his brother was murdered. He has no intention of marrying anyone and every intention of returning to his quiet country life just as soon as he discovers the identity of the fiendish culprit."

"And Modesty is helping him," Kitty said, as if July's sun was now shining on a field of daisies.

As she dropped her head, Modesty's stomach turned over. *St. Columba's bones, Mama will lock me in Stack Castle's tower for certain.*

Everything went silent. Even the carriage stopped jostling while Modesty glared at her dratted least best friend in the world. How did Kitty find out Modesty was involved in the murder mystery? Modesty hadn't even told Charity about that.

"Exactly what is going on between you and His Lordship?" Martin asked, his face clearly taking on high color akin to a man who was about to explode.

Mama again nudged Modesty's sore elbow. "Please tell me your assistance in this matter had nothing to do with his request for not one, but two waltzes."

"Verra well, the murder has absolutely nothing to do with waltzing." *Or kissing.* Usually Modesty smiled when thinking about Berwick's kisses, but given her present state of discomfort, she had no trouble hiding her emotions for a change.

Martin scratched beneath his top hat. "I dunna give a rat's arse about waltzes, a man like Kenneth Davenport kens better than to involve a lady in investigating a crime of any sort. For the love of God, why has he taken the inquest upon himself in the first place?"

As the carriage again got underway, Modesty didn't feel well enough to explain all the details—the clues they had uncovered, their visit to the apothecary, and discovering Alfred intended to propose to Lady Philomina. Heaven forbid she ever admit to posing as a man and entering a gambling hell. Her brush with death at Waiter's would send Martin into a fury of rage. So, she kept her reply simple, "I was rather persistent about helping him."

"You?" blurted everyone in the carriage.

"Well, I havena been of much assistance—just found out who Alfred was courting."

"Alfred?" asked Mama with alarm.

"Och, I only refer to him in the familiar because Lord Berwick doesna like me saying 'the former' or 'the deceased.'"

"I may burst a spleen before we arrive home where I will promptly strangle the damned viscount." Martin used the silver handle of his cane to knock upon the carriage ceiling. "How much longer?"

"We're turning onto Bond Street now, Your Grace," replied the driver, his voice muffled.

Modesty sat forward and winced. "I dunna want you take out your anger on Lord Berwick."

"Nay?" Martin barked. "You are bruised from head to toe, and canna walk without assistance. Not only are you on the precipice of being utterly ruined, you could have been killed! And mark me, I will tell His Lordship exactly what I think, and demand he never speak to you again."

Julia patted her husband's hand, whispering something indecipherable into his ear.

However, it seemed her words did nothing to calm the raging lion.

"I would like to speak to Lord Berwick as well," said Mama.

Martin shook his head. "I am master of this family and what I have to say is not meant for the ears of the fairer sex."

"Very well," The Dowager replied. "I shall be nearby and I *will* speak to His Lordship after you have had an opportunity to flay strips off him with your vulgar tongue."

The carriage rolled to a stop. "We've arrived, Your Graces!"

~

KENNETH STOOD at the bottom of the stairs while he watched the retreating form of the doctor, the butler leading him to Modesty's bedside. If only he could follow, but he'd been met with a rather unpleasant glower from the old Scottish butler. It took but one glance at the elderly man's rheumy-eyed expression and Kenneth knew he wasn't welcome—not even to darken the duke's opulent entrance hall.

Damnation, with Lady Modesty's every idea, a hundred reasons for refuting each one had come to the tip of his tongue. But had he been able to refuse her anything? *Evidently not.*

Kenneth heaved a sigh as he took in the black-and-white tiled floor, the recessed rococo painted ceiling, the life-sized portrait of Martin in his red Parliamentary robes, wearing a kilt beneath, of course. Along the far wall a Grecian marble of Athena in her military regalia stood recessed in an arched egress flanked by two Corinthian columns. The piece was pristine, and doubtlessly original.

"My Lord Berwick," said a footman entering the hall, his expression as dour as the butler's had been. "His Grace has requested your presence in the library."

A stone of lead sank to Kenneth's toes. If only he could offer his apologies and make a hasty exit. But that was an act of a coward. Rather, he nodded to the footman and was led up the stairs to the first floor and down a corridor to a library, it's maple shelves filled with leather-bound books.

"His Grace will be with you shortly."

Kenneth stepped inside, the doors closing behind him and booming as if they were prison gates. He wandered inside, noting the tall, lace-clad windows, ushering a glimpse of daylight peeking through the storm clouds. The library was partly furnished in the Grecian style with low-backed settees and upholstered chairs. In one corner an ornate writing table more reminiscent of Louis XIV vintage was situated where it could make use of the afternoon sun. Near the hearth were two leather wingback chairs with a matching settee between them.

At the far end, the door opened and the Duke of Dunscaby stepped inside. "Berwick," he said, his fists curling. "I'll have you know the only reason I havena had you thrown out of my house is because I need answers."

"You Grace." Kenneth bowed, overlooking the duke's irascibility. After all, the man had every right to chide him with a bitter tongue. "Is Lady Modesty all right? What has the doctor said?"

"My physician is still with my sister—behind

closed doors, mind you, which is why I am not presently standing at her bedside."

"Yes, of course. If you please, I would like to see her—t-to express my—"

"I dunna please. Not in the bloody least." His Grace poured himself a dram of whisky, then turned, not offering Kenneth a nip. "Exactly what is going on between you and my sister, under my verra nose, mind you?"

Kenneth had expected this question and had considered any number of quite rational answers, but presently, his mind didn't seem to be working. "N-nothing is going on between us."

"Nay? Modesty rode your horse in a sanctioned race, and if the Jockey Club finds out you entered a woman, you will be fined and most likely suspended from placing a foot on every racecourse in the Kingdom."

Rubbing the back of his neck, Kenneth looked longingly at the crystal decanter on the sideboard. "I figured you would be the first in line to see to my expulsion."

"I ought to be and if you dunna tell me why the devil my sister was riding your racehorse, I bloody will."

"It was all rather spontaneous, I suppose."

"Explain yourself."

"Well, I was visiting Venom at the stables and Lady Modesty was attending one of her lessons with Mr. Willett."

"Can you tell me why she was taking jockey lessons—astride, mind you?"

"Though you will have to ask Her Ladyship directly, I do believe she has the ambition to one day oversee her own stud farm."

"Breeding horses—even Thoroughbreds—and racing them are two verra different things."

"Agreed, though Lady Modesty is rather gifted at handling a high-spirited mount."

"That still doesna explain why you allowed her to ride your stallion in a race attended by all manner of society! You are a viscount, a peer of the realm, an educated man, yet you seem to be rather lacking in the execution of affairs where an iota of judgement is required."

If that wasn't a verbal slap in the face, Kenneth didn't know what was. Nonetheless, he refused to allow his pride to send him into a rage. "We had a bit of wager, you see..."

"Good God, you mean to say you allowed a wee slip of a lass to bamboozle you into wagering? Modesty never wagers on anything she might possibly lose."

"Truly? I wish I would have known—"

"Regardless, the absurdity of her wager ought to have given you pause."

"I assure you it did. I even refused... at first. The problem is your sister is impossible to deny."

"My sister is far younger than you are, sir, and thus overly confident and ridiculously cavalier. You are a gentleman. You are older. You shouldna have given in to her bloody whims."

Kenneth looked to his toes. "No. I should not have."

"Exactly. You are the one responsible for this ill-fated state of affairs. If anyone discovers my youngest sister is the jockey who took a spill in the first race at Primrose Hill, she'll be ruined for certain. Do you have any idea how difficult it is to find a suitor for a strong-willed, opinionated, Scottish lass with flaming red hair?"

"She has expressed a certain amount of vexation with the predicament."

"To you?" Martin tossed back his drink. "God's stones. In addition to posing as a jockey and appearing in a sanctioned horse race. I understand she has assisted you with your investigation into your brother's death."

Though Kenneth was the same height as the duke, he felt two feet smaller. Had Modesty told him about Alfred? Why did he suddenly feel betrayed? "That was a mistake."

"Bloody oath it was. Have you no sense of propriety, sir? The sister of a duke has no business flitting about Town asking questions to assist you in some futile investigation."

Kenneth's stomach twisted into knots. How many times had he told Lady Modesty he didn't need her assistance? Of course, he'd be lying to himself if he said she hadn't been helpful. "Though you are correct on the first account, I do not believe my inquiry into Alfred's passing is futile. There are too many suspicious circumstances surrounding his death for me to brush the issue aside without asking questions first."

"Such as?"

"What happened to the sapphire ring Alfred purchased the day before his death? I found the empty box beneath his bed yet there was no sign of a struggle. The servants didn't see anyone enter his bedchamber, yet the ring is missing." Of course, there were a host of other circumstances, but it was best not to elaborate. If His Grace found out Her Ladyship had donned a man's suit of clothes and passed herself off as a gentleman at Waiter's, Kenneth would be hung in the town square by his ballocks regardless of whether he'd told her to don the disguise or not.

"If you believe there is skullduggery afoot, then why did you not report it to the magistrate?"

"I did and was subsequently told there would be no investigation because the coroner deemed Alfred died of natural causes."

"What about hiring a detective or a Bow Street Runner?"

"Before doing so, I wanted to find out about the ring. Find out if Venom's race at Epsom Downs was rigged. Find out if Alfred..." Kenneth pursed his lips.

Dunscaby squinted. "Do you believe your brother was involved in something nefarious?"

"No! But I want to be certain he was not before I take the risk that my family's name will be dragged through the mire."

"Fair enough, though I insist Modesty's involvement stops forthwith."

Kenneth nodded. "Agreed."

The duke ground his fist into his palm. "In truth I ought to take you to Jackson's Saloon and beat your face to a bloody pulp."

Evidently, His Grace wasn't finished with his reproach.

With a soft click, the library door opened. "Hello, Lord Berwick," said the Dowager Duchess of Dunscaby, her tone genteel without a hint of malice. How she managed to come across as undaunted and absolutely collected after watching her daughter hurled from a horse was astonishing. But then, she was a duchess.

Kenneth bowed. "Your Grace."

"Mother," Dunscaby growled, *his* discontent, on

the other hand, was still quite discernable. "I wanted a word with Berwick before you intervened."

"Yes, and that is why I gave you plenty of time for you to have your say, dearest." She looked at the empty glass on the side table. "Has Martin offered you a refreshment, sir?"

"I didna offer him a wee dram because he nearly got Modesty killed this verra day!"

"Fortunately, the doctor says she's badly bruised, and her knee is quite swollen, though miraculously no bones are broken. And goodness, Martin, you can blow things out of proportion." Her Grace appeared to float to the sideboard where she poured two drams of whisky. "I'm quite sure Lord Berwick did not intend for her to fall off the horse. After all, you know as well as I my youngest daughter is the best equestrian in the entire MacGalloway family."

"Her skill in the saddle has nothing to do with the fact that His Lordship allowed a wee—"

"Martin, please lower your voice. Shouting doesn't become you, dear. After all, you are a duke." Her Grace gave Kenneth a glass. "Please tell me, why you chose to waltz with my daughter on two separate occasions."

"Ah... " Kenneth blinked, quite stunned with the sudden change in subject matter. "I enjoy waltzing?"

"Oh, please, Berwick." The dowager offered the second glass to her son. "You cannot tell me you have no affinity for Modesty. After all, she is fetching— dancing blue eyes, a radiant smile."

Martin shifted his hands to his hips. "By the way you leapt over every barrier leading to the racetrack, ye didna look indifferent in the slightest."

"I agree," said Her Grace. "I was quite taken aback when you embraced her—even though I thought her a man at the time—until Kitty informed us the poor jockey was none other than my youngest daughter."

Kenneth recalled now. Kitty was renowned for not keeping secrets. He took a healthy swig of his whisky. "I was concerned for Lady Modesty, certainly. After all, she was in command of my horse and the jockey who rode Wild Ben clearly struck her in order to win the race, the blasted fiend."

"*He's* the fiend?" bellowed Martin.

Her Grace raised her palm. "Please, dear. I'm sure as three well-bred adults we can devise a solution to this predicament."

"Aye, I can take the bastard to the boxing ring and thrash him." His Grace seemed to have grown more agitated since his mother entered the library.

The Dowager collected her skirt and sat on the settee facing the hearth. "Not necessary."

The duke glowered. "Then I'll demand a wedding by the point of my musket."

"First of all," said Her Grace, ignoring her son's outpouring of ire. "We must allay any hint of scandal."

Kenneth managed to nod while the duke threw out his arms. "What about wee Modesty's hair? If that doesna in itself create a scandal, what will? Everyone at Primrose Hill saw it." He glared at Kenneth. "Was that your idea?"

"Not at all." Kenneth chopped his hand through the air. "I forbade her to cut her tresses when she suggested doing so."

"Forbade?" The Dowager asked with a hint of humor. "Truly, short hair is quite fashionable in Paris and now that the war is over, I believe Modesty will be the envy of the *haute ton*. Furthermore, she will look darling in a bandeau. We can order one to match each dress."

Dunscaby lowered himself into one of the wing-backs, then dropped his head against the leather upholstery. "Mayhap we ought to send her home to Scotland."

"Excellent idea." Kenneth nearly smiled, happy to have finally managed to slip a word in.

Her Grace glowered. "Horrible idea."

"What about her injuries?" asked Dunscaby. "She willna be able to go out for a fortnight or more."

"Perhaps waltzing will be out of the question for the time being, but if I know my daughter, she will go mad if we force her to remain indoors whilst the weather is fine."

"What do you suggest?" asked His Grace.

"Berwick will court her," the woman said with no indication she might be jesting.

"What?" both men blurted at once.

"Don't you see? His Lordship can take her on carriage rides through the park, bring her flowers and—"

Kenneth downed the remainder of his dram. "I'm not writing sonnets."

Inhaling loudly, the duke crossed his knees. "Dear God, I wouldna want to hear a word of lovesick sap from the likes of you!"

"Your Grace," Kenneth said, facing the dowager and ignoring Dunscaby. "As you may be aware, I am quite overwhelmed with the responsibilities of assuming my brother's mantle."

"Hogwash." Her Grace snapped open her fan. "You had time to loiter about the stables, giving Modesty the opportunity to convince you to allow her to ride Venom. And I'll venture to assume my daughter was properly chaperoned at your every encounter."

Kenneth looked toward the shelves of books. "Of course," he mumbled.

"Good. Then I will expect flowers. On the morrow, mind you."

Kenneth recognized her order for what it was. "Yes, madam."

"And furthermore, as head of this family," said His Grace, standing and giving his mother a dour frown. "I insist on proper chaperones at all times. Understood?"

Not quite understanding, Kenneth cleared his throat. "So, I am to merely court Her Ladyship for how long? Until the end of the Season?"

Her Grace stood and floated toward the door, her skirts lightly rustling. "Until all pretense of scandal has vanished."

19

Kenneth sat at his writing table reviewing the notes he'd made regarding the investigation when Freddie popped his head into the library. "I 'ave the flowers you requested, milord."

Kenneth gestured to the low table. "Very good, please set them there."

"Ye're no' courtin' one of them 'ighbrow ladies, are ye?"

The lad's question could have been taken as insolent criticism, but by the sparkle in his eyes, Kenneth figured Freddie quite admired women of quality. "You must learn not to question my authority. Besides, gentlemen purchase flowers for any number of reasons."

"Aye, sir," the boy replied with a sly grin, one indicating he knew the flowers were for a lady—a special one.

Kenneth sifted through a neatly stacked pile of slips of paper until he pulled out the drawing of the sapphire ring he'd received from the clerk at Phillip's. "My brother purchased this ring before he died."

Freddie gaped at the picture. "Cor, that must 'ave cost ten pounds."

"Indeed, it was very dear." Truly, the lad had no

grasp of monetary affairs, but the ring's exorbitant price mattered not. "And I believe it might have been stolen."

"Someone picked 'is pocket, did they?"

"Perhaps." If only it were simply a case of light fingers. But how and where the sapphire was stolen was not important at the moment. "I found the box but no ring."

"Do ye know who stole it?"

"At first I thought it might have been Mr. Crockford but—"

Freddie scratched his mop of sandy brown locks. "I don't reckon Crocky the Shark would steal anything like *that*."

Kenneth's brow pinched as he considered the boy's words. Indeed there were many ways in which a person could be intelligent. When it came to the gutters, Freddie seemed to be very astute, indeed. "Why?"

"First of all, 'e'd 'ave one of 'is cronies pinch it. Secondly, someone already done 'im in."

"I beg your pardon? The coroner said Crockford died of asphyxiation."

Freddie snorted, batting his hand through the air. "Aye, and me ma is a saint."

Perhaps Freddie had spent a little too much time on the streets. "How do you know Mr. Crockford was murdered?"

"Everybody knows."

"Everyone?"

"Well, most folks in St. Giles."

"I see." Then again mayhap Kenneth hadn't been speaking to the right people. "Let us back up for a moment. My understanding is Ward Crockford engaged in smuggling of sorts."

Freddie nodded. "I'll say."

"You are familiar with his operation?"

"Everyone—er—" The boy tugged on his collar as if his neckcloth was a bit too tight. "I suppose I might have been privy to a transaction or two on account of me ma."

"Hmm." The deeper he probed, the more sinister Crockford's operation appeared to have been. "Tell me about the dealings between Ma and Crocky, if you please."

Freddie blanched, his eyes fearful and wary. "If I do, will ye throw me out?"

"Of course not. You have a new life now and you are under my protection."

The lad glanced over his shoulder as if he needed assurance that no one was listening in. "Well," he said, lowering his voice. "If one of Ma's boys *found* somethin' of particular value, she'd send 'em to Crocky."

"And what did he do with these valuable items?"

"'e'd make coin by the flour-sack full."

"By selling them?"

"By smuggling 'em."

Kenneth sat back in his chair, eyeing the boy. How much did Freddie know about smuggling? "Do you mean to say he shipped and then sold them?"

"I dunno. Everyone said Crocky could make anything disappear."

"Well, now he has disappeared, so to speak." Kenneth handed the lad the drawing. "If I were to ask you to search for this ring, do you think you could do that for me?"

Freddie's lips twisted "Do you want I should nick it?"

"Not at all. Do not say a word. Do not give any indication you're looking for the piece. Just browse."

Freddie scrunched his nose. "Browse?"

"Use your eyes, boy. You know how to keep to the shadows. Have a look around, then report back to me. Can you do that?"

~

"There you are, m'lady," said Randolph, patting the bandeau she had just secured with a bow.

Still on bedrest enforced by Martin's physician, Modesty held up the silver mirror and studied her new hairstyle. "I do like it."

"The cut is absolutely darling," said Kitty, sitting on the bed and tweaking one of the curls. "And Harry said there wasn't a mention of your spill in the *Gazette*."

Modesty had already read the newspaper, thanks to Randolph saving it before the other servants managed to mangle the pages beyond readability. "Perhaps they didn't specifically name me, but there was an entire paragraph about the underhandedness amongst the ranks of the jockeys. They challenged the Jockey Club to put an end to it after a fellow was knocked from his mount on the final leg of the first race."

"See?" Kitty beamed. "You were not mentioned."

"Aye, but Mr. Modistie was entered into the books as Venom's rider. Sooner or later they will approach Mr. Willett to find out who I am."

"And he'll say something along the lines of, 'a young man from France who has returned home to recover from his injuries.'"

Yes, that was what Berwick told the trainer to say, but what if the trainer made a mistake? After all, Mr. Willett nearly revealed Modesty's identity when the viscount had first appeared at the practice track. Modesty set the mirror aside. "Perhaps, but a great many people attended the race. What if someone looks at my hair and realizes I was Venom's jockey?"

"They will not because they were too far away to really see you." Kitty clapped her hands excitedly. "But if you are so unfortunate to be named, then your brother will insist you marry Lord Berwick at once."

Groaning, Modesty let her head fall against the pillows. "I am planning to become a spinster. Besides, His Lordship doesna want to marry."

Kitty adjusted her fichu, spreading it wider to reveal a tidbit of cleavage. "Then His Grace will challenge him to a duel and shoot him dead."

Goodness, the lass could act the flighty, feather-brained nitwit. "I canna abide duels. First of all, Mama had one of her spells when Marty challenged Prince Isidor to a duel, and then when all of my brothers rode off in the dark of night, it had to be the most unbearable three hours of my life. I would never forgive myself if Marty was shot on my account—and the same goes for Lord Berwick."

Charity popped her head inside. "Modesty, dear, you have a caller."

Kitty hopped off the bed, batting her eyelashes. "I told you."

"Och, ye dunna even ken who it is."

No sooner had the words left Modesty's lips when her sister widened the door, revealing none other than Viscount Berwick.

Modesty shrank beneath the coverlet, pulling it up to her chin. "But I'm in no condition to receive a caller of any sort."

Charity ushered His Lordship inside. "Mama says otherwise, as long as I act as chaperone."

"Me as well," said Kitty as if she were well-qualified for the role.

"Nay," Charity replied. "Wait for me in the parlor with Auntie Patience."

The lassie's shoulders dropped. "Aw, that is no fun at all."

Charity escorted Kitty to the door while Berwick moved to Modesty's bedside. There was a furrow etched in his brow, his lips tightly pursed.

"Has something happened?" Modesty asked.

"Ah… " He glanced back to Charity who smiled in her lovely way and slid onto the settee facing the hearth. "I apologize for not visiting you after the doctor left yesterday. But Dunscaby insisted you were not to be seen."

Modesty could only imagine the choice words which must have spewed from her brother's lips. "I hope he wasna overly harsh."

"Oh no, he was well and truly incensed, but it was your mother who was… might I say surprising."

"Aye?"

From behind his back, Berwick produced a bouquet of red roses interspersed with dandelions. "For you."

As Modesty reached for the flowers, Randolph quickly captured the stems and wrapped in white lace. "I'll put these in a vase straightaway, m'lady."

"You remembered," Modesty whispered as the lady's maid took her leave.

"Of course. Pollinators and whatnot." Berwick grinned—och, the mood grew instantly lighter. In fact, he ought to smile more often. The man gestured to Charity who was pretending not to eavesdrop. "Wasn't it your sister who compared you to dandelions?"

"Aye, it was my sister—but the middle sister. Grace now lives near Loch Lomond with her husband."

"Ah, yes, the princess."

"Former princess," said Chairty.

Ears piqued, Modesty scooted up in the bed a bit. "I beg your pardon?"

"I received a letter a few days ago. Grace has decided to assume the title of Lady Buchanan."

Modesty's jaw dropped. "I am in awe of that Highlander and how he tamed the haughty shrew."

"Modesty!" Charity chided, though she was unable to hold in her subsequent laugh. "I suppose it is a verra good thing Grace was rescued by His Lairdship."

"Rescued?" asked Berwick.

"'Tis a long story," Modesty explained. "But the short of it is she married a prince who died of consumption. Then after her carriage slid off the road and plunged into a ravine, Grace was pulled to safety by a proper Highland laird and married him."

"That is an unbelievably abridged version. Neither were the circumstances in the right order," Charity said.

Modesty tossed a pillow at her sister, only managing to send the projectile to the foot of the bed. "I thought you were going to mind your own affairs."

"Oh, yes, there is something of great import to which I must attend." The eldest MacGalloway sister stood and hastened toward the door. "I willna be but a moment. I'm counting on you to act the perfect gentleman, Lord Berwick. I shall return momentarily."

As the door closed, His Lordship sighed, the tension in his shoulders easing before Modesty's eyes. "How are you feeling, my lady?"

"Do you not believe it is time for us to stop with the formalities?" she asked, avoiding his question, at least for a moment.

"If you believe it is best."

"I do." Modesty gestured to the chair beside the

bed. "Please sit before my neck begins to ache from looking up so high."

Kenneth complied.

She quite liked thinking of him as Kenneth. "As for my current state of wellness, I dunna believe there is a square inch on my body that isna bruised or scuffed or swollen."

"I am so sorry. Had I realized how underhanded jockeys could be I never would have allowed you to race."

"Then I'm glad for your ignorance on the matter."

"I beg your pardon?" He took her hand between his warm palms. "You must know it was devastating to see you thrown, and at such great speed."

Modesty was so angry with herself. Not only was she hit once, she didn't learn the first time, and the fiend had smacked her again. She had been too intent on winning to pay attention to the other jockeys, a lesson sorely learned. And now she'd never have another chance to prove herself. "What was devastating was I didna win."

"Are you so competitive you would prefer winning over everything else including your health?"

Modesty opened her free palm, revealing the scrapes on the heel of her hand. "Had I won, I wouldna be in this predicament at the moment."

"Yes, but racing is dangerous."

The corners of Modesty's lips tightened. Perhaps racing was dangerous, but entirely worth the risk for a chance to experience the thrill of galloping at breakneck speed on the back of one of the fastest animals in the world. *Kenneth wouldna understand.* "You will be pleased to know I found out the name of Alfred's mistress. Isna that worth a wee spill?"

"You did?" he asked, quickly schooling his features

into a stern frown. "I say, a bit of sleuthing might have been fortuitous, but not worth all your bumps and bruises."

"Bless you for being so perseverant." He drew her hand to his lips and kissed it. "What is her name? Who told you?"

"Evelyn it is. One of the jockeys told me—said he frequently saw her with Alfred at Primrose Hill."

"Evelyn, hmm? Another piece to the puzzle," he mused, seeming to ponder the news.

"So," she said, glancing down to the hand still clasped between his. She hadn't noticed before, but Kenneth had very masculine hands—rough with the callouses of a man who toiled regardless of his breeding. A pleasant stirring awakened deep inside her as she considered how much she liked his hands. "Um… thank you for the flowers. They are lovely and a surprise."

"Oh? Did your mother not tell you?"

The stirring altered to a stone sinking in her stomach. "What is she up to now?"

"I'm courting you."

"Courting? Me? That is preposterous!"

"I don't believe it is all that unusual. After all, it is what men and women do."

"Aye, but you dunna *want* to court me."

"Hmm." He kissed the back of her hand, then turned it over and applied a lingering kiss to her palm, gradually sliding his lips up to her wrist. "But court you I shall."

Good glory, how could a man's lips applied to the sensitive skin on the underside of a woman's wrist give her such a thrill? It was nearly as riveting as riding a racehorse. "Ye dunna have to act the hero because I'm ruined," Modesty said, her voice a wee bit breathless.

Kenneth scooted closer, staring directly at her. "I didn't realize you've been ruined."

Of course, the man had looked at her dozens of times, but presently there was a certain hunger in those half-lidded blues. "I will be if anyone figures out who Mr. Modistie really is. And you are partially responsible."

"I see." He kissed her lips—just a peck.

Needing something more substantial, Modesty slipped a hand around his neck and drew his lips to hers, taking full advantage of his proximity. "And my mother doesna have any say in who courts me or who doesna," she managed to say, resisting every fiber of her body urging her to tug the viscount onto the bed.

Kenneth leaned forward and nibbled along her jaw line. "Is that so?"

Dropping her head back, she fought to remember why she needed to resist the whole issue of courting. "Aye. I'm to be a spinster and you'll be heading home to Northumberland soon."

He clasped her cheeks between those masculine, warm hands. "My oath, you are vexing but by the life of me, I enjoy every moment of it. Now stop arguing and kiss me, woman."

A flood of overwhelming passion gushed through her as Modesty closed her eyes. For once in her life she did as she was told without asking why, without questioning anything, but simply allowing herself to react, to feel, to think of nothing but this moment and the man kissing her as if she were the most precious being in the world.

Kenneth's hands slid to her shoulders and lower.

Modesty grabbed his wrist, her eyes meeting his. Unspoken understanding coursed between them and together they moved his palm over her breast.

"Ahhh," she sighed, her breath hitching.

"You are so soft, so feminine. I want to kiss you here."

She arched her back. "Aye."

A loud clearing of a woman's throat came from the corridor. Kenneth jolted back to his seat while Modesty grabbed the coverlet and again yanked it up to her chin.

The door creaked as it slowly opened. "Forgive me, dearest. I'm afraid I was occupied a wee bit longer than I intended." Moving inside, Charity held up a vase full of white gardenias. "These are from Lord Roxburgh."

Modesty sneezed. "At the mention of Roxburgh it appears I've developed a sniffle."

"That's why I had Giles tell him you were abed with a megrim."

"Is Roxburgh courting you as well?" asked Kenneth.

"He most definitely is not," Modesty replied.

Charity placed the gardenias on the mantle. "He'd like to be."

Modesty adjusted her bandeau which had fallen askew while she was kissing His Lordship. "Well, I hope you told him to set his sights on women a wee bit nearer to his age."

"Evidently you already did that," said Charity.

"He told you?"

Kenneth chuckled. "You did? You are a vixen."

"I told him to court Mama."

"Modesty," Charity chided. "You didn't."

"Well, he's much nearer to her age, and she has been a widow for seven years. Dunna ye think it is time she was courted, as well?"

"I think you need to focus on your own circumstances and let Mama worry about hers," said Charity. "Goodness, after that horrendous fall, you're lucky to be alive."

"Agreed." Kenneth stood. "I'd best be going and leave you to your healing."

"So soon? But you havena told me about the investigation."

"Not much to say, really. Though I have happened upon another idea."

"What is it? You canna leave without telling me."

"Oh, but I can. And I shall." Kenneth kissed Modesty's hand, bowed to Charity, and slipped out the door.

20

Kenneth dressed in his "shabby" farm clothes, consisting of knee breeches, a pair of scuffed Wellingtons, grey waistcoat and coat, along with an old John Bull top hat—the same clothing he wore when traveling, which was an act of self-preservation. If a man looked more like a pauper than a peer, he was far less apt to be set upon by highwaymen. He walked the distance to the corner of Piccadilly and Bolton Row, where he stood for a time and watched the comings and goings at Waiter's which, according to the papers, had reopened for business.

He couldn't tell Modesty what he was planning for two reasons. First of all, he didn't have much of a plan and secondly if he told the woman about his next steps, she would somehow don a disguise and slip out of her brother's house, regardless of the doctor's orders for her to stay abed for at least three days.

The last thing Kenneth wanted was to be responsible for further injury to Her Ladyship's person. Since Ward Crockford's death, she had been skewered by a shard of glass, and then flung from a horse that would have killed most men, let alone women. Who knew how many near-misses she had left?

A hackney stopped in front of the gentleman's club, and Kenneth moved sideways for a better look at the fare. A single footman greeted a dandy as he emerged from the carriage. There had been two footmen outside on the day of the chess tournament. Waiter's had seemed a great deal busier at that time as well.

Above on the first floor, a curtain parted, revealing the face of a woman. Kenneth took a step forward. Was she Evelyn? He had to find out.

Rather than approach the front door, he made his way around to the alley where the murder had played out.

Everyone in St. Giles knows he didn't die of natural causes.

Well then, it was nigh time to play a different role. After all, if Modesty was successful at it, then Kenneth ought to at least be able to garner a few answers.

He leaned against the wall beside the back door and pretended to pick the dirt from beneath his fingernails. And by the time someone actually exited the door, Kenneth's already pristine nails were well and truly spec free. "'ello, guvnor," he said, mimicking Freddie's accent. "I was wonderin' if ye might pass along a note to my sister."

"No' likely. Who is the bloody wench?"

"Last I 'eard she was livin' 'ere. One of Crocky's girls."

"Crocky's dead."

"Aye, but Waiter's 'as reopened." Kenneth almost said he recognized the chap as one of the footmen, but that might have given away his ruse. "And I saw a woman peerin' out a window above stairs."

"Ye did, did ye?" The man narrowed his eyes. "What's your sister's name?"

"Evelyn."

"Applewhite?"

Ah-a! "Of course," Kenneth said. "She in?"

"No, she don't live here no more."

"That's a bleedin' shame." He scratched beneath his hat. "'ow long ago did she leave?"

"The wench left when most of the others did, right after Crocky met his end."

Kenneth noted the man hadn't used the word murdered. Then again he also hadn't mentioned the cause of death reported by the coroner. "Do ye know where she went?"

"Your sister thought she was too 'igh and mighty to talk to the likes of me. She might have been pretty, but she was a loose glove just like the others. Can ye believe she set her sights on marryin' one of them 'igh-brows she was shaggin'?"

"Do you think she did?" Kenneth rolled his hand, urging the fellow to say more. "Marry one of 'er... ah... gentlemen friends?"

"Nah." The footman batted his hand through the air. "I reckon she was increasing with one of their by-blows and she slipped away to 'ide somewhere in the country."

"You believe she is with child?" Kenneth asked, forgetting the accent for a moment.

The man eyed him. "Where'd ye say ye're from, gov?"

"North." Kenneth pointed upward while kicking himself. "Near Scotland."

"Well then, ye might have a look there."

"I will," he said as the man started away. "But I 'ave one more question, if I may."

"Aye?" The fellow regarded him over his shoulder.

"Ye'd best make it fast, I've an appointment with a schooner of ale."

"You indicated my sister had many partners. But by 'er correspondence, I assumed she fancied one in particular."

The man shrugged. "Dunno. She seemed to favor Viscount Berwick, I s'pose. 'e came 'round enough, too."

"But was 'e no' killed?" Kenneth asked, holding his breath, anxious for an affirmative reply.

"That's not 'ow the papers reported it. The fop drank 'imself to death, I reckon."

Kenneth nodded as the man strode away, heading for the tavern, no doubt.

Evelyn Applewhite thought to marry Alfred? Hmm. Did the mistress know about Philomina? Kenneth couldn't imagine she would. Alfred most likely would have waited to break off their affair after his proposal had been accepted.

With every new tidbit of information, a whole barrage of questions came with it. Why did Miss Applewhite leave London? Was she in fear for her life, somehow caught in the middle of the rift between Crocky and Alfred? She must have been utterly bereft when Alfred died.

He opted to take a different route home, and as he walked along Berkely Square he spotted a shingle reading: *JJ McGrath, Sleuth.*

Without hesitation, Kenneth entered the small, somewhat dim office, a bell ringing above his head.

Inside, a rather grizzled man was stretched out on a fainting couch, his hands clasped over a rotund stomach, his snores nearly deafening.

"Ahem." Kenneth stood expectantly for a moment, but then realized if the bell on the door hadn't awakened the man, why would the clearing of his throat do so? "Mr. McGrath?" he said rather loudly.

When shouting didn't work, he tried shaking the man's shoulder, which brought an inkling of a stutter, followed by lighter snoring. Not about to give up, Kenneth half-filled a glass with water from the pitcher on the washstand and tossed it in the man's face.

"Jesu, Mary, Joseph, and all the saints!" Sputtering, the disheveled chap shifted his legs over the side of the fainting couch and shoved his hands up his face, making his hair stand on end. "Why the devil did you have to go and ruin a perfectly good dream?"

"Are you JJ McGrath?" Kenneth asked.

The man eyed him with distrust. "Might be. Who's askin'?"

Kenneth produced a card. "Berwick here, and I'd like to enquire as to the nature of your sleuth services. After all, it is a rather far-reaching vocation."

"I'm a sleuth. The word means detective."

"Yes, well it also means bloodhound."

McGrath smirked. "I've been called that a time or two."

"Ah-a. I thought as much. Tell me, can you find a missing person?"

"Who's missing?"

"I'm not sure if the lady believes she is missing or not, but I'd like to find her."

"A woman, aye? Let me guess..." Scratching his day-old beard, McGrath looked at Kenneth's card, then scowled at his shabby suit of clothes. "She's a rum-blower and she nicked something of import."

"Somewhat correct on both accounts, but there's more. Evidently she was my late brother's mistress. And I do believe she might have stolen a ring from him. However the story has a sinister bent."

"Oh?"

"If my hunch is correct, she may also be in possession of information regarding my brother's murder."

THE SUN SHONE with warmth while Modesty and Charity walked the short distance to Lord Berwick's town house where they had been invited for luncheon. "I wonder why His Lordship sent an invitation to me and not to Kitty," said Chairty.

Though the swelling in her knee had eased, Modesty still suffered a faint limp. "You didna tell her, did you?"

The breeze caught the ribbons on Charity's bonnet, blowing them into Modesty's face. "Of course not. Doing so would only hurt her feelings."

She brushed them away. "True, but if I were Berwick, I'd invite you and not Kitty as well."

"Whatever led you to arrive at such a conclusion?"

"Oh come now, sister, you ken as well as I Kitty canna keep mum about anything."

Charity's lips formed an O, her eyes wide. "Lord Berwick harbors secrets?"

Modesty's toe caught on a raised brick in the footpath, sending her stumbling forward. She quickly regained her composure, smoothing her skirts and glancing about to ensure no one was watching. "My goodness, canna they keep the path even? This is Mayfair of all places."

Charity stopped beside her. "Did you twist your injured knee?"

Modesty shifted her weight between her feet. "Nay. Fortunately, I am resilient."

"I certainly can concur with that." Charity looped

her arm through Modesty's elbow. "However, I'll not take any chances when crossing a busy street this close to the noon hour."

Lord Roxburgh in his phaeton rode past with his nose in the air, followed by a hay wagon, the driver tipping his hat. "Good day, ladies."

At a break in the traffic, the two sister's raised their skirts ankle-high and hastened, zigzagging through the assortment of horses, carriages, and wagons slogging their way along Charles Street as if a quarter of the conveyances in London chose this very hour to travel on this road.

"See there," said Modesty as they stepped onto the footpath. "No harm came to life or limb."

"Then might I suggest you watch for loose bricks on the footpath throughout the remainder of the journey?" Charity chuckled and gave her sister's arm a pat. "Now, you didna answer me about Berwick's secrets."

"He doesna have secrets so much as he doesna want everyone to ken his affairs."

"You are referring to his inquiries regarding the death of his brother?"

"Aye, and Kitty already told everyone in the family I was riding Venom at the race. Had she kept mum, you would have been none the wiser."

"Except you would have had a difficult time explaining how you ended up bruised from head to toe and needed to spend three days abed."

"Verra well, then I assume he asked you because you were the one to chaperone us when he came to call. After all, you told Kitty to go visit with Mama in the parlor at the time." Modesty puzzled for a moment. "Why did you do that if you werena worried about her gossiping?"

Charity shrugged. "Mama's idea, not mine."

"Our mother was worried about Kitty's proclivity for gossip?"

"Who kens what was on her mind. It's just…"

"Hmm?"

"Never you mind." Charity stopped in front of the tall brick town house with its ornate sandstone façade before them. "We've arrived."

Modesty stood back while her sister gave the knocker two raps. *Did she ken Berwick would kiss me if she left us alone for a moment? Did Mama? Were they scheming?*

A boy dressed in footman's livery opened the door. "Ye must be Lady Modesty and Lady Brixham."

"Aye," said Charity. "We've come at Lord Berwick's invitation."

"I know ye did. And I knew 'is Lordship was courtin' quality." With a grin practically touching his ears, the lad opened the door wider. "Come in… *er*… please… *um*… ladies."

Modesty gave the lad a nod as she stepped across the threshold. *So, this is the young pickpocket?* "Are you Freddie?"

He bowed with an exaggerated flourish. "At your service, milady."

A throat cleared and a man dressed in a butler's costume stepped forward and offered a modest bow. "Thank you ladies for allowing Frederick to practice his footman's skills." The man clasped his gloved hands over his black waistcoat. "I am Mr. Welch, Lord Berwick's valet and butler, more frequently referred to as His Lordship's manservant."

"You perform both duties?" asked Charity. "My heavens, isna that a bit overwhelming?"

"Not at all, my lady." Welch gestured through the entrance hall to a parlor. "I would have answered the door myself, but Lord Berwick insisted Freddie give it a go. I hope you are not offended."

"Why would they be offended?" asked the lad, though when Welch gave him an unamused frown, Freddie pursed his lips closed.

"We are not offended in the slightest," Modesty replied. "In fact, Frederick's welcome was endearing."

Charity nodded and tweaked his nose. "Though as a countess, I must say it isna proper to spread gossip about the lord of the house."

A pinch formed between the lad's eyebrows. "I never gossip."

"Away to the kitchens with you," said Mr. Welch, ushering Freddie through a small door. "And tend to your letters before you set out for St. Giles today."

Modesty glanced over her shoulder. *Why St. Giles?*

"Lady Modesty, Lady Berwick!" Kenneth descended the stairs, his smile reminiscent of Freddie's. "Thank you for coming."

He strode directly to Charity and kissed her hand, then applied a slightly longer kiss to Modesty's.

"Thank you for inviting us," she said, dipping into a curtsey.

Charity turned full circle. "I say, m'lord, your home is lovely. You ought to entertain more often."

"Should I?" he asked. "I'm afraid I'm rather uncomfortable with the *ton* and whatnot."

"Oh? You have the breeding and the connections," said Charity. "Why uncomfortable?"

"As you may well know, before I was so swiftly thrown into filling my brother's shoes, I was quite content to be a farmer."

"A farmer?" Charity asked.

"Bees and sheep," Modesty replied. "However,

Berwick is a scientist as well. Tell my sister about your sheep."

"Certainly, but perhaps we ought to move to the dining hall first."

Though she had been there before, this time Modesty took in everything. Unlike the duke's residence, Kenneth didn't have a row of footmen at the ready to cater to their every whim. There was but one footman who served them efficiently. The dining hall was a bit smaller than the one at Martin's town house, though it was of ample size, the table seating a very respectable twelve. The crystal in the chandelier overhead was polished to a shine. The sideboard was hewn of maple, and inlayed with bronze. The chairs looked to be newly upholstered with gold damask and were quite comfortable. Of course, she couldn't overlook the silver cutlery, crystal glasses, and china plates. In effect, the viscount's presentation was as ostentatious as any in London.

But Modesty hadn't expected it to be. Though Kenneth had given her no reason to believe so, she expected something rather more provincial. Perhaps she wanted something rather more provincial. As the footman took away the dishes for the third course and replaced them with petite apricot and almond tartlets —three per guest—she studied the flaky pastry. "This looks too delicious to eat."

Kenneth licked his lips. "It is delicious and Cook would most definitely be taken aback if you did not indulge."

Charity slid a bite from her fork, then grinned as if she'd just tasted mana from heaven. "Oh, my. You are quite fortunate to have such a skilled cook in your kitchen."

Modesty destroyed one of the dainty works of art

by cutting it with the side of her fork and taking a bite. She sighed audibly as the sweet concoction slid across her tongue. "Mm. I do believe we need this recipe."

"Yes, we do."

"I'm certain Cook would be happy to send it over."

"Nonsense." Charity removed her serviette from her lap and placed it on the table. "May I venture below stairs and speak to your cook myself? I'd like to give him my felicitations."

Kenneth sipped his cordial. "Do you promise not to steal her away?"

Modesty's eyes popped wide. "Her? You have a lady cook?"

"I do."

"Then I am duly impressed." Chairty looked between the two of them. "I promise not to steal her as long as I have your word to behave while I am gone."

"Of course," Kenneth replied, looking to the footman. "James, would you please escort Lady Brixham to the kitchens?"

As soon as Charity slipped away, Modesty reached for Kenneth's hand. "Why is Freddie going to St. Giles? You're not having him pick pockets are you?"

"You wound me." He raised her hand to his lips and kissed her knuckles. With a dark glint in his eyes, he urged her off her seat and onto his lap.

She was growing a bit too familiar with his lap. But it decidedly was the most comfortable seat in the dining hall. Sliding her arms around his neck, she licked her lips and looked into his bonny eyes. "Why, then? Is it not dangerous?"

Kenneth toyed with her curls, his lips nearing. "The boy spent his life there. Freddie knows the streets better than me and he can blend in without being noticed."

Modesty wriggled in her seat, her heart thumping as she anticipated the viscount's next move. "Not wearing livery with a red coat."

A throaty chuckle rumbled, setting her heart afire. "Well, he doesn't wear his livery in St. Giles."

"Tell me," she said, running her little finger over his bottom lip. "Is he looking for Evelyn? Have you found out more about her?"

"He's searching for the sapphire ring. Only looking, mind you. If he sees anything that resembles the piece, he's to report back to me." Kenneth caught her finger between his teeth and licked it before he let her go. "As for Evelyn, I went back to Waiter's and discovered her last name is Applewhite. She was indeed in some sort of relationship with Alfred, and—"

"You mean she was his mistress?"

"It does seem so. She also left Waiter's along with several other girls after Mr. Crockford's death."

"Interesting. I believe I encountered one of his ladies of easy virtue when I first arrived at Waiter's on the day of the chess match."

Kenneth slid his hand to Modesty's nape, finally drawing her in for a kiss. He took his time, exploring her mouth while he emitted a satiated moan. "Did you? What did she look like?"

"She was verra pretty, though there was a rough edge to her face as if her life had not always been easy."

Closing his eyes, he pressed his cheek against hers. "I doubt any moll would have had an easy time of it."

Modesty arched against his chest, needing to be closer. "The wee tart winked at me."

"She did?" He slid his fingers into her hair, knocking her bandeau askew. "Perhaps she thought you an attractive man."

"Perhaps she kent I was a woman."

Kenneth trailed kisses from her shoulder to her neck. "Now that I can believe."

"Mm." Closing her eyes, Modesty melted into the gentle nibbles of his lips. "How do you propose we locate Miss Applewhite?"

His hand slipped to her waist, his thumb lightly brushing her breast. "I'm kissing you, madam. It is very difficult to think of anything else at the moment."

The room spun as her breathing became more labored. "Your kisses take me to the edge of unfettered bliss, but we still have a murder to solve."

"Not to worry. I've hired a sleuth."

"To find her or the murderer?"

"Her. One thing at a time, love."

Love? The word gave her pause. "Kenneth?"

"Hmm?"

"Are you only playacting at courtship?"

Before he could answer, the sound of feminine footsteps resonated from behind the servants' door.

21

———

K enneth dipped his quill for what seemed like the hundredth time:

Tenth July 1819

Your Graces,

In fulfillment of your wishes I have been courting Lady Modesty for nearly a fortnight now, and I believe it is time to end the charade. It seems clear Her Ladyship well and truly has yet again escaped being ruined by scandal.

He groaned, drawing a line through the words "yet again." Also, "charade" sounded awfully insensitive. After all, courting Modesty had not been entirely unpleasant.

Actually, it had been too pleasant.

Overly so.

Every time he found himself in her presence, she managed to turn him into a simpering swain. He was too taken with the woman's lips, her hair, the feminine curves of her body. Moreover, the Highland lass wasn't a bore as so many of the mindless young ladies of the *ton* had proven to be.

But all this lovey-dovey rubbish had come on far too quickly. He was a scientist, not a Casanova.

And it needed to stop.

He was still learning to be a viscount. Alfred was the elder brother who had remained at Papa's side, learning what was required of a peer. Kenneth had never once considered he might succeed to the post. Afred was supposed to marry and produce an heir.

Kenneth supposed the responsibility now fell onto his shoulders, but not yet. He had his own affairs to settle in Northumberland. He needed to visit the viscountcy estates and set them to rights. Lady Modesty deserved to be courted by someone who was ready to marry, someone who could tame her, someone who didn't utterly lose his mind when she was in the room. Someone whose sole desire was *not* to slowly strip her of every piece of clothing and worship her naked body, not for a few hours, but for days—perhaps weeks—perhaps an eternity.

Lady Modesty could not possibly be his ideal wife. When he found her, Kenneth's wife would be demure and quiet and she would listen to whatever he said and obey him without question or argument.

He crumpled the slip of stationery and then threw the ball into the hearth's fire.

The Season was nearly over and, with it, most of the members of polite society would return to their country seats for the hotter months of summer. Doubtless, Modesty would travel to one of Dunscaby's estates somewhere in Scotland. Kenneth also needed to head home to his bees and his sheep. Well, he'd have to stop by his castle near Berwick upon Tweed and ensure everything was in order there. And then there was Kiedler Equine, which was quite a bit larger than his farm in Rothbury. It wouldn't be inconceivable to move his affects there, even though bees were not easy to relocate. And if he did move them, he'd have to ensure plenty of pollinating flowers were about. Perhaps he could establish new hives at Berwick Castle as well? The estate certainly had ample land for it.

Now that Kenneth had time to think about his inheritance, Kiedler not only had acres of land tilled by tenant farmers, it had a rather large stable complete with a racetrack.

It is best not to tell Modesty about that.

The prospect of becoming mistress of the Kielder Equestrian estate might attract her interest more than the prospect of marrying Kenneth. He was not like other peers in the slightest, interested in marrying to increase their holdings. In addition to needing a demure spouse, when he did decide to wed, he wanted a woman who loved him unconditionally. He wanted to love his wife as well. And, by the saints, his never-ending desire to ravish Lady Modesty exceeded the boundaries of love.

But I do not wish to marry. I must first complete my work on the Northumberland Longwool.

Kenneth dipped his quill again and groaned as a blob of black ink soiled his next sheet of stationery.

"Fie."

What did it matter if he traipsed around London for a fortnight or two pretending to court Modesty? True, it tied him in knots to be in her presence, but he truly didn't want to hurt her feelings. Perhaps she might tire of him—realize he was dedicated to science and a very dull conversationalist. Kenneth might handle the ribbons of a phaeton well, but he was far too large to race horses. Of course, horses interested him because he was a scientist and chiefly interested in exceptional breeding programs. However, he had no interest in the racing industry with all its wagering and underhanded skullduggery.

In fact, I ought to sell Venom. Or perhaps turn him out to stud.

Modesty was too naïve about such things. She was a skilled rider, but Kenneth could never see her fighting with other jockeys and knocking them off their horses. *Besides, once she marries, no husband in his right mind would allow her to race, or ride astride for that matter. I most certainly would not allow my wife to go about wearing jockey's silks and racing horses like hellfire and brimstone.*

Though, when in command of the reins she certainly did pose a magnificent sight. Who knew a woman could handle a horse so deftly? Not just any woman, but a lass who had been bred into a dukedom, a lass who ought to be courted by the most esteemed gentlemen in the Kingdom.

Which Kenneth was not. Yes, he had a title and lands, and was reasonably wealthy. But he was a country squire in his heart. London, ballrooms, and tea parties caused him heartburn. Modesty might think she preferred horses and stables, but she was raised in a family at the center of polite society. Anywhere Dunscaby went so did the newspaper reporters.

As he crumpled the ruined piece of paper, Welch stepped into the library. "It seems Freddie has returned from today's escapades, my lord."

Kenneth removed his pocket watch and noted it was only ten o'clock. "He found the ring?"

"Not exactly. But he has someone with him who insists upon speaking with you."

"Who?"

"A Mrs. Lewis. I refused to allow her above stairs and she is waiting in the kitchens."

Kenneth envisioned a woman covered in mud. "Tell me, does Freddie refer to this woman as Ma?"

"That would be the one, and though it pains me to add, she's holding the lad by a leash."

"A what?" Kenneth sprang to his feet and hastened through the servants' entrance. "Why the devil have you not released him?"

Welch followed. "Because Mrs. Lewis threatened to stab the boy if I didn't fetch you immediately."

"Her words?"

"Not precisely." Welch stammered. "Sir, watch your—"

As he smacked his forehead, stars crossed Kenneth's vision as he reeled backward. "Ballocks, that hurt," he growled under his breath.

"I tried to warn you, sir."

Kenneth glanced up at the enormous oak lintel. "I suppose the last time I used these stairs I was a bit shorter."

"Do you need a moment?" asked Welch. "You have quite a knot forming already."

He pulled a handkerchief from his coat pocket and dabbed the wound. At least he wouldn't be meeting Mrs. Lewis with blood streaking down his face. "I'll be fine."

Leading his manservant around the corner into the kitchens, Kenneth stopped short.

A woman wearing a filthy apron atop a brown dress stood beside Freddie with one hand holding a hemp rope tied around his neck so tightly, the boy was standing on his toes, his chin tilted upward. She held a dagger to the throbbing vein at his neck.

Kenneth's heated ire rushed through his veins. Not only was she treating the lad worse than a dog, crusty remnants of blood were caked at his mouth, a clear sign she'd struck the lad.

"Lord Berwick, I presume?" she asked before Welch had an opportunity to make the introductions.

Calculating his next move, Kenneth took a step nearer. "You are correct."

Freddie barely made eye contact, his face twisted in a cringe. "I'm sorry, milord—"

Mrs. Lewis yanked on the rope, practically strangling the boy. "Shut up!" she snapped, her hateful gaze arresting Kenneth's advance. "Ye take another step and I'll do 'im in, I will."

He stopped, though didn't step back. "I take it you are here because you want something?"

"Damned right I want somethin'. I want me due. Ye stole this boy from me."

"I stole nothing," Kenneth said cooly, watching the hand holding the dirty blade. "I simply offered Freddie a better position."

The blade pressed but drew no blood. "But 'e's mine! I taught 'im everythin' he knows."

"Do you mean to say you taught him the art of light fingers?"

"Oy, ye toffs are all the same. Ye live in fancy 'ouses with all this finery and take no mind of the poor souls who 'ave to work for a livin'."

Kenneth remained still, staring directly into Mrs. Lewis' grey eyes. "I believe I was taking considerable note of Frederick's circumstances. In fact, Mr. Welch is teaching him to read. Is that not right, Welch?"

"Y-yes, sir," the manservant stammered.

Kenneth dared to take another step forward.

"Stay back, or I'll run this knife right across Freddie's throat! Sharp it is, too."

If the blade was sharp, the lad would already be bleeding.

Ready to strike, Kenneth clenched his fists and

forced himself to breathe deeply. "No, I do not believe you'll do that."

The woman's mouth dropped open. "Huh?"

"Two reasons. Firstly, if you kill Frederick, he will be dead, and thus his corpse will be worth nothing to me. Secondly, if you commit murder, I'll have no recourse but to lock you in the coal cellar and send for the magistrate. Then I will make it my life's ambition to see to it you will be tried and hanged for your crime."

Mrs. Lewis bared her yellow teeth. "Ye bloody swine!"

Kenneth sniffed, the pall in the air quite unpleasant. "You are wrong on that count, madam." He did not want to put Freddie's life in further peril, but he wasn't about to roll over and allow this wench to come into his home and start making demands.

Out of the corner of his right eye, he spotted the call bells. Using a trick he'd learned as a lad who could descend the servant stairs without hitting his head, he stamped his foot, making them ring. As the woman's attention shifted, Kenneth lunged for the knife, bent her wrist away from Freddie's throat, then twisted her arm up her back, making the blade clatter to the floor.

"Ye'll break me arm!" Mrs. Lewis shrieked.

Freddie hastened to pick up the knife and faced her, his hands trembling as he pointed the weapon. "I ought to—"

"Silence!" Kenneth warned, giving the boy a wink. He had her in a hold no one could escape unless they did indeed want a broken radius. "You will leave my house and never come back. If you ever see Freddie again, you will turn and go the other way. If I hear from anyone in all of England that you have mistreated any child no matter how young or old, I will have you arrested. Have I made myself clear?"

"But I—"

Kenneth twisted Mrs. Lewis' arm until she shrieked in pain. "Am I clear, madam?" he asked through clenched teeth.

"Ye are a 'eartless, vile brute!"

"I believe of the two of us, I'm the only one in possession of a beating heart." He pushed her away. "Now go before I change my mind."

Mrs. Lewis stumbled forward, but as she regained control, she looked to Freddie and narrowed her eyes. The boy raised the knife, scooting away, his entire body shaking.

"Go!" Kenneth bellowed, taking a menacing step toward her.

The woman had the gall to grab a loaf of bread off the counter before she hastened out the door.

Freddie tossed the knife onto the timbers, blinking, his face contorted as if he were about to burst into tears. "I-I'm sorry, milord. Please don't send me away."

Kenneth pulled the boy into his arms and crushed him to his chest. "I told you before and I'll say it again. Your home is here now. I'm not ever going to turn my back on you."

"I 'ate 'er."

"She is vile. I almost wish she'd tried to stab me, because then I could send her to prison where she belongs." Kenneth held Freddie at arms' length and loosened the hemp noose. "I never want to see a rope around your neck again."

"You've been rubbed raw," said Welch. "I'll fetch a salve from Mrs. Fielding straightaway."

Kenneth spotted a flagon of water and poured Freddie a glass, then urged him to sit beside him at the kitchen table. "Now, tell me how you ended up in that woman's clutches."

Shaking his head, Freddie stared at his lap. "I shouldn't of done it."

"What?"

"I never should of showed the drawing to One-Eyed 'enry."

"Who is he?"

"'e's a devious cur, that's who."

"Help me to understand… " Kenneth rolled his hand, requesting a more thorough explanation.

"The fella makes fine things disappear—just like we talked about. Like Crocky but not as shifty. When I spotted 'im near Covent Garden, I asked if he knew about the ring."

"Did he answer?"

"Aye, but 'e's the one who tied the noose around me neck, then he dragged me to Ma's corner—said I 'ad no business mullin' about askin' questions either."

"Do you think he had anything to do with the ring?"

Freddie shook his head and sipped his water. "If he did, ye've no chance of findin' it now."

Kenneth draped his arm across the boy's shoulders and gave him a squeeze. Freddie's words rang true. Doubtless the ring already adorned the finger of a new owner who had no idea the man who'd initially purchased the sapphire had lost his life. *Did Alfred die because of the ring? Because of the incident at the Epsom Derby? Perhaps he was indeed rubbing elbows with the likes of Ward Crockford. Was Crocky the murderer? Did the owner of Waiter's die from a salve of his own poison?*

~

MODESTY CARESSED the shiny black paint with the tips of her gloves. "I wasna aware you had a phaeton."

Kenneth offered his hand. "It came with the viscountcy, of course. Usually I drive a simple curricle."

"Well, thank you for the invitation to go riding today." She allowed him to hand her up to the bench "Mama was especially thrilled."

He joined her and took up the ribbons. "Just your mother?"

"Well, I ken you're only courting me to allay any damages to my reputation."

He drove the matched pair into traffic. "Do you now?"

"Aye, and I ken Mama and Martin colluded to *encourage* you to make a good showing."

"Told you, did they?" he asked, one eyebrow arching.

"There was no need." Modesty patted her bonnet. "It will take some time for my hair to grow," she said. After all, someone still might connect her with the jockey who took the spill in the first race at Primrose Hill.

"I'd assume so. But you'll soon be heading back to Scotland, will you not?"

"Thank heavens. We always summer at Stack Castle. Up there no one gives a rats arse about my hair."

"Doesn't your mother host a great many house parties."

Modesty regarded Kenneth's mouth out of the corner of the corner of her eyes. He looked so strong and confident driving a team. If she were to actually marry someone, he would be the sort of man with whom she might be content. "She has in the past—for my sisters. However, I think I have convinced her that I have no interest in parties of any sort."

"Such a shame," he said, tapping with his whip, cueing the team to turn the corner.

Is he siding with Mama and Martin? "Why do you say that?"

"Well, you are quite an accomplished dancer."

Modesty snorted. "Wallflower is more apt."

"And you are a very skilled conversationalist."

"Ha! Even if I didna speak with a Scottish burr, most gentlemen would take one look at my hair and turn on their heels, never engaging in a single word."

"Then they do not deserve you."

This time, Modesty didn't hide her stare as she studied the man beside her. He oft said the most astonishing things—things that turned her insides into levitating clouds and made her feel weightless. How could he make her feel so effervescent inside when he wanted nothing more than to return to the north of England and dally with his bees and sheep?

Kenneth deftly steered the carriage around a cart laden with barrels and pulled by two oxen. "By the way you handle a team, you dunna seem like a country curricle driver."

"I don't recall saying I hadn't driven this phaeton. I just was not her owner."

"I see," she said folding her hands atop her reticule while Kenneth maneuvered a corner, making her slide until she was stopped by his hip. Glancing downward, the yellow muslin of her day dress contrasted with his black trousers. "Excuse me."

She put her hand down to push away, managing to place her palm on Kenneth's thigh. Good glory, his muscles were as solid as iron. He grunted as her fingers dug in a wee bit. "Och, I didna mean to hurt you."

He gave her a sly glance out of the corner of his eye. "You didn't."

"Then why the grunt? I swear your leg is as solid as the leather on my saddle. I wouldna be surprised if you were impervious to a strike from a jockey's crop."

Modesty's comment not only drew a glance, he grinned and looked at her as if she'd just paid him the finest compliment he'd ever received. "I'll try to be more careful when taking the corners lest you end up in my lap."

"Oh?" She glanced downward, the memories making her smile. "Your lap isna any place I havena been before."

"But not in public."

"Aye, well, I suppose the first time doesna count."

"First time?" he asked as they entered Hyde Park.

This being the time of day where the members of the *ton* came to the park to be seen, heads turned their way—women gawked, then gossiped behind their fans. Modesty didn't care. "When Crocky fell out his window. I canna for the life of me remember how I got there, but I did end up on your lap."

"I suppose you did." Kenneth tipped his hat at a couple of pedestrians. "I was wondering how you fill your time when you're not riding a horse."

"How do I fill my time or how do I *prefer* to fill my time?"

"Both."

"As you are aware, I am officially out, which means my mother is largely in charge of my social calendar. She insists I go to every ball, soiree, luncheon, opera, theater, Vauxhall, shopping, dress fittings... " Modesty drew in an enormous breath. "Shall I go on?"

He tweaked one of the curls Randolph had carefully styled to frame her face. "I would think you've had a bit of a reprieve of late."

"I was allowed to send my regrets whilst I was

healing, but no longer." Modesty gave him a quizzical glance. "Is that not why we're out riding today? Because Mama wants everyone to see us together and assume you are courting me?"

"That may be a byproduct of our little jaunt through the park, but I assure you, this ride was solely my idea."

"But courting me wasna. And dunna deny it."

"Perhaps the dowager duchess and His Grace twisted my arm but—"

Modesty didn't care to hear any tall tales at the moment, however there was something making her insides churn ever since she and Charity were Kenneth's guests for luncheon. "Tell me one thing and I'll leave it be."

"Very well, what do you want to know?"

"Since ye didna want to court me in the first place, why do we always end up kissing?"

He slowed the horses to an ambling walk. "I suppose you would know if I tried to hide the truth."

"Please tell me the truth. I'm ever so conflicted."

After heaving an enormous sigh, he faced her, his expression most serious. "It shames me to admit it, but I cannot help myself."

"You too?" she asked, biting her bottom lip. Perhaps she hadn't have sounded so joyful.

Kenneth lightly tapped the reins. "I suppose that is why young ladies require chaperones."

"Aye." Modesty twisted the strings of her reticule around her finger. He couldn't help himself from kissing her just as she couldn't resist kissing him? Holy Moses, if that wasn't a disastrous calamity for a man who wasn't ready to marry and a woman who wanted to remain a spinster.

"So," she said, altering the subject. "Have you uncovered anything new in the investigation?"

"Nothing of any use."

"What about the sleuth you told me about?"

"Well, there might be something brewing there. Right before I left my town house, I received a letter asking me to stop by his offices."

"Then why the blazes are we ambling through Hyde Park?" Modesty reached over and tugged on the ribbons, turning the horses back toward Town. "We've a sleuth to see!"

22

___

"Once we go inside, I shall do the talking," Kenneth said, handing Modesty down from the high seat of his phaeton.

The hem of her skirt caught on the iron step, revealing a slender, feminine ankle, but to Kenneth's dismay, she quickly flicked it down as if she had practiced the maneuver hundreds of times. "Why must I keep mum? Do you still not trust me?"

He sighed. After all, this was the headstrong Scottish lass he'd come to adore, not the demure rose he wanted to adore. "Trust has nothing to do with it. I am the man who engaged Mr. McGrath to carry out an investigation on my behalf. It is only natural for me to take charge of any conversation that might ensue."

Her Ladyship tossed her head, as if his request didn't sit well. "Verra well, if you insist."

Together they stepped inside, making the bell above the door tinkle.

Kenneth first looked to the fainting couch, somewhat surprised not to see the man sprawled atop it. As he stood, Mr. McGrath cleared his throat from behind his writing table. "I see you received my missive, milord."

"Indeed." Kenneth made the introductions, some-what pleased the sleuth had combed his hair and donned an ironed shirt. Even his neckcloth was fairly tied. "Your letter said you have news."

The chap eyed Modesty. "Do you reckon you want to hear it with a lady present?"

"She—"

Modesty stood taller. "I assure you, sir, I am not a shrinking violet like so many of my contemporaries."

Kenneth gave her a hard stare before schooling his expression and nodding to the investigator. "Please do continue."

Mr. McGrath resumed his seat, gesturing to the two mismatched chairs opposite his writing table. "Let's see here," he said, rummaging through slips of paper.

Kenneth held a chair for Her Ladyship, then took the smaller, straight-backed chair, which looked sim-ilar to the one his governess had used for punishment when he was a lad.

"Ah, yes. It seems your Evelyn Applewhite used an alias. Her real name is Mary Cole—let me tell you that wasn't easy to find. It seems she quite prefers to go by Applewhite."

"Where did you discover her true identity?" Mod-esty asked.

Mr. McGrath looked up with a dead-eyed scowl. "I never reveal the tools of me trade, else I'd run meself out of business."

"Good work uncovering her name, but what of her? Where is she?" asked Kenneth.

"Well, that is the question of the hour, is it not?" McGrath held up a note from an unorganized pile of them. "Here it is. Her mother was Agnes Toombs—the record shows she was arrested and died in Newgate of —" He glanced at Modesty and frowned.

She rolled her hand through the air. "Go on, if you please."

"The pox."

She drew a hand to her chest and coughed. "Oh my."

"It seems Mary was fourteen years of age at the time and was placed in the custody of her father." The sleuth found another slip of paper on the other side of his writing table. "Here it is, Josiah Cole. He was a sailor in in the Royal Navy."

"Was?" asked Kenneth. "Is he dead?"

"Might as well be. He was injured in the Battle of Trafalgar and sent to Bethlem."

"The lunatic asylum?" Modesty asked.

"The one and the same. Most everyone calls it *Bedlam*." Mr. McGrath turned the paper over. "A couple of years past Mr. Cole was transferred to Haslar—the new asylum they built for naval lunatics."

"What is wrong with him?" asked Kenneth.

"Insane for certain. You are aware many naval men go mad from all the cannon blasting?"

Though he shifted in the chair, the straight back proved impossible, so Kenneth scooted forward. "Do you have anything more about Evelyn—er—Mary? Where is she living now? Has she ever been convicted of a crime?"

"All I know is no one in London has seen her since she left Town after Ward Crockford fell out of the window at Waiter's. But that goes for several of his other lady birds as well. As for any criminal record, there was none to be found."

"For Evelyn Applewhite or Mary Cole?" asked Kenneth.

"Neither."

Kenneth wasn't surprised to hear Alfred's mistress had kept her nose clean. *But someone must know her whereabouts.* "You mean to tell me she has disappeared without a trace?"

"It seems that way."

"With whom did she stay when her father was at sea?" asked Modesty.

"I could always make inquiries with the boarding schools around town, though given a sailor's wages, it is more likely a lass of fourteen would have been left to fend for herself."

Still uncomfortable, Kenneth stood and began pacing. "Can you find out? And what about her mother? What was the reason for her imprisonment? Debts? Prostitution? What?"

"I'll make some inquiries, but my fee... "

"You shall be compensated fairly." Kenneth scanned the collection of notes haphazardly spread across the writing table. "Do you think Miss Cole is still in London?"

Mr. McGrath swept the pieces of paper into a pile. "I don't believe so. You see, the day after Crocky met his end, the mail coach headed for Basingstoke left with five passengers—all of them ladies and not a one of them entered her name on the manifest."

"Why not?" asked Modesty.

"Because each one signed with an X."

Kenneth picked up the top slip of paper, but the man's handwriting was as readable as the scribble of a toddler. "Did you follow the trail?"

"To Basingstoke?" Mr. McGrath snorted loudly. "Did you read my terms, sir? I do not take on assignments more than an hour's ride outside of Town. Besides, who knows where they might have traveled from there?"

Modesty cleared her throat. "Where is Hasler?"

"I understand it is near Britain's largest naval base," said Mr. McGrath.

"Portsmouth." Kenneth glanced from one dingy wall to the other. "Have you a map of England?"

"Certainly." Behind him, the investigator pulled out map after map, unrolling it and frowning until finally he said, "Ah-a."

Kenneth exchanged eye rolls with Modesty. If Mr. McGrath were even slightly organized he ought to have been able to go straight to it. The chap might be capable at finding people, but he obviously didn't perform his duties from behind his writing table.

All three of them bent over the map, but Kenneth was the one who spotted a clue across the harbor from Portsmouth. He planted his fingertip on the Gosport Peninsula. "I'll wager the asylum is here near the Haslar Sea Wall."

~

"Do you reckon Mr. Cole will be well enough to speak with you?"

"How will I know unless I try?" Filled with unease, Kenneth paced the floor of the Duke of Dunscaby's front parlor while the dowager duchess sat in the bay window pretending to be fixated on her embroidery, but doubtlessly listening to every word they said.

"When do you think you'll go?" asked Modesty, pretending to sew, though her needle wasn't even threaded.

"There's no need to wait. I'll leave on the morrow."

"But Lady Northampton's masquerade is the next

day," said Her Grace. "My dear Berwick, there's no chance you'll make it back from Portsmouth in time. And it is the last momentous event of the Season."

Modesty gripped the embroidery hoop on her lap. "Her Ladyship willna notice if Lord Berwick isna there, just as she'd not notice if I was missing as well."

Mama hummed as she did when she wasn't entirely convinced of something. "But I thought it would be a good opportunity to introduce your new hair style to the *ton*."

"I've decided to wait until next year to show my face again. After all, Lady Northampton's masquerade marks the end of the Season. And it will ensure there is no chance of creating a scandal because my hair will be long enough by then."

"I thought this was to be your one and only Season," said Kenneth.

The Dowager's eyes grew round as she lowered her needle and thread. "My good sir, you have proposed?"

Modesty sprang to her feet, waving her palms. "No, Mama. Why must everything be about marriage?"

"Because that is why we go to all the expense and trouble of putting on airs for the London Season. You ought to be able to recite the reasons in your sleep, sweeting."

"Aye, but I dunna want to marry. I want to train racehorses."

"I am aware." Her Grace folded her hands atop her lap as serenely as if a butterfly had landed on her shoulder. "That is why Berwick is such a good match for you."

"I beg your pardon?" they both blurted at once.

Kenneth shook his head and looked sternly at the Dowager while Modesty gaped directly at him. Never in his life had he felt so exposed. If only he could ask

Her Grace exactly what she was scheming and reiterate that this courting farce was of Her Grace's own concoction, but doing so would hurt her daughter's feelings and he wouldn't venture that far.

"Mama!" Modesty threw her arms wide. "To what are you referring?"

"Why, Kiedler Equine, of course."

Modesty's lips parted with her gasp. "In Northumberland," she whispered as if she suddenly realized Alfred's equestrian dream now belonged to Kenneth.

His face burned as his gaze darted between the two women. Could things grow more awkward? He hadn't yet decided if he was going to keep the estate in the viscountcy. Kiedler had been Alfred's indulgence because the eldest brother was the racing enthusiast in the family. And he had turned the estate into a renowned and respected horse training facility. At a complete loss for words, Kenneth's mind whirred. Her Grace may have lured him into thinking he was play-acting at courting her daughter, but the woman had obviously been scheming all along.

"What is happening?" Modesty asked, inching toward the door. "Mama, have you been meddling?"

The dowager duchess appeared as unruffled as her portrait hanging above the mantel. "Of course I have. It is my duty to meddle to ensure you make a fine match."

Modesty shook her finger beneath Kenneth's nose. "And you! You've been in on it all along?"

"No—well, it's not what you think," he replied, suddenly filled with the desire to drop to his knees and beg for her forgiveness.

"Oh? So, what is it, then? Am I supposed to fall in love with you? Or is it the other way around?" Realization crossed Her Ladyship's face as she gaped at her mother. "How could you? Am I so hideous I canna charm the right sort of gentleman?" She turned on her heel and hastened for the parlor doors. "Forget the masquerade because I'm not setting foot inside Carlton House. And for you, Berwick, never speak to me again!"

"Modesty!" Kenneth called out as he followed her into the corridor, but she was already gone, dashing up the stairs, heading for rooms where he was not allowed.

"Never mind my daughter's temporary ire." The Dowager came up beside him. "She thinks we've ruined the plans she has set for her life."

"Haven't we?"

"Absolutely not. She is naïve. Only a foolish young woman would wish to be a spinster and spend her days among a plethora of smelly horses."

Kenneth considered Modesty's dreams not to be strange in the slightest. After all, he spent most of his time with sheep. Bees to a lesser extent.

"You go on to Portsmouth and find the fellow with whom you want to speak. I'll wager by the time you return, Modesty will have forgotten this conversation ever happened." Her Grace floated back toward the parlor. "And I suppose it isn't a horrible idea to miss the masquerade. After all, so many people forget themselves when wearing a mask."

23

———

Modesty sat in the window embrasure and watched the passing traffic while Randolph flitted about the bedchamber packing her things. "I dunna understand why Her Grace is so anxious to leave for Scotland. Were ye not planning to attend Lady Northampton's masquerade?"

"I told her I refused to go." Modesty groaned at the image of Kenneth's face when she'd realized he had colluded with Mama. Though she suspected it all along, it stung to have him admit to it. "I doubt I'll show my face at another London social affair again in all my days."

Randolph folded a shift. "Och, it canna be as bad as all that."

"Believe me, when your own mother conspires against you, it is verra bad, and utterly disconcerting."

"But what will you do? Ye ken the Dowager will insist you return again next year."

Modesty pulled an embroidered cushion onto her lap and hugged it. "I have the entire summer and autumn to convince her otherwise, do I not?"

She had already decided to enlist her sister-in-law,

Julia's assistance. Martin's wife was ever so industrious and forward-thinking. If anyone in the family could help her achieve her dreams, it would be the duchess. Drat it all, she should have spoken to Julia before she and Marty left for Stack Castle.

Down below, a young boy dressed in livery darted across the street, straight for the town house door. Recognition tickled the back of her neck as she leaned forward for a better look. "Is that Freddie?" she mumbled while her lady's maid continued to pack.

Has something happened to Berwick? But he ought to have departed for Portsmouth yesterday.

Modesty slipped her feet into her slippers, then headed out the door.

"Going to take some air, m'lady?" asked Randolph, holding out a bonnet. "You'll want this."

Though Modesty wasn't certain if she might venture outside or not, she took the hat. "Thank you."

As she tiptoed to the banister, a child's anxious and alarmed voice resounded from the marbled entryway. She sped her pace, dashing down two flights of stairs. "Freddie, is something amiss with Lord Berwick?"

Giles turned from the door while the lad slipped past him and marched up to her directly. "I didn't know where else to go, milady. A man named McGrath came to the 'ouse and said 'is Lordship could be in grave danger if 'e goes down to Portsmouth, but I told 'im 'e was already too late. The lord left yesterday morn."

Modesty grasped the lad by his shoulders. "Why does Mr. McGrath believe Berwick to be in danger?"

"On account of the ma."

"Mary Cole's mother? Agnes Toombs?"

Freddie nodded his head. "That's 'er. She went to prison for makin' poison and sellin' it to murderers."

Modesty's blood turned cold. "Wolfsbane," she whispered, hauntingly.

"What do ye ken of this, m'lady?" asked Giles. "Did you say wolfsbane?"

"I surely did. 'Tis what Mr. Ruthford at the apothecary shop thought the former viscount might have been poisoned with—Crocky as well."

"But did they not die of natural causes?" asked Giles.

"That is what Kenneth is trying to find out." Modesty donned her bonnet, tying a bow beneath her chin and looking at the lad. "Can you ride a horse?"

The butler stepped between them. "I beg your pardon?"

"Aye, I reckon I can," said Freddie.

"You canna be thinking to ride all the way to Portsmouth!" Giles insisted.

Making her decision, Modesty squared her shoulders. She hadn't been brought up in a duke's household to turn her back on a wee bit of danger. "That's exactly what I'm going to do."

"I canna allow you to leave the house with a footman. Her Grace will have my hide for certain."

"Nay, she'll have mine." Modesty grabbed Freddie by the arm. "Come with me."

"I forbid you to take another step," Giles said, trying to sound as if he had any authority whatsoever.

"And I forbid you to stop me!" She thrust her finger toward the stairs. "I'm going whether you approve or not. And if you want to be any help at all, go tell Randolph I need proper riding attire and a satchel that I can affix to the back of my saddle."

Giles flailed his arms. "But you'll be ruined, m'lady!"

As Modesty pulled Freddie into the corridor, she grinned over her shoulder at Giles. "Now wouldna that be a shame? Nonetheless, I'm bringing along this wee footman as a chaperone. When Mama returns from playing whist with the Wayward Widows, please do let her know where I've gone. I shouldna be more than a day or three. Now go on and tell Randolph to bring my things out to the mews."

"Modesty Alice MacGalloway!" Giles boomed, but she was already halfway through the house and heading for the mews. If Kenneth was in danger, it would take a lead ball from a musket to stop her and she was certain the family's butler wouldn't go that far.

"Your ma is with a mob of wayfaring widows?" asked Freddie as they stepped into the courtyard.

"Wayward. And it is a name I made up for her gathering of friends. Just be glad she's not here at the moment, else it would take an act of God to saddle the horses and ride south."

~

KENNETH THOUGHT DRIVING HIS LIGHTWEIGHT, two-wheeled curricle to Portsmouth was smart. It enabled him to stow a small trunk with his effects in the rear as well as offer more comfort during a long journey than a saddle. Moreover, if he encountered a bit of weather, he could put up the cover and remain reasonably dry. But he had been ever so wrong.

After driving the rig through Milford, he'd thrown a wheel and there wasn't a blacksmith nor a farmer for miles. He'd ended up riding his horse back to Milford and finding a smithy there. By the time the wheel had been fixed, he'd had had no choice but to let a room at the only inn in town where he was quite certain he shared his bed with all manner of vermin. Kenneth was accustomed to farm environs and haylofts full of insects, but the straw mattress upon which he tried to sleep must have been fifty years of age with growing colonies of moving pests from midges to gnats to beetles and Lord knew what else.

As he continued on his way, Kenneth twitched and scratched at the innumerous welts and bites he'd sustained. Thank the stars Lady Modesty hadn't devised a way to accompany him. He would have been mortified if she had been forced to endure such shoddy accommodations.

Before he reached Portsmouth, he took the western road and then continued south to Gosport where Haslar Beach was located. It wasn't difficult to find the Haslar Asylum. It was a new, enormous brick building overlooking the water. It also wasn't surprising to find the hospital staffed by nuns.

"May I help you, sir?" asked a veiled sister seated in the front hall at a rather plain-looking writing table.

Kenneth gave her his card. "I understand you have patient by the name of Josiah Cole here."

She looked at the card and set it aside, smiling. "That is correct, Lord Berwick."

"Might I gain an audience with him? I'd like to ask him a few questions about his daughter."

"You can certainly see Mr. Cole, but I'm afraid he won't be able to answer your questions."

"Oh? Why?"

"The poor soul hasn't spoken since the Battle of Trafalgar."

Kenneth rubbed the back of his neck. "I see."

"But it would be ever so generous of you to visit with him. So few of the patients here receive guests."

"Does Mr. Cole ever have visitors?"

"Not often."

"But he does. His daughter perchance?" Kenneth gripped his hands together. "Do you know her?"

"Not really. She has only come in a few times." The nun stood, the keys around her belt jangling. "Come with me and I'll take you up to Mr. Cole's room. Do you have a book?"

"Book, madam?"

"He seems to enjoy it when we read to him." She collected a volume from a shelf behind her. "This might suffice."

He accepted the book and looked at the spine, relieved she hadn't given him a novel.

The nun led the way up the stairs, which seemed sterile and abandoned. She showed him into a room with four beds, the men in them silent and cadaverous. "Mr. Cole," she said to the man closest to the door. He had a strip of gauze tied around his eyes. "Lord Berwick has come to see you."

"Hello, sir," Kenneth said rather stiffly.

The only sign that Mr. Cole had heard him was a slight incline of his head.

"Go on and have a seat." The sister gestured to a chair. "He won't bite."

Kenneth did as asked and opened the book. "I'm told you like it when people read to you."

A bit of spittle leaked from the corner of the old sailor's mouth.

"I've come from London. At least I have today. I'm actually from the north of England. I dabble in a bit of farming and whatnot."

The spittle oozed down to the man's clean-shaven chin.

Unable to tolerate it, Kenneth found a cloth and wiped away the drool. "There you are. I'll wager it's maddening not being able to wipe your mouth." He waited for a response but when there was none, he continued, "My brother is—was Alfred Davenport, Viscount of Berwick. Are you familiar with his name?"

Nothing.

"I thought not," Kenneth mumbled wondering why the devil he was in a lunatic asylum trying to carry on a conversation with a man who had gone mad. "How about a bit of Byron?"

"*She walks in Beauty...* "

Kenneth looked up. How would Mr. Cole be able to distinguish between poetry and anything else? "Well, it seems my brother was acquainted with your daughter. Evelyn Applewhite."

Nothing.

"That isn't quite correct. As your daughter, you would have called her Mary Cole."

The man's finger's twitched as did his lips.

"You know her, do you not? Mary?"

The twitching stopped and Kenneth leaned near Mr. Cole's ear. "I am searching for your daughter, Mary. Her mother's name was Agnes Toombs."

Spittle ran down both sides of the old sailor's mouth. He might not be able to speak, but it was clear he held Agnes in low esteem.

Not certain if his visit to the asylum had proven useful or not, he returned his attention to the book and read Byron's poetry until the nun returned. "I'm sorry, but it is time for the patients to eat supper."

"Of course."

"Did you find what you wanted?" she asked, leading him back down to the hall.

"Unfortunately, no. I'm afraid I came all the way down from London for naught."

"Well, if it might help, I checked the records for his daughter's address. Considering your rank of viscount, I believe that makes you an official of sorts." She handed him a slip of paper. "Miss Cole recently moved to Portsmouth across the harbor."

Perhaps being a viscount does have its benefits.

24

They weren't out of London before Modesty realized Freddie was about as skilled at horseback riding as she was at attracting suitors. When they were held up due to congestion at London Bridge, she connected a lead line to the lad's gelding.

Pulling him alongside her mare proved to be much faster than waiting for Freddie to figure out how to control a horse, and Modesty wasn't about to be slowed down from reaching Portsmouth—or Gosport where the hospital ought to be located.

They rode until dusk and stayed in a roadside inn. After a second day of hard riding, it was nine o'clock at night when they found the asylum, at which time they were told visiting hours were over and had been for quite some time.

"But we dunna want to see anybody," Modesty explained in a rush. "Lord Berwick should have been here earlier looking for Mr. Cole."

There was enough surprise in the nun's expression for Modesty to realize Kenneth had indeed paid a visit. "It is not our policy to divulge—"

"Do you care if your policy gets a man killed?"

"I beg your pardon? It is late and—"

"She's a lady." Freddie stepped forward. "The sister of a duke, so ye'd best 'ear 'er out."

Modesty clapped her hands over her heart, determined to continue. "Lord Berwick came here because he's investigating the murder of his brother who evidently was courting Mr. Cole's daughter, Mary Cole who also uses the name Evelyn Applewhite."

Freddy threw out his arms. "And the sleuth who discovered Evelyn's real name come to 'is Lordship's town 'ouse and said she was murderin' people with wolfsbane."

Modesty glanced at the lad, knowing he'd deviated from the truth a wee bit. As far as they knew, Evelyn hadn't murdered anyone—but her mother had made a profession of it. "You see." Modesty urged the boy to move behind her. This was too important to be spouting half-truths to a woman of the cloth. "Lord Berwick's life is in grave peril. We must find him forthwith!"

The sister pursed her lips and glanced over her shoulder. "The addresses of the patients' families are confidential."

"But you gave Mary Cole's address to His Lordship, did you not?" Modesty hedged. "Please dunna make me ride all the way back to London to fetch my brother. Mind you the Duke of Dunscaby is seventh in line for the throne as well as the most powerful peer in Scotland. Furthermore, if Lord Berwick dies because of your negligence I—"

The nun threw up her hands. "Very well. But I must caution you not to pester Miss Cole. My guess is she is living peacefully and would prefer to be left in solitude."

"If she is truly doing so, I shall be overjoyed to

leave her in peace." Modesty clapped a hand to her forehead. *I pray we are not too late.*

"Well," the nun said, leading them inside. "The hour is late and the ferry across the harbor has shut down for the day."

"Did Lord Berwick take the ferry?"

The woman thumbed through a journal, stopping a quarter of the way through, and reached for a slip of paper. "I have no idea where the viscount went after he left the hospital." She held up a finger. "Though he did drive a curricle. The ferry is too small for a carriage of any sort. 'Tis only for passengers on foot or those on horseback, so he must have driven around the harbor."

Modesty eyed her young chaperone. "Then we've no time to spare."

"It isn't safe to ride up the Gosport Road after dark," said the nun. "If you want my advice, you'll stay here and take the first ferry come morn. To be perfectly honest, it is such a long journey to navigate the shore, you will not arrive at Miss Cole's door any faster."

Modesty glanced out the window, catching a magnificent sunset in hews of orange and fuchsia. She might be daring, but she wasn't daft. Besides what good could she do if she and Freddie were set upon by highwaymen and left for dead? "You did say Berwick visited this afternoon, did you not?"

"That's correct. During proper visiting hours, mind you."

Then he'd most likely be arriving in Portsmouth about now—much too late for a social call.

Making up her mind, Modesty rubbed her hands. "I say, madam, if I promised a sizable donation to the hospital from the Duke of Dunscaby, might you consider finding us two beds for the night?"

~

FOR THE SECOND time on this journey, Kenneth rued having driven the damned curricle from London. This time it wasn't a problem with the rig, but his horse came up lame. Fortunately he'd spotted a farmer's cottage a few hundred paces from the road where he was able to buy a new horse and turn the old one out to pasture for a rest. He didn't blame the gelding. Hell, if Kenneth had to live in a tiny stall and pull a carriage across London's cobblestoned streets, he'd most likely end up lame as well.

By the time he made it to Portsmouth, it was too late to call on Mr. Cole's daughter. Once again, he was forced to spend a night in a roadside inn. However, he found a lovely boarding house on the outskirts of town with tasty fare and fresh linens. He was even able to order a bath.

After a night of sound sleep, Kenneth was ready to confront Miss Cole and, Lord willing, get to the bottom of Alfred's death.

Except he wasn't ready. Not really. Yes, he wanted to uncover what had led to Alfred's end, but he hadn't liked some of the things he'd uncovered about his brother thus far. His curious association with Ward Crockford aside, Alfred was courting a young lady yet entertaining a mistress. If it had been up to Kenneth, he would have ended things with the mistress before entering the marriage mart.

Of course, he wouldn't find that surprising behavior for men like Bull Brummell, but Alfred had been brought up in a well-bred family with solid values. Had he really thrown in with Crockford? Or had he fallen in love with the wrong sort of woman and Waiter's was one of the few places he was comfortable being seen with her?

I suppose the stables at Primrose Hill as well.

After receiving directions from the inn's patroness, Kenneth asked the stable's groom to hitch up his horse and curricle, then ambled toward Miss Cole's cottage. How should he address her? Miss Cole or Miss Applewhite? Of course, he ought to tread delicately so as to not upset her sensibilities. As Alfred's lover, the woman might be quite sorrowful at losing him. Is that why she left London abruptly?

Was she bereft?

He turned onto Thicket Road, where there was only one cottage. Rather than a small hovel which Kenneth expected, the home was rather large with two floors and a thatched roof. He stopped the rig in front of the cottage, tied the reins to the brake lever, and checked his pocket watch. Having timed his visit perfectly, he hopped down and then started up the flagstone path.

A man exited the front door, donning his hat. And though the chap walked right past Kenneth, he took no notice of him.

Odd fellow. Kenneth was accustomed to tipping his hat to folks when he passed them. Unless he was in a crush of people at which time hat-tipping became ridiculous. Nonetheless, the chap should have at least nodded his head.

Putting the slight behind him, he proceeded to give a few raps of the brass knocker, then pulled a card from the pocket of his waistcoat.

Expecting to be greeted by a butler or a maid, Kenneth's jaw nearly hit his chest when a woman wearing nothing more than a dressing gown loosely tied at the waist, opened the door and casually leaned against the jamb. Her brown hair was a riotous mess, appearing as though she'd slept with it pinned up, only to have a hive of tresses escape said pins. Her gaze slid from the tip of his head, meandering to his toes. "Ye're a bit late for the party, luv."

"Party?" he asked, glancing in the direction of the retreating man.

She started to close the door. "Come back tonight at ten. That's when the toffs show up. And bring a sack of coin. Not a one of us is cheap."

"I beg your pardon, madam." Kenneth moved his foot forward to keep the woman from shutting the door in his face. "But I believe the proper way to answer a door is to allow the caller to state his name and purpose before you rudely dismiss him. And mind you, this *is* an appropriate hour to call. However, ten o'clock in the evening is not."

This time, she looked him directly in the eyes her brow furrowing. "You're not lookin' for a buttock ball?"

Now that was a term he hadn't heard since his Cambridge days. He did his best not to guffaw. After all, he was on a serious errand. "No. I'm looking for a woman named Evelyn Applewhite."

The lady's lips thinned as she leaned out and looked both ways. "Why would ye be searching for 'er?"

"Because I have reason to believe she was attending a *buttock ball*, as it were, with my brother."

She plucked the card from his fingertips. "So, ye're the new viscount?"

"A title I never dreamed of inheriting. Is Miss Applewhite in? I'd like to ask her a few questions, if I may."

"Why?"

"I'm not certain, but there might be a chance she was the last person to see Alfred alive."

Another scantily dressed woman traipsed down the stairs, took Kenneth's card, and gaped. "Cor."

They both studied him without an iota of affability. "'ow'd ye find us?" asked the second woman.

"Us? Would there perchance be five of you?" Kenneth could be a tad thick-headed at times, but after being snubbed by the man outside this house and now being given the third degree by women who were so unconcerned with their state of dress, this had to be a covey of prostitution, he was on the verge of losing his patience. "I beg your pardon, *ladies*, but I'm merely here because I didn't believe my brother, who was vital and fit, died of asphyxia. I simply desire to ask a question or two and then I'll be on my way."

"Show 'im in," said a woman from the top of the stairs. Her voice was deep and coarse as if she'd been in a smoke-filled room all night, but at least *she* was wearing a dress.

The two other women disappeared. "Miss Applewhite, I presume?" he asked.

"That would be correct."

"Or do you prefer Miss Cole now that you have moved closer to your father?"

If Kenneth had blinked, he would have missed the flicker of surprise in the young woman's eyes. With lightning speed, she schooled her features into an expression of calm affability. "Next of kin information is confidential."

"Is it?" Kenneth glanced to the parlor, noting the gaudy and outdated furniture. "Shall we sit?"

"Is it manners ye're lookin' for?" Miss Applewhite

smiled beautifully as she gestured to a settee. "'ave a seat, milord."

Kenneth waited for her to sit in a chair before he took the settee. Though Miss Applewhite's smile was stunningly beautiful, he'd sensed no warmth in it. "Can you tell me the last time you saw my brother?"

She plucked a silk rose from a vase, then removed the lid of a porcelain bowl shaped like a swan and tapped the rose's petals inside. "I do so like the fragrance of roses," she said, not answering his question.

"As do I," he agreed, playing along. Perhaps it was best if they engaged in small talk before he started asking difficult questions. After all, she loved Alfred as well. "Is that rose oil? I can smell the bouquet from here."

She waved the artificial rose through the air. "It is. Your sense of smell is quite discerning," she said, shifting to the settee beside him. "I miss Alfred ever so."

"As do I, madam. He passed long before his time." Kenneth picked at the frayed upholstery on the armrest. "Were you aware that he purchased a ring the day before he died?"

This time, Miss Applewhite closed her eyes before giving him a chance to observe her expression. "First, please tell me how you discovered I was his mistress."

Kenneth frowned. Why was she being so damned elusive? "A footman at Waiter's told me."

"Oh? What was his name?"

"I don't believe I asked."

"What else did he say about me?"

"Only that you and a parcel of other women left Waiter's employment after Mr. Crockford's death."

"But I made it very difficult for anyone to find me

—'aven't used the name Mary Cole in over a decade, yet 'ere you are."

Kenneth nodded while the stuffing on the armrest began to bulge from the small hole.

"No footman from Waiter's would 'ave known my former name. 'ow did you come by it?"

He shoved his thumb atop the fluff. "To be honest, I hired an investigator."

"Because Alfred purchased a sapphire ring?"

Though he hadn't mentioned the stone in the setting, Kenneth winced at her use of his brother's given name. "Because the ring was missing."

"Didn't 'e give it to his intended?" she asked, cooly smiling again, the rose twirling in her fingertips.

"I assumed so, but the young lady was the first red herring I encountered."

"I imagine you 'ave all this information well-documented?"

Kenneth patted his inside coat pocket where he kept his notes. "Indeed."

"Who is this investigator? Someone from St. Giles, I presume?"

"Actually, no." Kenneth eyed her, deciding to keep Mr. McGrath's identity to himself. "He's a friend of the family."

"From Scotland Yard, perchance?"

He merely nodded. "So, tell me, when did you last see Alfred?"

Miss Applewhite held the rose steady and stared at it. "I'm not certain. After all, it was some time ago. I've moved away from London and started anew since."

"But—"

She brushed the rose across his nose. "My dear Lord Berwick, don't you see? By coming 'ere, I cannot possibly allow you to leave."

"I beg your pardon?" Kenneth asked, his nose tingling. He removed his handkerchief from his top pocket and wiped it. And though ungentlemanly to do so, he blew out with force. "What aside from rose oil is on your flower, madam?"

This time, a devious, sly smile spread across her lips, one you might expect from Medusa. "Why, sir, if you 'aven't figured it out by now, I'd say your power of deduction is quite lacking."

Kenneth gulped, his nose growing number with every tick of the clock standing by the hearth. His cheeks burned while Miss Applewhite leaned forward, rolled the carpet away from the tips of his shoes, and placed a chamber pot between his feet. "Your brother promised to marry me. When I found out he was planning to propose to some 'ighborn toff, I took my revenge."

Keneth lurched forward and heaved, losing his breakfast. How much of the poison had he inhaled? Dear God, he was going to die. A cold sweat broke out across his skin.

Miss Applewhite slid her hand into his coat and removed his notes. "Girls! Help me escort the viscount to his carriage," she hollered.

"What about Crocky?" Kenneth asked, his throat closing as he gagged. "Did you murder him too?"

"The thievin' bastard never gave us our due. Sure, I touched him with my rose oil concoction as well—right after he paid me for your brother's sapphire." The two girls who had answered the door appeared and the three of them pulled Kenneth to his feet and all but dragged him out the door.

"Where is the ring?" he garbled.

"I took it, of course. Then sold it again to—"

"Some devious cur n-named One-Eyed-Henry?"

Kenneth managed to mumble while drool trickled from the corners of his mouth.

The women grunted and groaned under his weight, but the three of them managed to shove him onto the floor of his curricle. "Ye reckon you know everythin', don't ye?" seethed Miss Applewhite. "Ye're a damned fool. Ye're going to die just like your brother and nary a coroner in all of England will ever be able to trace your death back to me."

The rocking motion of the horse pulling the curricle away brought on unbearable dizziness as well as a violent fit of heaves.

25

"That's 'is Lordship's 'orse cart!" shouted Freddie.

Modesty dug in her heels, demanding a canter. As they neared, the blood in her veins pulsed cold at the sight of two shiny black boots dangling over the curricle's floor. "Kenneth!" she shouted, quickly dismounting, then tossing her reins at Freddie.

"Kenneth!" she shouted again, climbing onto the bench beside him and clamping his face between her hands. "Please, God, tell me ye're still alive!"

White foam bubbled from his lips as his eyes opened and rolled back.

"Merciful saints, ye've been poisoned!"

Freddie started to dismount. "Is 'e going to be all right?"

"Stay where you are!" Modesty took up the reins and slapped them on the horse's rump. "We need to find a doctor straightaway."

"Ye want me to follow?"

"Aye," she hollered over her shoulder. "You've had nearly two days to figure out how to ride. Dunna fall behind, else ye'll be lost forever."

Modesty drove the curricle southward, keeping a

white wooden cupola in her sights. Situated atop a stone tower, it had to be the largest church in Portsmouth, and most likely near the center of town. Still lying on the floor of the rig, Kenneth groaned, the sound miserable, yet filling her with hope. "Hang on, darling. We'll find help soon."

As she approached the seashore, she spotted a sailor tying the line of a fishing boat. "Hello, sir!" Modesty hollered. "Can you tell me how to find the town's physician?"

He glanced up from his work, his brow creasing when he saw Kenneth's feet hanging over the side of the curricle. "My oath, what's wrong with him?"

"Poisoned," she snapped. "Please. The doctor!"

He pointed along the shoreline road. "Take Pembroke until it ends at High Street. Turn right and you'll see his shingle up on the left before ye reach the courthouse."

Modesty slapped the reins, shouting a thank you as Freddie came into sight. At least he'd see where she turned. But she hadn't been joking when she told the lad to keep pace. For heaven's sake, Modesty would never forgive herself if anything happened to Kenneth. She shouldn't have stayed in Hasler. She shouldn't have let Kenneth travel alone. At least he could have taken Freddie or his valet. If only they had been married, he would have been able to take her.

She drove the curricle as if she had a demon on her shoulder. But nothing could be fast enough, not even Venom or Poseidon would be fast enough. If only she had gone straight to Portsmouth. If only Mr. McGrath would have been more thorough and found out about the true nature of Mary Cole and her mother *before* Kenneth hastened away to find her.

By the time Modesty stopped the horse and engaged the brake, she was overwhelmed with all the things that should have been done. She blamed herself the most, of course. She should have been smarter, faster, more assertive. And she never should have doubted him. Bless it, if it meant saving Kenneth's life *she* would have taken the initiative, proposed to him, and hastened for Gretna Green.

If he'd have her, of course.

She hopped down from the rig, ran to the door, and pushed inside. "Help! A man's been poisoned. Help us please!"

The doctor emerged from a rear room, wiping his hands on a linen cloth. "Calm down."

She stamped her feet and balled her fists. "I'll no' calm down until His Lordship is set to rights!"

The doctor's gaze shifted out the window. "Poisoned, did you say?"

"Aye. He's hardly breathing."

"Matthew!" hollered the doctor as Freddie reined his horse to a stop behind the curricle. "Help me carry this chap into my surgery."

An enormous fellow ducked under the lintel of the back room, his sleeves rolled up, his forearms larger than Modesty's calves. "Thank you," she said, holding the door as they carried Kenneth inside with Freddie on their heels.

The expression on the lad's face was as grief-stricken as she felt.

"It might be best if you remain out here," said the doctor as they opened the same rear door from whence the two men had come.

Modesty surged after them. "I will not remain behind."

"Suit yourself." After they placed Kenneth onto a

cot against the wall, the doctor faced her. "You are Lady...?"

"Berwick," she replied without hesitation. Though Modesty was fed up with fibbing, posing as Kenneth's wife was far less likely to usher in a scandal than if she admitted to her true identity.

"Aren't the Berwick lands in the far north of England?" he asked, washing his hands in the washstand's bowl. "How the devil did an earl—"

"Viscount," she corrected.

"A viscount become poisoned in Portsmouth of all places?"

Modesty exchanged glances with Freddie whose livery was smudged with grime. In truth, Modesty's costume wasn't in much better condition, though that's not why the hairs of warning were needling at the back of her neck. If she told this doctor about Mary Cole, the woman might hear of it and come to High Street to ensure Kenneth met his end.

"The reason is of a sensitive and confidential nature. If I were to tell you, I could put His Lordship's verra life in danger."

"I assure you, his life is already dangling on a precipice."

"Cor," mumbled Freddie.

"And this young fellow is?"

"Our footman, Frederick," Modesty replied, making the introduction.

The doctor looked to the lad. "You may wait outside."

Modesty gave the boy a curt nod and he reluctantly stepped back while the big man followed and closed the door.

The doctor lifted Kenneth's eyelids and peered

closely. "Do you know with what Lord Berwick was poisoned?"

"I assume it was wolfsbane."

"Oh? Do you know the person who administered the poison?"

"No, we havena met."

"Please tell me *you* didn't poison him," the doctor said, moving to shelves filled with jars and bottles of various sizes. "Was it an error perchance?"

"Och, how can ye say such a thing?"

He selected a jar and removed the cork stopper. "It isn't unusual for a woman to poison her husband. However what I don't understand is if you wanted to kill him, why did you bring him to me?"

"I didna try to kill him. Canna ye understand, I'm trying to save him!"

The doctor faced her. "I'm afraid I'll need a bit more of the truth than that."

Modesty quickly launched into an explanation of how Kenneth's brother was found dead and why.

All the while, the physician dropped a few pieces of coal from the jar into a small bowl, added a bit of water, and proceeded to grind them with a pestle.

She left out all of the details except for the visit to the apothecary shop and the information provided by Mr. McGrath, which led Kenneth to Hasler. When the doctor proved shrewd and continued to ask questions, Modesty finally gave in and told him about McGrath's discovery about the poison.

He stopped grinding. "If there is a murderess living in Portsmouth, she must be reported to the magistrate."

"I promise she will be. And just as soon as Kenneth is able to rise off this bed I shall give you her name."

"If he rises, *he'll* be able to give it to me."

Modesty clasped praying hands beneath her chin. "Then cure him!"

"Aside from feeding him charcoal, there isn't much we can do except wait while his body fights the poison."

"Wait? Isn't there an antidote? Something, anything to stop the progress of wolfsbane?"

The doctor stood holding the mortar and pestle, studying Kenneth as if he were some sort of specimen in a laboratory. "He seems to be in his prime, and rather fit."

"Of course he is." Modesty moved to the shelves containing vials of potions while her mind whirred with the list of remedies she'd learned from Miss Hay, her governess who'd helped Modesty gather the necessities for her medicine basket. "Surely you have something to give him. Cod liver oil? Willow bark tea? The oil of avens? Mallow root?"

The large man who helped carry Kenneth into the surgery popped his head inside. "Sorry to bother you, sir, but Mrs. Watson has gone into labor."

The doctor handed her the bowl now half-full of sludgy black charcoal. "I take it you haven't made arrangements for a place to stay?"

"No."

"Then you may remain here until I return. Brush his lips and tongue with this every quarter of an hour or so and try to encourage him to swallow. If he manages to survive the night, chances are he'll recover."

"Chances? What are the odds?"

"Right now?" The doctor removed his coat and hat from a peg on the wall. "No more than a quarter. But that could change to half by morning."

Modesty brushed the charcoal over Kenneth's lips. "I'll take the half. Ballocks to your quarter."

"I pray you are right."

~

MR. MASON, the doctor's manservant who helped to bring Kenneth in from the curricle had brought in bowls of pottage and bread. Though Freddie ate his fill, Modesty had no appetite. She maintained a vigil beside Kenneth's bed, brushing his tongue with spoons of charcoal and praying.

Once Freddie curled up in front of the fire and fell asleep, she started talking. "I have decided that you cannot die. You are going to open your eyes right now."

She held her breath and waited. But when Kenneth remained motionless her eyes welled with tears. "Please dunna die," she whispered, her throat grating with the strength of her conviction. "I will never forgive myself for not telling you—"

She bit her bottom lip. Why did she always have to be so headstrong? Why couldn't she be more like her sister Charity who was winsome and lovely and affable? Or why couldn't she be like Grace who was commanding and stunningly beautiful and ever so self-assured? But Modesty was born with a keen sense of competitiveness. She was unattractive, and overbearing, and too chatty. And far too ambitious.

What fool would ever allow me to be a jockey?

"Tell me what?"

For a moment Modesty thought she imagined Kenneth uttering the question. Her gaze snapped to his face. His eyes were closed, his mouth smeared black and slightly parted.

"Kenneth?" she probed. "Did you say something?"

"Tell… " His sooty tongue slipped across his mouth. "…me w-what?"

Tears spilled from her eyes. "So many things," she said, kissing his cheek, his forehead, his eyes. "How are you feeling, my love?"

"A-as if someone has shoveled the c-contents of the hearth into my m-mouth," he garbled, his every word strained as if talking caused undue agony.

"'Tis charcoal. It helps to counteract the wolfsbane."

His nod was slight but he most definitely had nodded. "I was foolish."

She dipped a cloth into a bowl of water and cleaned his lips. "Mayhap too trusting, but certainly not foolish.

He trembled as he reached for her hand. "What did you wish to tell me?"

Modesty's heart nearly leapt out of her chest. She couldn't say it—not when he didn't feel the same. "It doesna matter now."

"It matters to me."

Pursing her lips, she spotted a speck of black she'd missed and dabbed it away.

"Please?"

"I canna utter it."

"But y-you can. You can say anything to me—especially if it will make me f-feel better."

As she drew in a deep breath, she gazed into his eyes. Though they were bloodshot and half-cast, there was an intensity to his stare that said far more than a thousand words—hope and trust were there for certain, but the strongest emotion he imparted was that of love.

She knew it.

He did as well.

Taking his cheeks between her palms she brushed her lips over his, carefully, adoringly. "Och, ye ken I've loved ye since our first waltz."

"Yet you've known I own a stud farm since the day I visited Venom at the track."

"Aye... " She twirled a lock of his hair around her finger. "What are ye saying, m'lord?"

A slow grin turned up the corners of his mouth. "If you agree to marry me, it shall be yours."

She blinked, her heart beating out of rhythm. How could he talk such nonsense when he dangled on the precipice of death. "Mine alone?" she whispered.

"If that is what you w-wish." He urged her to his lips, stealing another gentle kiss. "I am yours to command."

"What of your bees and sheep?"

"I believe they'll be quite content at Kiedler Equine."

"Och, I do love you."

"Enough to m-marry me?"

She gave him a sly wink. "I suppose since I told the physician I'm Lady Berwick, I canna refuse."

26

_____

Though every fiber of Kenneth's body tortured him as he fought to overcome the poison, remaining abed for another day was not an option. Firstly, if Modesty's family didn't break down the doctor's door within the day, they most certainly would by the morrow. She had crossed a fragile line by chasing after him, and he needed to set things to rights quickly.

But first, there was the matter of a murderess to confront.

After washing at the bowl and a penny shave given by Mr. Mason, Kenneth managed to don his clothes. Though as he tried to tie his neckcloth, his hands trembled like a frightened puppy's.

"Are you ready?" As if Modesty had anticipated his need for assistance, she opened the door to the surgery and stepped inside. "Allow me."

Kenneth snorted. "You?"

She slid the long linen cloth from his fingertips. "Dare you forget I posed as a man? Moreover, I have five brothers and I am verra observant."

He stretched his neck and allowed her to take charge. "Now that I believe."

He savored her closeness, her cool breath on his throat as she carefully tied a barrel knot. How the devil did he once consider her impishly cute? She was magnificent and multifaceted and highly likely the most intelligent human being he'd ever met. "Is there anything you cannot do?"

Her smile was all-knowing and mature beyond her years. "I'm afraid I'm not verra skilled at flirting."

He slid his hands to the enticing arc of her waist. "I beg to differ. You have flirted with me mercilessly."

Those crystal blue eyes sparkled with the reflection of the candlelight as she met his gaze. "Och, ye ken I havena."

"My dear woman, you merely need to be within my presence to render me dumbstruck with love." He'd spent so many hours arguing with himself over what type of woman he thought he wanted, he'd overlooked the fact that Modesty MacGalloway was exactly the type of woman he *needed*.

Dipping his chin, he kissed her, watching her eyes flutter closed while his heart swelled with the enormity of his love.

With a soft chuckle, she caressed his cheek. "Och, if ye keep doing that, I'll never finish."

He glanced to the narrow bed. "We could lock the door."

"And have the magistrate beat it down?" She patted the completed barrel knot. "Now that would be an unmitigated scandal."

Perhaps he still wasn't quite thinking clearly. He snorted. "One to make the headlines of the *Gazette*."

"One to give my mother a gargantuan spell that would send her to bed for an entire year." Modesty stepped back and brushed her hands over his shoulders. "Perhaps that wouldna be such a bad thing."

Though she was jesting, Kenneth felt the need to vindicate the dowager. After all, if she hadn't intervened, he never would have courted Modesty, and she mightn't have hastened to Portsmouth to save his life. "As soon as this ugly business is over, we must go to your dear mama and set her mind at ease."

Modesty grazed her teeth over her bottom lip, batting her eyelashes. "Must we?"

"There you go flirting again."

"'ere we are!" said Freddie, coming through the door with nary a knock. "This is Mr. Ball, the magistrate."

Aye, the magistrate's arrival indeed would have created a scandal the *ton* would not be able to resist gossiping about.

Kenneth bowed and made the introductions.

"Freddie gave me some of the details, but can you tell me why this woman poisoned you? And how the devil you ended up here?" asked Mr. Ball.

It took a bit of time, but Kenneth went through every detail of his research and his reason for being in Portsmouth, including the fact that Miss Cole had stolen his notes.

"Have you any proof aside from your word?" asked the magistrate.

Freddie removed his cap and dipped into an exaggerated bow. "'e's a bleedin' viscount."

"Watch your tongue," Kenneth chided the boy. "To your question, sir, I have plenty of evidence. As I mentioned before, I employed Mr. McGrath in London as a private investigator. Furthermore, I have reason to believe Miss Cole also murdered Ward Crockford, the former proprietor of Waiter's."

"The notorious gambling hell?" asked Mr. Ball.

"Notorious, I'll say," Modesty added. "Did ye ken he rigged the Epsom Derby?"

Mr. Ball jotted a note in his leatherbound book. "It seems there's a great deal of skullduggery afoot."

Kenneth fought against his overwhelming exhaustion, taking the pitcher from his bedside table, and pouring himself a glass of water, drinking half before he replied, "Yes, and I intend for it to end here and now."

"Very well, I'll take my men to Thicket Road and we shall see what we find."

"I would like to go with you," Kenneth said, finishing the water.

"It could be dangerous."

"I know it is." Refreshed, he returned the glass to the beside table. "The woman is a calculating murderess, among other things."

Modesty removed her gloves from her reticule. "Freddie and I will come along as well."

Kenneth stepped between her and the magistrate as if to protect her. "Absolutely not."

"Och aye?" She stepped around him. "And we are to remain here, imposing on the doctor and Mr. Mason?"

"I'm sorry, my lady, but the viscount is right," said Mr. Ball. "Since Miss Cole has already successfully murdered two men that we know of, there's no telling what dangers we shall face when we apprehend her."

~

NO SOONER HAD the men left, when the doctor returned, looking tired. "Ah, Lady Berwick, how is His Lordship faring?"

"It seems he's well enough. Though he was trembling too much to tie his neckcloth, he just left with the magistrate to apprehend Miss Cole."

"The person responsible for the poisoning?"

"Aye."

"Very good," He strode across the floor to the surgery door. "Mr. Mason! There's a boy in my carriage with a broken arm. Can you please assist?"

The doctor again faced her. "Forgive me, my lady, but duty calls. You are welcome to remain here, though bone setting isn't for the squeamish."

Modesty looped her arm through Freddie's elbow. "I believe we have overstayed our welcome. Thank you ever so much for your assistance."

"Where are we off to?" Freddie whispered as they headed for the public stables.

"Need you ask?"

"I didn't reckon ye'd be able to stay behind."

It didn't take long to saddle the horses and ride to Thicket Road. Modesty reined her horse to a stop a good fifty paces from the cottage.

"The 'ouse is just a bit farther," said Freddie, stopping beside her, his skill in the saddle having improved markedly.

"You heard the magistrate, it isn't safe. We shall remain here."

"But I can't even see anybody."

Modesty rested her hands on her horse's withers. "I stopped to ensure you remain out of harm's way."

"But I'm a lad." Freddie tapped his heels and rode in a circle around her. "Ye're the one who needs protecting, milady."

Heaving a sigh she cued her mount to walk on. "Perhaps a little closer, but His Lordship will burst his spleen if either one of us is harmed in any way whatsoever, and I dunna want him upset. Not until he is feeling completely well."

"Aye, but it's not difficult to rankle 'im." When they stopped again Freddie held his hand to his ear. "Why is it so quiet?"

The silence brought with it an eerie chill. "I wish I knew."

"Don't ye think Mr. Ball would have knocked down the door and grabbed the ladies?"

"I hope it was that simple." She startled when a shrill scream pierced through the air. "Where did that come from?"

"Dunno." Freddie leaned to the side. "It didn't sound like it came from the cottage."

Modesty rode ahead a few paces, catching sight of yet another roof. "There's a carriage house out the back."

Together they trotted around the cottage, just as a team of horses pulling a wagon piled with a jumble of furniture came barreling toward them.

"Watch out!" Modesty shouted, giving Freddie's horse a slap with her riding crop. The gelding side-stepped, just barley escaping a collision.

A beautiful woman handled the ribbons, a determined bent to her expression. Modesty had seen her face before—the woman had even winked at her at Waiter's.

That's Evelyn Applewhite?

"Stay here!" she shouted at Freddie as she reined her horse into an about face. Leaning out over the mare's withers, it took one slap of her crop to cue the horse for a gallop. This was no racehorse, and she was hampered by a sidesaddle, but Modesty could not allow the woman who had nearly killed Kenneth escape.

Even with a team of four horses, a wagon was no match for a trained jockey.

"Stop!" she hollered, coming up alongside Evelyn.

The woman sneered, drawing back her whip, the tine hissing through the air as she aimed it at Modesty's face.

Ducking beneath the vicious strike, the draft from the whip's force sent a shiver down her spine. "I've been struck by a heartless cur before, and I'm not about to let it happen again!"

She had but two choices to stop the wagon. The first was akin to suicide, and the second would see her whipped mercilessly.

Out of the corner of her eye, a rider galloped toward them as if chased by hellfire.

Kenneth!

Her decision made, Modesty leaped from her mount, flinging out her hands, barely grasping ahold of the wagon's backrest while her shins collided against the edge of the floor.

"No!" Evelyn screamed, drawing her arm back for another strike.

Too enraged to feel pain, Modesty bore down, commanding every fiber of strength in her arms to hoist herself onto the bench beside the vixen. Grabbing the brake lever with both hands, she gnashed her teeth and pulled hard, while the bedamned Miss Applewhite struck her with the butt of her whip.

The wheels screeched, the team of horses whinnied, their manes flailing, but they gradually slowed. Unable to fight back, Modesty maintained her grip, dipping her head between her elbows to protect herself from the onslaught of vicious strikes.

"Enough!" Kenneth bellowed, jumping from his galloping horse onto the bench, and wrenching the whip from Evelyn's hand. "I ought to whip you into shreds!"

"Do it!" the woman seethed, her teeth bared.

"Not today," said Mr. Ball, stepping beside the wagon. With Kenneth's help, he pulled Evelyn down, then locked her in irons along with the other two women.

Kenneth surrounded Modesty in his arms, his breathing still a bit shallow. "Please tell me you are not badly injured."

She winced, not caring about the pain. "Merely a few wee bruises."

"Thank God. The way you leapt into the wagon scared me to death." He cradled her head to his chest, kissing her forehead. "I told you to stay behind."

"I ken, but you were feeling so poorly and the doctor returned and had to set a lad's arm, and Freddie and I had nowhere else to go."

Kenneth's shoulder's shook with his chuckle. "Is that the lot of it?"

"Aye, and the truth, mind you."

As they alighted from the wagon, Evelyn faced them, her hands bound behind her back, not looking nearly as fierce or even as beautiful as Modesty had previously thought. "I know I 'ave no grounds upon which to ask, but the only person in my life who ever showed me a lick of kindness was me father."

"Not Alfred?" Kenneth asked, white lines forming around his lips.

"Alfred?" she asked, her voice filled with sadness. "'e said 'e wanted to marry me—make me 'is viscountess. But that was nothing but a lie uttered in the midst of passion."

Stepping nearer, Berwick crossed his arms. "Tell me true, was my brother in collusion with Ward Crockford to throw the Derby?"

Evelyn snorted with a rueful laugh. "Aside from lyin' to me, I don't believe 'is Lordship ever connived an ill-fated plot in all 'is days."

"What about Venom's jockey?" Modesty asked.

"One of Crocky's men." Evelyn kept her gaze focused on Kenneth's face. "I say 'ere and now, I'm no fool and I've never been close to being a saint. I'll meet my end just as me 'ateful mother did. Me father is a good man. 'e lost everything on account of his service to King and country. I don't deserve your compassion, but Papa does. I only ask that ye look after the old man."

"He likes stories," said Kenneth, oddly compassionate, given the woman murdered his brother and nearly sent him to an early grave.

"'e does. Tell 'im I've gone abroad. Tell Papa I shall always love 'im."

"Do you think he'll understand what I'm saying?" Kenneth asked.

"'e will. 'e understands far more than anyone realizes."

"Enough chatting," said Mr. Ball, leading Evelyn away.

Modesty stood baffled. "My heavens, it appears the woman actually is in possession of a heart." Modesty watched as the magistrate and his men locked the three women into a barred wagon. "I wonder what happened to the other two ladies Evelyn was supposed to have left London with?"

"Mayhap she poisoned 'em," said Freddie, riding up beside them, leading the mare.

Kenneth patted the horse's shoulder. "I'd like to

think they followed their dreams and are now in situations far better than they endured under Mr. Crockford's employment."

Modesty took his hand and squeezed. "I'd like to think so, too."

27

They were fortunate to catch the ferry for Hasler without much of a wait. All three of them visited the old sailor. Modesty read to him, Freddie sat beside him on the bed, and Kenneth relayed his daughter's message. Afterward, Kenneth made arrangements to pay for someone to read to the sailor daily.

"Ye ken, ye didna have to do that," Modesty said as they climbed into his curricle, now pulled by two horses with Freddie riding alongside. "Even though it was quite philanthropic of you to do so."

Kenneth looked ever so tired as he took up the ribbons. "That man fought in a war against a tyrant. If it weren't for chaps like him, we might very well have been annexed to France and governed by a despot. It isn't his fault his wife and daughter are murderesses."

Modesty was still pondering how Mr. Cole's daughter could be so vicious yet have such tenderness for her father. *She must have had a traumatic upbringing for certain.* "I wonder what Evelyn would have turned out like if she had been raised in my family."

Kenneth chuckled. "Perish the thought."

"Och?"

"I've seen and heard enough of the MacGalloway

women to know not a one is to be underestimated. God save us all if one of you turned out to be homicidal."

Modesty scooted closer to him, looping her arm through his elbow. "You are a smart, man, Kenneth Davenport, verra smart."

"Perhaps."

He slapped the reins, his expression pleasant yet far away.

"What are you thinking about?" she asked.

"Alfred can now rest in peace."

Contentment washed through her as she rested her head on his shoulder. "Because ye ken he was a good man?"

"Yes. A principled peer who may have made a few ill-fated choices, but he honored the title. By selecting Lady Philomina as his bride, I believe he was trying to set the viscountcy to rights."

"Though he ought to have parted ways with Miss Cole first."

Kenneth kissed her cheek. "Agreed."

The rest of the day's journey progressed quickly with few stops. Even the weather was reasonably fine aside from a sprinkle or two. But when they turned onto the London road, all bliss was forgotten.

Modesty was familiar enough with the Earl of Brixham's carriage to immediately recognize it as it approached with its team of matched bays. "Oh no," she mumbled sliding down on the bench.

"Please don't tell me that's His Grace," said Kenneth.

"Nay, Marty and Julia have already headed to summer at Stack Castle in the north. That is the Earl of Brixham's carriage. Doubtless Mama, Harry, and Charity are within."

"Not Kitty?"

"She may be as well." Modesty pointed to a passing place on the side of the road. "We had best stop there."

"I pray Brixham won't shoot me first," said Kenneth, reining the horses over.

"Pistols are not his weapon of choice."

"Oh, that's right. He was a boxer."

Modesty cringed. "A verra talented one."

After signaling to Freddie his intention to pull over, Kenneth stopped the curricle and engaged the brake. "I suppose it is best if I do the talking."

"Aye?" Modesty looked at her intended as if he'd grown two heads. "That is if being poisoned by Evelyn Applewhite wasna enough and ye want to be pummeled to within an inch of your life."

Kenneth regarded her out of the corner of his eye. "Brixham may give me a clock to the muns, but are you not afraid of repercussions?"

"I'm kin. The worst Mama might do is lock me in a tower and feed me bread and water."

"Wonderful." Kenneth gestured for Freddie to ride up beside them. "It seems Modesty's family is approaching. I suggest you remain at the rear of the curricle until we've had a word."

"But I'm the one who chaperoned 'er on the way to Portsmouth. I reckon they ought to 'ave a bone to pick with me."

The viscount placed his hand on the lad's shoulder. "I shan't allow any bone picking. Your actions were nothing short of heroic, lad. Now do as I say and wait behind the curricle."

Modesty stood beside Kenneth as the Brixham carriage rolled to a stop. Of course, two footmen hopped down from the rear and placed a stepstool on the ground before they opened the door. The earl emerged first. Though a large man, Modesty had forgotten exactly how large.

As he strode forward, he loomed over Kenneth, by a good two inches. Brixham slammed his meaty fist into his palm. "You'd best explain yourself quickly, Berwick, else I'll have no recourse but to thrash you senseless and leave you alongside the road for buzzard fodder."

Modesty forced herself in between the two men and poked the earl in the shoulder. "I beg your pardon, Harry, but that is no way to speak to your future brother-in-law!"

"Brother-in-law?" Mama asked as a footman handed her down from the carriage. "Is this true, Lord Berwick?"

Charity followed. "I knew it!"

Kenneth held Harry's gaze, his expression grave as if he didn't dare shift his eyes. "It is. Lady Modesty risked her life as well as her reputation by riding to Portsmouth to warn me that Alfred's mistress was a murderess."

"Murderess?" Kitty echoed, the last to exit the carriage.

"Aye." Modesty slipped beside Kenneth and waggled her fingers, urging him to hold her hand. "The woman used a salve of wolfsbane to kill her victims because it doesna kill the coroner's dogs when he feeds them the contents of the deceased's stomach."

Mama fanned herself. "Oh, that is utterly vulgar."

"Indeed," said Kenneth. "And not an acceptable topic for conversation when among delicate ears."

Brixham took a step away, his snarl softening into an affable grin. "So, we have a wedding to plan?"

Stepping forward, Mama eyed Modesty, and then

Berwick. "Given the circumstances, I do not believe it is advisable to endure a long engagement."

Modesty bit the inside of her cheek. Kenneth hadn't mentioned anything about the length of the betrothal. She'd just assumed...

"I have no need to wait at all," he said, thank heavens. "Shall we all hasten to Gretna Green?"

"Absolutely not," Mama replied. "We shall hasten to Newhailes. I'll send word to Martin so he and Julia can come down from Stack Castle. Of course, we'll need to send out invitations and—"

"Your Grace." Kenneth squeezed Modesty's hand rather tightly. "With all due respect, I would prefer as small, family wedding."

"As would I," Modesty agreed.

"I would think so, since my daughter galloped out of London, chasing after a viscount regardless of if her reasons were virtuous or not." Mama patted Kenneth's shoulder. "We shall have a family wedding at the family church with merely one hundred and fifty guests or so. It should not take long at all to set a date, send out invitations, and have Modesty's gown made."

Kenneth turned a tad pale. After all, he was still recovering from Evelyn's wolfsbane salve.

Perhaps he might feel a wee bit better if I make an attempt to curb my mother's enthusiasm. "Why do we not simply invite the immediate family?"

"Perish the thought." Mama returned to the carriage. "Come everyone. We all have a great deal of work to do!" She clapped her hands. "Modesty, since Lord Berwick is driving an open curricle, you may continue to ride with him."

28

The wedding had been a grandiose affair, akin to a royal coronation. And no matter how much Modesty had tried to rein her mother in, it had been an act in futility. The dowager insisted since Modesty was her last daughter to be married she was going to ensure it was the most magnificent spectacle Scotland had seen in decades.

By the time they reached the Newhailes estate, the guest list had ballooned to five hundred and Modesty had given up trying to dissuade her mother, which made Kenneth enormously happy. While Her Grace proceeded to orchestrate the wedding, he and his intended spent lazy summer days looking for seashells along the shore of the Firth of Forth and taking long walks from Newhailes into the small towns of Musselburgh and Leith. They went to the theater in Edinburgh with the Duke and Duchess of Dunscaby. They entertained Lord Richter when he paid a visit to Miss Kitty, though she was quite disappointed he didn't propose. Alas, it seemed Modesty's dearest friend was to prepare for her second Season.

Kenneth would have been lying if he said it wasn't pure torture to be so near Modesty while keeping his hands to himself. In fact, a week before the wedding date, he feared he might lose his mind. But in the end, the breathtakingly monumental passion they enjoyed on their wedding night proved to be worth the weeks of agonizing abstinence.

And now, he had the pleasure of taking his bride to Kiedler Equine.

Modesty inclined her head out the carriage window. "Oh my heavens, I can tell the stables are bonny already."

"I should have known you'd remark on the facilities first." Kenneth shifted to the opposing bench so he could gaze at the estate with her. After all, he'd only visited the place a half-dozen times. "The sables alone are twenty thousand square feet and there are three entire rows of horse stalls. Of course, there's a carriage house in back of the manor, but you cannot see it from here."

She clapped her hands, bobbing up and down. "All that and a racetrack as well!"

Simply watching her excitement filled Kenneth with contentment. He kissed her cheek. "But you knew that, my love."

"Aye, though I never dreamed it would be a full-sized track."

"Kiedler lacks nothing for the serious Thoroughbred breeder."

She threw her arms around his neck and peppered his face with kisses. "I canna believe this is real."

"Believe it. There is nothing I would deny you."

Sitting back, she schooled her enthusiasm and folded her hands. "And what about your sheep?"

"They are already here. Though I've hired an overseer to care for the bees."

"Why didna you tell me about the bees? I thought beekeeping is your elixir for relaxation."

"It is, which is why I've already purchased new hives to establish a colony of honeybees here."

"You had time to do all that in the midst all the wedding preparations?"

"Ah, but you forget, the Dowager Duchess of Dunscaby is not my mother. I also wasn't required to stand for hours during dress fittings."

She chuckled. "I suppose we're going to be so busy with our endeavors, we'll never have time to visit Mama."

Kenneth did like Modesty's mother, but the idea of not seeing her for quite some time gave him no remorse. "Perhaps she'll visit us *after* we're settled."

The carriage stopped in front of the enormous, red brick manor while Modesty craned her neck. "It looks verra similar to Newhailes."

"It is, though larger."

"I do not need a home larger than Newhailes."

Near the east corner, Kenneth caught a glimpse of the servants filing out to greet them. "You may not need it, but it is yours."

"I thought the stables were mine."

He gave her one last fleeting kiss. "What is mine is yours, my love."

Freddie hopped down from his perch at the rear of the carriage. The lad had grown at least four inches since Kenneth had met him at the Covent Garden markets. It was amazing what good eating could do for a child. "We're 'ere at last!"

"That we are." Kenneth handed Modesty down to the drive. The manor's servants were all now standing at attention in a long, tidy row. "Allow me to introduce Mrs. Wilking, the housekeeper."

The woman curtseyed. "Lovely to have a matron of the house, my lady."

Modesty's lips twisted. "I hope so, though you might find me a tad unconventional."

Of course, Kenneth knew this to be an understatement, but the servants would come to love her in time. Together they meandered along the queue of servants, some expressing belated condolences, others excited to begin a new chapter in the manor's life.

Freddie had already taken a spot at the end of the line and bowed gallantly as Mr. Welch had taught him to do. "Am I to be a footman 'ere, too?"

As Kenneth opened his mouth to reply, Modesty held up her hand. "Laddie, after you rushed to His Lordship's rescue, I believe you should decide. Would you prefer to learn the intricacies of a great house, or do horses suit your fancy more?"

The boys eyes popped wide open. "'orses? But I thought ye said I rode like a flour sack."

"You did at first, however you learned quickly."

Freddie looked to Kenneth. "Would ye be awfully disappointed if I gave the stables a go?"

He riffled his fingers through the lad's hair. "Her Ladyship said the choice is yours and I heartily agree."

"Whoop, whoop!" the boy shouted, jumping and clicking his heels together.

"A little less enthusiasm," Welch chided. "After all, you are an Englishman."

"Would you like me to give you a tour of the house, my lady?" asked Mrs. Wilking.

"Och, nay." Modesty grasped Kenneth's hand. "The stables first, then we'll have a wee peek at the house."

Kenneth gave the housekeeper an apologetic shrug as he happily followed Freddie and his wife to the barn.

~

As nervous as a nesting puffin, swarms of butterflies danced in Modesty's stomach. She hadn't been this anxious since she was introduced to the Queen. Now, after a whirlwind of a morning, she needed to find her husband.

It was difficult to believe a year had passed since her frantic ride to Portsmouth. Her life had changed so much since then. The best part? All changes had entirely been for the better.

She and Kenneth had made quite a few modifications to the estate including the construction of a sheep paddock and outbuilding for scientific testing. To their joy, all the tenant farmers were now raising Northumberland Longwool sheep, which were destined to grow in popularity across the Kingdom. And though the majority of his hives were still at their estate twenty miles to the southwest in Rothbury, he enjoyed donning his beekeeper's costume and harvesting honey in the dozen hives they had installed in a paddock far away from the horses.

The gardener had planted numerous flowering pollinators, and never once did anyone dare pull a single dandelion from their lawn.

Most mornings Modesty headed straight for the stables after breaking her fast, though she hadn't done so today. Instead, she chose a lovely white muslin dress, donned a straw bonnet, and headed out to hives.

Except as she strode past the library, the rustle of a newspaper caught her attention. "What are you doing in here?"

Kenneth peered at her over the top of his *Gazette*. "Rain's coming, so I thought I'd have a leisurely morning like most aristocrats. Besides, the honey will still be there on the morrow. Care to join me?"

A new wave of butterflies began to swarm. "I would."

She tiptoed across the floor and stood before him, clasping her hands.

His brow furrowed. "Is all well?"

"Aye."

When she didn't move, he folded the paper and put it on the side table. "Why do I sense you have something to say?" he asked, taking her hands and pulling her onto his lap.

She settled comfortably atop his thighs and removed her bonnet.

Kenneth toyed with her hair, his eyes shining. "It isn't like you to reply to me in monosyllables. Why do I sense something is amiss? Is it one of the horses?"

"Naaaay," she cooed, lacing her arms around his neck, growing bolder as she inclined her lips to his ear. "You're to be a father."

Gasping, he clamped her cheeks between his palms, his smile splitting his handsome and ever-so-caring face. "A father?"

She nodded, squirming and too excited to hold still a moment longer.

"When?"

"Before Yuletide for certain!" Hopping to her feet, Modesty pulled her husband with her. Together they danced in a circle in the middle of the Persian carpet.

He led her into a pirouette beneath his arm. "Are you sure? Are you feeling well? Should you be so rambunctious? Do you not need to take to your bed?"

"One thing at a time, dearest!" Laughing, Modesty fell into his arms. "The doctor just left. He said I looked well and only need to make a few modifications to my daily duties."

Kenneth lifted her into his arms and kissed her. "What sort of modifications?"

"Well, I'm not to ride horses."

"Truly?" He looked more bereft than she had felt when the doctor gave her such news. "How will you survive the next..." Looking to the ceiling he paused for a moment. "Seven months?"

"I ken it is a monumental sacrifice, but it simply must be done."

A slow smile spread across his lips. "Oh... ?"

She nestled into the soft place where his neck met his shoulder. "You see, Mama was right. She told me that after I married, I'd look back on my Season and wonder what all my fussing was about."

"Do not tell me you agree with the Dowager Duchess of Dunscaby?"

"Perhaps in this instance."

He kissed her nose. "And why the change of heart, my dearest?"

"Because I love you. Because I want a family."

With Modesty still in his arms, he turned in a slow circle. "And what of your dreams of being a horse breeder?"

She patted her belly. "I reckon I can breed horses as well as barins!"

"Yes, you can, and do you know what else?"

Staring into her husband's loving eyes, Modesty slowly shook her head.

"I'll be beside you forever. You are not only my viscountess, you are my most astonishing, quite industrious, and stunningly radiant dandelion."

THE MACGALLOWAY FAMILY TREE

To view a larger version of this, click here.

ALSO BY AMY JARECKI

The MacGalloways

A Duke by Scot

Her Unconventional Earl

The Captain's Heiress

Kissing the Highland Twin

A Princess in Plaid

Charmed by a Wily Lass

The King's Outlaws

Highland Warlord

Highland Raider

Highland Beast

Highland Defender

The Valiant Highlander

The Fearless Highlander

The Highlander's Iron Will

Highland Force:

Captured by the Pirate Laird

The Highland Henchman

Beauty and the Barbarian

Return of the Highland Laird

Guardian of Scotland

Rise of a Legend

In the Kingdom's Name

The Time Traveler's Destiny

Highland Dynasty
Knight in Highland Armor
A Highland Knight's Desire
A Highland Knight to Remember
Highland Knight of Rapture
Highland Knight of Dreams

Devilish Dukes
The Duke's Fallen Angel
The Duke's Untamed Desire
The Duke's Privateer
The Duke's Secret Longing

ICE
Hunt for Evil
Body Shot
Mach One

Blitzed

Defenseless
Unintentional
Tackled

Celtic Fire
Rescued by the Celtic Warrior
Deceived by the Celtic Spy

Lords of the Highlands series:
The Highland Duke

The Highland Commander
The Highland Guardian
The Highland Chieftain
The Highland Renegade
The Highland Earl
The Highland Rogue
The Highland Laird

The Chihuahua Affair
Virtue: A Cruise Dancer Romance
Boy Man Chief
Time Warriors

ABOUT THE AUTHOR

Known for her action-packed, passionate historical romances, Amy Jarecki has received reader and critical praise throughout her writing career. She won the prestigious 2018 RT Reviewers' Choice award for *The Highland Duke* and the 2016 RONE award from InD'tale Magazine for Best Time Travel for her novel *Rise of a Legend*. In addition, she hit Amazon's Top 100 Bestseller List, the Apple, Barnes & Noble, and Bookscan Bestseller lists, in addition to earning the designation as an Amazon All Star Author. Readers also chose her Scottish historical romance, *A Highland Knight's Desire*, as the winning title through Amazon's Kindle Scout Program. Amy holds an MBA from Heriot-Watt University in Edinburgh, Scotland and now resides in Southwest Utah with her husband where she writes immersive historical romances. Learn more on Amy's website. Or sign up to receive Amy's newsletter.

www.ingramcontent.com/pod-product-compliance
Lightning Source LLC
Chambersburg PA
CBHW010535100726
47903CB00011B/3009